THE WEEPING

Preface

I first wrote *The Weeping* back in 2010. When I started querying agents, any response I got contained some variation of, "A horror novel with a gay male lead will never sell." Disheartening? Yes. Surprising? Not really. Back then, people were more comfortable with gay characters as side roles. A gay male lead in horror was almost unheard of.

Wanting my book to sell, I rewrote it. Heath became straight, and I gave him a female love interest. I still didn't land an agent, so in 2012 I decided to self-publish. Since it was the most polished version, I went with the "straight version." It did okay. Not a bestseller, but it found readers. Still, it never sat right with me. I had put out a book I was only half proud of. Eventually, I pulled it.

The version you're holding now is the one I always wanted to tell. The core story remains, but Heath is once again gay, as he was from the beginning. I've modernized the setting and cleaned up the prose. Be sure to read my note at the end for a deeper dive into what changed and what inspired me to write this book.

If you read the earlier version, I hope you enjoy this new and improved one. If you're meeting Heath and Catherine for the first time, leave a light on.

THE WEEPING

Kallum Rytting

ECHO HOUSE

PRESS

For those who lived by someone else's script,
and then found the courage to make it their own.

Acrid smoke clawed at Catherine's lungs, searing them with every breath. Through the screams, a man with a deep, booming voice instructed everyone to stay calm and move toward the exits.

"Phillip?" Catherine's ragged voice was barely audible over the chaos.

When the smoke started billowing onto the stage, her panicked cast mates scattered. Bodies slammed into her from all sides, knocking her to the ground. She crashed to the floor, the air punched from her chest. Feet pounded against her ribs as they rushed to safety, leaving her to fend for herself.

The stage lights glared off the wall of black haze that surrounded her. She had no idea which direction she faced. She crawled toward what she hoped was stage left. There was an exit backstage. If she could just get to the exit.

"Catherine?" Through the terror-stricken screams of those rushing to safety, someone called her name. It was Phillip. It had to be.

He'd come back.

"Phillip!" His name caught in her throat as her lungs protested against the influx of smoke.

She pulled the skirt of her costume over her face, but the fabric offered little protection. Toxic smog pressed down, stabbing at her eyes, scraping her chest raw.

Crushing. Smothering.

Move toward the screams, she told herself.

An intense blast of heat, furnace hot and hungry, hit her in the face. She recoiled, hair singeing, skin tightening as flames leapt before her. If she didn't get out soon, she would die.

Stay below the smoke.

She flattened herself against the stage, and dragged herself forward. Sweat poured from her blistered skin, carving hot trails down her soot-blackened face.

The stage lights above her popped and hissed, briefly lighting up before shattering into white-hot glass. Like grotesque paparazzi, each flash lit her death crawl in cruel snapshots.

Glass jutted from her palms like shattered bone. Blood dripped steadily. She dragged herself forward, marking her path in crimson handprints.

She would not die.

He's not coming back. You're pathetic. Stupid!

He doesn't care about you. He never did.

Sirens wailed. The promise of rescue almost too intense to hope for.

Keep fighting! They'll save you. Someone will rescue you.

A thunderous crack split the air. Something massive crashed to the ground, missing her by inches. The entire stage convulsed beneath her. The decades-old theatre was collapsing, determined to make her its final performer. She clawed at the splintering wood, fingernails tearing from their beds.

Faster.

Choking.

Burning.

Pulling.

Every inch that much closer to safety.

The stage floor vanished in front of her. She caught herself before dropping into the yawning orchestra pit. Her lungs tried to force their way out of her body, away from the thick smoke threatening to suffocate her. The flames grew closer.

Too close.

The heat pressed against her skin, relentless. She could almost taste the sulfurous tang of burning wood and the unmistakable stench of her own hair charred at the roots.

There was only one choice: down.

With a choked breath, she let go and plunged ten feet into yawning darkness. Pain splintered through her frame on impact.

To her right, a battered door beckoned from beneath a flickering exit sign. Its red glow guided her forward. Whimpering, she clawed her way forward, the smoke wrapping itself around her throat.

Stalking her.

Wanting her.

No!

A thunderous roar shattered the blaze's fury as the stage above her collapsed. Burning planks and smoldering beams crashed down, sealing the doorway, a dam of charred timber.

"Please, God. Help me get out of here. Please." A beam exploded in front of her, sparks lighting up her petticoat. She slapped at it with trembling hands, smearing soot into what had once been pristine white lace.

The flames closed in. There was nowhere to go.

"Help me!"

She edged toward the far corner, each inch costing her precious energy. Her tears burned like acid on her scorched cheeks. Why hadn't he come? Why had he abandoned her?

Because he doesn't love you, Catherine. He never loved you.

You're not good enough for him. You're trash.
She clawed at the walls.
He's one of them. They hate you.
Beating.
They've always hated you.
Pushing.
It should be them down here. Bodies cooking, hair melting.
Screaming.
You let them ruin your life.
She sank to the ground, defeated.
They killed you. And you let them.

The wall of flames licked at her, branding her skin with fiery kisses. Flames needled her toes, a thousand wasps attacking at once. She pressed herself against the corner, but the embers followed, patient and hungry, the crackle and hiss a lullaby of death. Despair clawed past her throat as the roaring blaze promised to strip her bones and turn her to ash.

She stopped fighting. She surrendered to the inferno and did the only thing she could do.

She wept.

CHAPTER ONE

Twelve weeks and two days. That's exactly how long it's been since I killed three of my closest friends.

Jake and Meredith were the first to die. It was quick and painless for them, or at least that's what I was told. Amy wasn't so lucky. She was conscious the entire time, completely aware that her body was shutting down as blood filled her lungs, suffocating her.

It was my 20th birthday. Spring break. All of us together again for the first time since Christmas. It was supposed to be a harmless weekend of fun. It was anything but.

Now they're all dead, and I'm trapped in this car, forced to endure five and a half hours of my parents' false happiness as they drive me to stay with my uncle for the summer.

"We'll be there soon, son. Maybe another hour tops." Dad adjusts the rearview mirror. "How you holdin' up?"

I pretend not to hear. I have my earbuds in, but nothing plays through them. I ran out of good music an hour ago. I stare out the window, watching the trees fly by in a blur of dark green. Looking at them through the rain-speckled windows, they appear to be melting.

My mom places her hand on my knee to get my attention, and I remove one of the buds from my ears.

"Are you doing okay, sweetheart?"

Why does she talk to me like I'm six? I'm literally an adult. She's done this shit for the last two and a half months. Like ever since the accident, I'm a child again. I bite back the words stinging my throat.

"Fine." That's all she's getting from me right now. One word. Fine.

I shift in the backseat, trying to ease the throb in my hip. Sitting too long sets it off.

"Do you need to stretch? There's a rest stop a few miles ahead. We can pull over."

Rather than answer her, I put my earbud back in. It's easier this way, not talking.

She stares at me with a sad look on her face, her standard response to my petulant behavior. Her blue-green eyes, my eyes, peer at me through eyelashes caked with mascara. They search my face, looking for someone who isn't there anymore.

Sorry, Mom. He's gone.

I wait for her to scream at me the way she did a few weeks ago. *Talk to me*, her eyes say. *I'm your mother. I love you. I'm here for you.*

I look away, pretending not to notice. She turns back, and I let the rain-spattered window and the blur of trees swallow me.

I know it bothers them that I act this way, but I can't help it. I love my parents, I honestly do, and until a few months ago, we had a great relationship. It's just that something broke inside of me, and I don't know how to fix it. I'm not the same guy anymore. My body may have made it out alive, but the son they knew died that night. A part of him lies curled in each of their graves, wrapped around his friends. Apologizing.

Always apologizing.

Dad hits the blinker and veers off the highway. The sign reads 'Trucks to the Right,' so he follows the pavement left.

My parents glance back at me, as if the big brown building ahead is some kind of mystery and the bathroom signs need explanation. I stay quiet. My hip makes the decision for me, flaring hot and sharp. Guess I'm getting out.

I step into the pouring rain despite my mother's objections. Her door opens, and she crawls out, opening her umbrella. She stands next to me, shielding us both from the cold, coastal wetness.

My hip catches as I move out from under the protection of the umbrella. I want to feel the rain. It pounds at me, reminding me that, despite my best efforts, I'm still alive. It's cold, and it hurts.

I deserve to hurt.

"Heath, you're getting wet. Let me walk with you." Her high heels click behind me as she dodges the same puddles I purposely drag my feet through.

"I have to piss," I mumble as I make my way toward the restroom.

The stench of urine, bleach, and mildew assaults me as soon as I push open the door. Nasty. I want to turn around and walk out, but my bladder makes the call. I finish up fast, eager to escape the smell. I wash my hands, running a finger over the scars on my wrists. Battle wounds from my war with grief.

They don't heal. They just remind.

My parents thought that getting me out of Northern Washington for the summer would strip the grief away.

It didn't. Still here.

"You're drenched." I turn to find my father shaking out his umbrella. People often mistake us for brothers. We have the same build: tall and athletic with thick arms and a bubble butt. Gray threads through his dark hair now, and lines crease the corners of his eyes, but strangers still do double-takes when they see us together.

I dry my hands without answering him and hobble out the door. There's nothing to say.

My mother stands guard outside, umbrella poised. She'll do anything to protect me. If it weren't for her book tour, she'd be happy to play the role of my personal bodyguard all summer. I walk past her, back through the puddles, moving as quickly as I can just to prove to her that I don't need coddling. I don't deserve protection.

Thunder growls overhead as the rain pounds us. I reach for the car door, then freeze at the screech of tires on wet pavement. A Prius fishtails across the highway and stalls. A horn blares. An SUV slams into it with a crunch that stops my breath. Metal on metal. My hand freezes on the handle. That sound.

I remember that sound.

Mom runs up beside me, placing the umbrella over my head as she opens the door for me, but I can't move. Momentarily thrown back to that night.

Why can't I get it out of my head?

"Honey, get inside. They'll be fine. Your father will call it in." She gently pushes me toward the car, and I crawl inside, shivering as she closes the door behind me.

I stare out the window, watching the drivers of the cars as they yell at one another in the pouring rain. They're fine. Pissed, but fine. No one died. They'll get over it in a few days.

I rest my head against the seat, shivering in my wet clothes. Mom doesn't even flinch at the thought of me ruining the leather in Dad's Range Rover. Before the accident, she'd have made me change on the spot. Now I could crawl in covered in mud and roll across the seats like a dog, and they'd only shrug.

Don't scold the boy. He's damaged.

I reach across and grab the blanket my mom keeps in the back seat for my baseball games. She didn't need it much this year. I wasn't able to finish the season. Still, there it sits, waiting to wrap around someone, offering them warmth and comfort.

The rain turns to a light drizzle as my father merges onto Highway 101 from OR-130. As we follow the road, cutting through the trees, the ocean appears in front of us. Beneath the ashen sky, the waves churn, pushing and pulling against the rocks. The view is at once stunning and intimidating.

I must have drifted off, because when I open my eyes, my father is navigating down Main Street in Rock Harbor, Oregon. The town looks exactly as it did when I was here five years ago for my grandmother's funeral. Untouched by modern chains that plague the larger cities, Rock Harbor appears to exist in an entirely different decade. Here, Starbucks, McDonald's, and Walmart don't exist. Instead, they have Rock Harbor Diner, Buck's Steakhouse, and Joe's Super Mart. There are no billboards announcing the upcoming summer blockbuster. No intrusive neon signs outside trendy nightclubs and no Space Needle. It's like someone hit pause on 1985 and forgot to press play again.

The power appears to be out. The streetlights are dark, the cobblestone sidewalks empty and quiet; the entire town shrouded in an eerie, blue-gray color.

"There it is." Dad slows the car in front of a large, dark building. It's much bigger than I expected.

The theatre and its lot stretch across the whole block. In the fading twilight, the three-story Art Deco facade looms, plucked straight from a 1930s photograph. Its stacked tiers rise from broad to narrow, capped by a triangular peak that juts like a ship's prow above the doors.

Before the fire, the Rock Harbor Opera House was the town's jewel, drawing both tourists and locals with live shows every summer. Afterward, the town tried to rebuild, but nothing stuck. For a while, it limped along as a dollar movie theatre, screening old classics, until that folded too. Two years ago, Uncle Vic bought it and, thanks to donations and investors, launched a full renovation to bring back its original look. Now, the place is fully restored, and it will reopen to the public this summer. Like it or not, I'll be part of its story.

With the power out, the sharp angles, intricate patterns, and casement windows make the theatre look more ominous than artsy. A sense of unease smolders in the pit of my stomach. I no longer want to be here. Before panic takes hold, Dad shifts into gear and pulls away. The theatre disappears behind us, but in one upstairs window, I swear I see it: a sudden flare. A light blooming into a flame.

We drive over the bridge, crossing Rock Harbor Bay to my uncle's house perched above the shore. Headlights flare against blank windows announcing our arrival. The small, white house still looks the same, but something about it feels hollow. It's strange not seeing Grandma waving from the top step. Instead, the vacant porch swing sways, pushed by invisible hands.

The rain has stopped, leaving behind a fine mist. A gust of wind pushes cool, salty air over us as Dad climbs the steps and knocks on the front door. Mom won't step past me, not until she's sure I'm steady, since I refuse to use my cane.

Dad knocks again before trying the doorknob. The unlocked door swings open, and he pokes his head inside. The familiar scent of cinnamon and apples greets us.

"Vic?" Dad's voice echoes off the walls of the empty house.

"Maybe he's at the theatre," Mom says when there's no answer.

"His truck is out front."

"It's not like it's a long walk. It's only a few blocks away," she says.

"But the front door was open. He wouldn't just leave the front door unlocked if he weren't here." They'll go on like this for hours, cordially arguing. Neither of them willing to admit they might be wrong.

My dad walks up the stairs, calling my uncle's name, feeling his way along the wall, Mom right behind him.

I find my way to the kitchen. Grandma's pots and pans still hang above the center island. Her apron rests on the door of the pantry, waiting for her to return. A cool breeze slides over me as if something just moved past, brushing through my hair, tickling my scalp. I notice the back door is ajar. I move to close it as a gust of wind bursts through the room, knocking the screen door open.

The air shifts, sharp and acrid.

Smoke.

Something's burning.

CHAPTER TWO

The screen door snaps, and smoke pours across my face. A figure waits beyond the threshold, knife dangling from their grip. My pulse hammers. I take a step back, fighting to keep my breathing even. I don't dare turn away.

Light stutters through the house as if the power is trying to find the courage to come back on. The porch lamp sparks, throwing the figure into view. The knife gleams, and a red flannel shirt glows in the burst of light.

Jake had a shirt just like that. He wore it all the time at the cabin.

But it can't be Jake. Jake is dead.

The figure moves faster, climbing the steps. My heart slams against my ribs as the lights flicker once more. I turn to run, certain he's seen me. I fall, dragging a bar stool down with me. A crash booms through the house. My hip ignites, forcing a cry from my throat. Light floods the room as I crawl toward my parents' voices. Footsteps close in behind me, each one louder than my pulse.

Jake.

Jake's going to kill me.

I close my eyes, waiting for the knife to hit.

"Heath? You all right?"

I open my eyes and roll to my side to see Uncle Vic setting down his knife. My hip screams at me for being so stupid.

"Yeah," I say, embarrassed.

My mom rushes to help me up. I start to push her away, but I know I can't do this by myself. I'm in pain.

"What happened?"

My dad moves to help her, and together they finally get me back on my feet and then to a chair at the table.

"I fell," I tell her. No way I'm mentioning the part about my dead friend chasing me with a knife.

"Did you trip?" Dad asks.

"Yes. I tripped. It was… dark."

"You're shaking." Mom places a hand on my back and her other hand on my forehead. "Panic attack? Do you need your medication?"

"He's probably in pain," my dad tells her. "Are you hurting, son? Do you need something?"

My jaw clenches. Why won't they get the fuck away from me? I shake my head. My hip throbs with each heartbeat, but if I tell them that, they'll just keep smothering me. I want them to back up and let me breathe.

"Nice to see you, too," Uncle Vic says as he places the knife on the counter. The smell of smoke rolls off him. He looks older than when I last saw him. His salt and pepper hair is cropped short, and with the flannel shirt and bushy beard, he looks more like a lumberjack than an acclaimed theatre director.

"Hey, Vic." Dad holds out his hand to shake, but Vic ignores it and pulls him in for a hug, instead.

"You haven't seen me in five years, little brother. You're not going to get away with a simple handshake."

"Victor, it's so good to see you." Mom walks toward him, her arms outstretched for her hug.

"You're as striking as ever, Carol," he says, kissing her on both cheeks. "I hope I look half as good as you when I'm your age."

She laughs and gives him a playful slap.

"Look at you. You're all grown up. The last time I saw you, you were only this tall." He holds his hand at chest level.

I try to smile, but it doesn't feel genuine.

"Don't say much, do ya?" He ruffles my hair like I'm a six-year-old before moving to the sink. "I've been smoking a brisket out in the smoke shed. Get your things in here, then get washed up, and we'll eat."

I stand, wincing in pain, and hobble toward the front door, but my dad stops me.

"I'll get your things. You go wash up for dinner." Rather than argue, I head toward the restroom. When I come out, my bags sit at the foot of the stairs. Hushed voices drift from the kitchen.

"We appreciate you doing this for us," my mom says.

This. Doing *this* for us. I guess it sounds better than, "Thank you for taking care of our fucked up son so we can enjoy our lives for a few weeks."

"Is he doing any better?" Vic asks.

"Honestly, I don't know. I don't think so." Her voice cracks. "He's so quiet all the time. I can't seem to get through to him. I wish he could just understand that no one blames him for what happened."

That's not true. *I* blame me.

"He's been through a lot, he's got a lot of anger inside," my dad reminds her. It's not as if she needs reminding. She knows all about my anger. She's been on the receiving end of most of it.

"I thought maybe he'd be better by now, or at least making progress, but he doesn't seem to be. The panic attacks are almost crippling at times despite his medication. I don't know what else to do. When we came home and found him bleeding on the bathroom floor, I thought for sure we were going to lose him. His psychiatrist said that getting away from everything would be good for him. This is our last hope. I hate leaving him, but we're willing to try anything." I think she may be crying. I hate that I've reduced her to this, but she doesn't understand. No one can possibly understand what I'm feeling or what I've been through.

"He'll be fine here. I'll keep him busy. I have a great group of kids working for me this summer. He's in good hands," Vic tells her.

I shuffle my feet so they know I'm coming. They don't need to know I've heard what they've just said. When I enter the room, everyone exudes smiles and happiness, hiding the fact that they're all worried about me.

My dad carves the brisket as my mom helps Vic place various food items on the table. My stomach growls when I see the corn on the cob, mashed potatoes, and gravy.

During dinner, the adults discuss the theatre, my mother's upcoming book tour, and Dad's latest award-winning architectural design. No one mentions the accident or why I'm really here. I'm predictably laconic, most of my answers consisting of no more than three words.

"I'm going to bed," I announce after the table is cleared.

I'm not tired; I just need to be alone. I'm afraid that if I stay here any longer, they'll guilt me into a game of Charades or something. I don't want to people right now. Or ever.

"Can you make it up the stairs?" Vic asks. "If your hip is bothering you, we can make up the couch."

"I'll be fine."

"I got your dad's old room ready for you. Clean sheets and everything. The dresser is cleared out."

"Thanks," I say as I limp toward the stairs.

I put the duffel bag on the rolling suitcase and sling my backpack over my shoulder. I start up the stairs, one at a time, the suitcase clumping behind me.

"Need some help?" Dad's voice stops me, and I can't help but roll my eyes.

"I've got it."

He watches me struggle with the bags, waiting for me to fall so he can rush to my aid. I want to turn around and tell him to leave me alone, but I bite my tongue. I remind myself that he's not trying to intrude. He just wants to be sure that I'll make it up the stairs okay.

When I hit the landing, I finally feel at peace. I drop my backpack and scan the room. Same model sailboats Dad built as a kid. Same autographed baseballs collecting dust. At least Uncle Vic repainted. The blue-gray tone is much better than that hideous green. There's a new comforter on the bed.

I immediately begin putting away my things. After I've showered, I prop open the window, letting in the cool, salty breeze. The rain has stopped, and slivers of clouds pass in front of the moon. The ocean crashes in the distance. I grab a blanket and sit on the window seat, doing my best to clear my mind. I tune out the murmuring voices coming from downstairs and focus on the calming sounds of the tide. For the first time in weeks, I remember what it's like to relax. Maybe this *is* a good idea.

An hour later, I hear the shuffling of feet as my parents climb the stairs. One of them, more than likely my mom, pauses outside my door. I consider crawling into bed and pretending I'm asleep. I wait, half expecting her to come in and check on me the way she usually does, but instead, her footsteps retreat down the hallway.

The stage lights glare down on the actors, bathing them in a soft, white glow. From the wings, I watch a young man deliver his lines. A girl in a wedding dress watches him wistfully as he crosses the stage in front of her. When the guy turns, I'm shocked to see that he looks almost exactly like me. If I didn't know better, I might think it *was* me, but I've never been on stage in my life.

Before I can look closer, chaos erupts. A veil of dark smoke descends on the actors. The girl in white is knocked to the floor as her terrified cast mates rush to safety. The patrons in the audience all begin to scream, and a man shouts for everyone to stay calm and move toward the exits.

The girl struggles to stand as the entire theatre clears out. She screams for help, but no one comes. I try to go to her, but I can't move. It's almost as if my feet are nailed to the floor.

"Somebody help," I scream. "She needs help!"

Flames leap from the wings, racing across the stage like starving animals. They snap and curl toward her, closer with every breath. Despite the smoke, I can see her perfectly. Her skin glows angry red, blistering as though she's been baking in the sun for days. Her blonde hair clings to her skull in wet strands. She drags herself on hands and knees, coughing, eyes frantic for an exit.

Then she vanishes. A sharp gasp escapes me as she drops into the orchestra pit, swallowed whole by the dark below the stage. I wrench against whatever holds me, but my body is stone. My hands twitch uselessly at my sides while the fire thickens, climbing higher.

The stage groans, then buckles. Wood splinters, beams collapse, and the blaze devours everything. The heat sears my face. The air tastes like ash. How am I even able to breathe?

And then, silence. The flames die out just as quickly as they arrived. Smoke thins. I blink and find myself standing alone in the husk of the theatre. A strange, ghostly blue light washes over the ruins, and pieces of ash fall from the sky like snow. The entire back wall is gone. The ceiling yawns open, exposing the night sky. The putrid smell of burning wood and plastic hangs in the air. It fills my lungs, thick and noxious, until my mouth feels like I've been licking the bottom of a barbecue grill.

Through the eerie silence, a fragile sound cuts across the charred remains. Someone is crying.

I clamber over the debris of the demolished stage, stumbling through the soot, tripping over fallen beams. Gray dust slides beneath my shoes. Broken beams snag my legs. The crying echoes, everywhere at once, bouncing off the ruins. My heart thunders as I scan the rubble, desperate for any sign of her.

"Somebody, help!" My voice cracks, echoing in the silence.

I drop to my knees and dig. Splintered wood shifts beneath my fingers. The crying grows sharper, closer, until it drowns out everything else. I dig faster, splinters biting deep, the heat of half-burned timber searing my palms. I ignore the pain, digging deeper until my arms give out. I collapse on the mound of soft ash, defeated.

But the crying doesn't fade.

It swells.

Louder. Harsher. Almost inhuman.

The rubble shudders beneath me. Boards jump. Ash cascades down the heap as if something below strains to break free. I reach out, fingers closing on a beam rattling in place.

That's when the charred hand bursts through.

Fingers like burnt twigs clamp around my wrist. Charred skin peels away, exposing raw flesh and bone slick with soot.

I yank back, but the grip doesn't loosen. The skeletal fist pulls, steady and relentless, dragging me toward the rubble.

"No!" I scream, voice breaking. I thrash, claw at the ash, but the pull is stronger.

She wants me.

The crying twists into a howl. And I know, even before my mouth tears open again, that it won't matter. No one will hear me.

"Heath?"

My eyes snap open. I'm standing on the front porch of my uncle's house in nothing but my underwear. For a moment, I don't recognize where I am. Fog coils around me, and gulls shriek in the distance, their cries syncopated with the pounding of the surf.

"Honey? What are you doing out here?" Mom asks.

I just stare at her, words stuck in my throat, skin prickling with goose bumps.

"Heath? Is something wrong?"

I shake my head, taking in my surroundings. "No. I'm fine."

"What are you doing out here without any clothes on?"

I search my brain for an answer. Any excuse that would seem logical, but I can't find one. So, I turn around and walk inside.

CHAPTER THREE

After breakfast, my parents drive me to meet my new shrink. Mom's even more wound up after the sleepwalking incident, and I can't blame her. She grilled me while we waited for Dad. I snapped.

Shocker.

The truth is, I don't know how I ended up outside. Nothing like that has ever happened before. I'm just glad I didn't wander past the front porch. Wandering aimlessly around the beach in your undies isn't the best first impression in a new town.

What would the neighbors say?

I'm dreading today's adventure. The therapist is Dad's old high school friend, which immediately puts me on edge. If she is anything like my brain coach in Seattle, I'm doomed to a long, annoying summer. I'm tired of talking about my feelings. I'm sick of discussing the healing process and the stages of grief. There's nothing left to say. Nothing will change what happened. It's not as if my feelings are a cavity that can be drilled and then refilled, the pain gone, the tooth good as new.

Dad parks the car in front of a small olive-green house. Great. My feelings dealer works from home. She's not even good enough to have her own office. I picture a woman in a "Live, Laugh, Love" sweatshirt, oat milk latte in hand, and cats everywhere. She'll probably tell me she "totally gets it" before quoting Taylor Swift lyrics back at me. Maybe we'll stress-eat cupcakes while watching episodes of The Real Housewives and baking competition shows. Peak therapy right there.

I reluctantly follow my parents up the sidewalk. The freshly mown lawn sparkles with morning dew, heavy with the smell of roses. A small plaque beside the door reads Melanie Plummer, MD.

At least she has a plaque. That's very important.

We step inside. No cats. No recliner. Just a friendly older woman behind a desk and the clean smell of professional competence. Mom gives the receptionist my name. Then a door opens and out steps a woman with dark hair brushing her shoulders, green eyes sharp enough to pin me in place. Attractive.

Way too attractive for a shrink.

"Oh. My. God. Phil?" Her voice is somewhat smoky, but not in a phlegmy sort of way. More of a sexy, sultry, cabaret entertainer sort of way. Jake would have eaten this up.

She's casually dressed in a powder blue top and cream-colored pants. She doesn't look stuffy or rigid or overly clinical. She moves across the floor and pulls my dad in for a hug. "It's been ages."

"Melanie. Good to see you. This is my wife, Carol, and my son, Heath."

"So happy to meet you." She shakes my mother's hand before taking mine, staring intently into my face, almost as if she's reading my every thought. "He looks just like you, Phil. It's like you went back twenty-five years and cloned yourself."

She leads us down a bright hallway and into a room resembling a library. Bookcases stacked full of hardbound books and periodicals line the walls. Two large, maroon wingback chairs sit in front of the only window, and a small, striped sofa lies against the wall closest to the door.

Dr. Plummer offers us a seat. My parents claim the sofa, which means I have to sit in one of the chairs across from Dr. Plummer. I feel like I'm on display. Like one of those ladies you would see on old talk shows who thought she was on the show to get a makeover, but then ended up being confronted by her husband and his much younger lover.

What sort of dirty secrets will Dr. Plummer uncover today?

"Let me just start by saying that I don't claim to have all the answers," she begins. "I'm here to listen and help work through this as best I can."

I'm not sure if she's speaking to my parents or to me.

"We just want him to feel like his old self again. We want our son back." Mom's voice becomes cloudy as she falls into her weepy, pleading story. I've heard it so many times I can practically recite it, word for word.

"Your son is right here," Dr. Plummer tells her. "He hasn't gone anywhere."

She doesn't move to hug my mother or offer her promises she knows she can't keep. "He's still your son, Mrs. Ingram, and he's lived through a horrible ordeal. I can only begin to imagine the rage and guilt he's dealing with. He's going to have to live with the loss of his friends every day for the rest of his life."

No one's ever said this to me before. My brain doc in Seattle always preached about finding myself and moving on. He constantly assured my parents he would give them back the son they felt they'd lost. Not once did he ever say the things Dr. Plummer just said.

"I just want to help. I just want him to be happy. I want to be there for him, but he won't let me." Mom's voice turns whiny, almost pathetic in its desperation.

"Heath? Do you have anything you would like to say?" Dr.

Plummer asks.

"Not really." There's a lot I *could* say, but I don't feel like getting into it right now.

"He won't talk to us," my dad says. "We want to help, but we can't seem to get through to him."

"Would the two of you mind waiting out front for a bit?" Dr. Plummer asks. "I'd like to speak to Heath alone."

"I think it would be better if we were all here. I think it's important that we all be on the same page. He needs us," my mom says, crossing her legs and clutching her purse in defiance.

"Mom, please. Just go."

Wordlessly, my parents stand and move toward the door. Mom turns to me with sad eyes and a trembling lip, shocked I don't want her here.

"We'll just be a moment," Dr. Plummer says as she closes the door behind them.

We sit in silence. I'm not sure if she's waiting for me to say something, or if she's waiting to make sure my parents are out of earshot.

"Wow, no wonder you have anxiety problems." Her lips quirk up.

The tight coil in my gut releases. Finally, someone who gets it.

In twenty minutes, I open up to Dr. Plummer more than I did in six weeks with my Seattle shrink. Not once does she promise to cure me. She just wants to help me heal, which is exactly what I need.

As we pull out of the driveway after my session, my mom immediately begins complaining about Dr. Plummer. "She seems too detached. Surely, he can see someone better while he's here. He needs someone more assertive. I don't trust her."

I put my earbuds in to tune her out. I don't care what she says. Today was the first time I've felt that someone heard what I had to say.

Later that afternoon, after hours of browsing antique shops

and lunch at a local diner, we pull up to the theatre. In the daylight, it doesn't look nearly as ominous. In fact, it looks drastically out of place. The pastel yellow paint is bright and cheery, a steep contrast to the lifeless brick buildings that line the nearby streets. The parking lot is empty except for Uncle Vic's old Ford, a newer truck, and a silver convertible.

Inside, fresh paint and sawdust fill my nostrils. Sunlight catches the lobby chandelier, scattering rainbow fragments across the walls. The high ceiling makes my neck ache as I crane back to take it all in. There's a large staircase in front of us that I assume leads to the theatre. Framed posters in the windows announce *Chicago* and *Our Town* as the summer shows.

"This is so exciting," Mom says as she walks around drooling over the decor, her heels clicking against the ceramic tile floor. I've grown used to the sound. She never goes anywhere without heels, wanting to appear tall and powerful instead of short and pixie-like. Dad likes to tease her that she has a Chihuahua complex.

"Isn't it beautiful, honey?" she asks my father, but he doesn't respond. He hasn't moved or said a word since we entered the building. He seems lost in thought. A shudder runs down his spine as if someone just tickled the back of his neck with a feather.

"So, what do you think?" Vic asks, appearing from a doorway to our right, flanked by a petite blonde.

"It's absolutely breathtaking," my mother gushes.

"Looks the same as before, huh, Phil?" Vic asks my dad, who still looks hypnotized.

"Yeah. Amazing," he says, finally coming to.

I barely hear a word of what they're saying because all of my attention is focused on the girl with Vic. She's about my age, average height, no more than five-foot-six with a slender build. Her blonde hair is pulled back in a ponytail. She wears gray, cutoff sweatpants rolled down, resting lightly on her hips. Sweat glistens on her chest, just above her light-blue tank top.

She looks almost exactly like Amy.

My breath catches as a vision of the last time I saw her alive flashes through my head. Trapped under the twisted metal of the Jeep, blood trickling from her mouth, reaching for me with desperate fingers. Amy. My 'girlfriend'. My cover story.

The lie that kept everyone from knowing about Jake and me.

She smiles when she notices me staring, and I turn away, embarrassed. I'm sure I gave her the wrong idea.

"Hi, I'm Molly," she says, walking toward me with an outstretched hand.

Before I can respond, the door swings open behind her. A guy steps through. Tall, dark reddish-brown hair, athletic shorts that leave little to the imagination. My breath catches. Wow. Haven't felt that in a while.

"Heath." I shake Molly's hand, but I can't take my eyes off the guy behind her. It feels like cheating on Jake. But I can't look away.

She catches my gaze and turns to acknowledge the guy behind her. "This is my friend, Cole."

He sticks his hand out. "Hey there."

I falter for a second, like I've forgotten how to shake hands. His eyebrows furrow, and suddenly I realize he's waiting for me to respond.

"Heath. I'm… uh… my name's Heath."

"Ah! You must be Vic's nephew," he says. His eyes are incredibly chocolaty. Dark and kind.

Inviting.

"Yeah, that's me."

His smile is warm and genuine. "Cool. I'm sure we'll be seeing a lot of each other this summer."

I nod awkwardly.

The two of them stand there, like they're ready to strike up a conversation. For some reason, my mouth has forgotten how to speak, so I look away. Mostly because I'm afraid that if I don't, I'll just stare at Cole and make things even more awkward.

"Well, we should probably get going," Cole says. "Early rehearsal tomorrow."

Molly waves and winks at me. "I'm sure we'll be seeing you around."

They start toward the door. "Bye, Vic."

"Good night, you two. Great work today." Vic turns to me after they've left. "She's single. Very sweet girl."

I watch Cole toss his bag in the back of the convertible. Vic follows my gaze and gives me a knowing smile. "He's single too. Also very sweet."

He winks. My face burns so hot it might explode. I duck down to retie a shoe that doesn't need it, just to avoid his gaze.

"You want a tour? Let me show you around," Vic says.

Dad shakes his head and backs toward the door. "I need to get back to the house and make a few phone calls."

"Oh, come on," my mother says, "I want to see the theatre."

"Go ahead. Vic can bring you back to the house. I've been gone all day. My email box is probably full."

Lame excuse. He's taken calls and typed on his phone all day. Something has him spooked. I've never seen him act this way.

"Want to join us, Heath?" Vic asks.

"Nah, I'm really tired. I think I'll go with Dad," I tell them.

We head back to the house in silence, the drive short but heavy. I spend the rest of the afternoon camped out in front of the television while my dad snores in the recliner. Vic and my mom show up an hour and a half later with buckets of fried shrimp, clam strips, clam chowder, and sourdough bread for dinner. I eat until I can't hold anything more. By the time I go up to my room, I feel as though I'm eight months pregnant. Or at least this is how I imagine it would feel.

I throw on a pair of gym shorts in the event I decide to sleepwalk again, crack open the window to let in the cool breeze, and crawl into bed. I doze off, thinking about Molly and how she reminded me of Amy. And Cole. His smile. His legs. The way his dark eyes crinkled at the corners.

Stop. You don't need to get involved. Look what happened to Jake.

I fall asleep hating myself.

CHAPTER FOUR

Something besides dreams of crashing vehicles and dead friends tears me from sleep. I bolt upright, lungs pumping. The room is freezing, and a sharp knot pulls at my neck as if I've been lying in one position for hours.

Then I hear it.

A voice.

It floats in faint and broken, carried on the wind. I crawl out of bed and move toward the window, rubbing at my eyes. At the far edge of the property, something pale flickers against the dark. A dress? A figure? Fog curls around it, swallowing details. Clouds smother the moon, leaving me blind to anything but impressions. But I know what I saw. Someone was out there.

Then she calls again.

"Phillip!"

Who is yelling for my dad?

I shove the window open, wood squealing in protest. A warm summer breeze pours over me, caressing my skin, the sounds of the nearby ocean greeting me.

"Phillip! Come down. Please?"

A woman's voice, sharp, urgent.

I lean out farther, scanning the yard. The figure is gone. Only the restless sway of the trees and the pulse of the ocean in the distance remain. I hold still, waiting for another word. Nothing.

Shaking, I slam the window shut.

And that's when I see her.

A face pressed against the glass. White skin stretched tight, eyes wide and unblinking. Her breath fogs the window in ragged patches. Her mouth opens in a silent scream.

I stumble backward and whip around, ready to confront her.

But there's no one.

Just me and the shadows.

When I look again, the glass shows only my reflection.

I crawl back into bed, pulling the covers up, whispering to myself that it wasn't real. Just my mind cracking in the dark. But the cold lingers, and I can't shake the weight of her eyes boring through me.

Eventually, my thoughts unravel, slipping loose one by one. The ceiling blurs, the dark folds in, and I drift off...

Water laps at my feet, jolting me awake. The fog presses in, thick as steam in a sauna. I shouldn't be out here. I need to go back inside, but I don't know which way to turn. I can barely see in front of me and have no idea how to get back to Vic's house.

"What are you doing out here?" A man's voice cuts through the mist. He must be talking to me, but before I can answer, another voice speaks.

"I needed to see you."

"I just saw you a few hours ago." His tone is clipped, weary. His voice sounds familiar, but I can't quite place it against the crashing waves.

"But you hardly talked to me. I've been waiting for you to come back for months, and when you finally do, you spend all your time with them," the girl whines.

"They're my friends. What do you expect?"

"What about me? I thought I was your friend."

"You are." His reply is flat and lifeless. Even I'm not convinced.

I stand frozen, caught between fear and curiosity. I don't want to eavesdrop, but I can't see through the fog, and I don't want to startle them.

"Is that all? Just a friend? I'm so tired of you jerking me around. I don't get you. Why do you do this to me?" Her voice cracks, and now she's sobbing.

He tries to soothe her. "I'm sorry you feel that way. I thought we had an understanding. I'm in college now."

"Oh, well, I'd hate to ruin your reputation," she spits through her tears. "Mister smart college man can't date the daughter of the town junkie. Is that what you're saying?"

"I don't know what you want me to say. Last year was fun, but we both knew it wouldn't last. I told you that. We agreed—"

"I don't care what we agreed," she snaps, cutting him off. "It's different now. I miss you, Phillip. I need you. Please? Can't we talk about this?"

My stomach drops. Phillip? Is she talking to my dad?

"It's over," he says firmly. "I'm sorry. I can't do this anymore. You have to go. You shouldn't be out here. It's late. Go home." His footsteps retreat as she sobs.

Panic drives me forward. I need to catch him before he makes it back to the house. I need answers.

"Don't leave me!"

A hand bursts through the fog and clamps on my arm, spinning me around. A young woman, no older than sixteen, stands before me, her ice-blue eyes smudged with black mascara. She latches onto my wrist, pulling me toward her. She's surprisingly strong.

"I'll change. I promise. I need you, Phillip. Please?" Her nails pierce my skin, drawing blood that glints in the moonlight. Where she touches me, my flesh burns. "Don't leave me. I need you."

I wrench against her grip, but she clings with desperate strength. Her bloodshot eyes bore into mine, refusing to let me look away. As I fight her off, her clothes shred and her hands blacken. Her eyes bulge, skin sloughing from her skull. Smoke spills from her mouth.

"Don't. Leave. Me. Again." The words rasp out, guttural, more growl than human.

My eyes flash open, and I bolt upright in bed. My mother stands over me, and I have to stop myself from smacking her. She scared the hell out of me.

"You must've been dead asleep." She sits beside me, the bed sinking beneath her small frame.

"Yeah, I guess," I say, trying to shake the image of the half-barbecued girl from my mind.

"Your father and I have to leave soon, and Uncle Victor needs you at the theatre today."

"Okay, I'll be down in a minute," I say, noticing the fresh scratches on my wrist.

"What happened?" Mom grabs my arm, worry etched into her face. I know what she's thinking.

"I don't know. I must have scratched myself in my sleep." It's the only plausible explanation.

She studies me for a long moment, lips pressed tight like she wants to argue. She sighs and releases my arm, then smooths the blanket on the edge of the bed. "Don't be long," she says softly before slipping out the door. Her eyes linger on me one last time, heavy with concern.

When she's gone, I drag myself out of bed and throw on some clothes before heading down for breakfast. It's going to be weird not having my parents around, but I can honestly say I'm looking forward to it.

"Pancakes or waffles?" Uncle Vic stands at the stove, a spatula in each hand. The smell of pancake batter and frying bacon fills the room. I'm surprised to find that I'm hungry after gorging myself last night. If I keep eating this way, I'm going to gain about fifty pounds. My father sits at the table, massaging a cup of coffee as he stares vacantly out the window. I pull out a chair and sit, snapping him out of his thoughts.

"Morning, son," he says as he lifts the cup to his lips and sips his coffee.

"Morning."

"How'd you sleep?"

"Fine. You?" A little small talk won't kill me. I won't see him for at least another six weeks.

"Not so well," he admits and leaves it at that. I want to ask if he heard the girl on the beach calling his name, but he couldn't have. It was a dream. Right?

"Eat up." Vic places two plates full of sausage, bacon, pancakes, and waffles on the table. There's enough food here to feed the entire town. I don't know who he thinks will eat all of this.

I pick at the pancakes, listening to my parents and Vic talk around me, their voices little more than background noise. My mind drifts elsewhere.

When the plates are finally cleared, I slip out the back door and down the steps, listening to the ocean. I scan the beach, focusing on the spot where I saw, or at least thought I saw, the girl in the white dress from my window last night.

"What you looking for?" I spin around at the sound of Dad's voice, almost losing my balance.

"Nothing, really. Just listening to the ocean." I walk over and sink onto the middle step.

He takes a seat beside me, and we sit in silence for what feels like forever. It's weird. We used to be able to sit and talk for hours.

"You'll be okay here."

Is that a question or a command?

I shrug. "I don't really have a choice, do I?"

"We're not doing this because we don't love you. We're doing it because we do," he explains, even though he doesn't need to. When I don't say anything, he continues. "I don't want you to feel like we're dumping you off. We want you to be safe, and honestly, we don't want a repeat of what happened... before..." He means when I slit my wrists while he and my mother were away at a dinner party. Why can't he just say it?

"Heath, we—"

"I know, Dad," I cut him off. "You don't have to explain. I'll be fine."

Just go already.

He looks at me like there's something he needs to tell me, but instead, he turns and looks back at the ocean. "Uncle Vic is doing us a huge favor, and it'll be nice if you don't give him any trouble. He has a lot on his plate right now. He could really use your help. That's why I thought this would be good for you."

I want to ask why he brought me here if he thought I was going to be trouble, but I just nod instead.

"Take this," he says, handing me a credit card. "I trust you with this. Only use it to buy things you need. Uncle Vic wouldn't take any money, but I can't expect him to pay for everything."

"Thanks."

"Promise me you'll take your meds and you'll keep your appointments with Dr. Plummer. If you feel overwhelmed or scared, tell someone. Call me. We're all here for you. You know we love you." He places a hand on my shoulder and gives it a firm squeeze.

"I know. I'll be fine, Dad. Really. I'm going to be fine." What I mean is I want to be fine. I hope that someday, I will be.

He stands, patting me on the back, and walks up the last step. "Why don't you come in and tell your mother goodbye? We need to leave soon."

Old boards clunk as he crosses the porch and enters the house. I sit for a moment longer, and then stand to retrace his steps.

"We need to get going, kiddo," my mother says as she moves

toward me. "I'm not looking forward to that long drive back."

Then why did you come?

"Okay," I say without moving.

"I'll see you in a few weeks." She pulls me in for a tight hug. I can tell she's crying. Her grip tightens like she's trying to memorize the feel of me in case something happens and she never sees me again.

"I'm going to be fine, Mom," I say, patting her on the back. "Don't worry."

It's enough to placate her for the time being. She wipes her eyes and smiles, then reaches up to kiss me on the cheek.

I follow my parents to the front door, my feet dragging against the hardwood. My neck and shoulders tighten with each step. When Mom reaches for another hug, I take a half-step back before catching myself.

I hate goodbyes.

Dad wraps his arms around my neck. "We'll see you soon, son. Be careful," he whispers.

Careful of what?

"See ya," I say as he pulls away.

"I'll call you when we get home," my mother tells me.

She's crying again. It seems like she's always crying.

I stand on the porch and watch them load their things into the car, more out of a sense of obligation than actually wanting to. I wave as they back out of the driveway and watch their car disappear around the bend. The knot in my chest loosens.

Suddenly, I can breathe again.

CHAPTER FIVE

I stand on the porch for a moment, almost expecting my parents to come back, the grief of leaving me too much for them, but it doesn't happen. I breathe in the salty morning air. The sky is clear, and the breeze cool, the miserable wetness from the day before a distant memory.

I feel invigorated. For the first time in months, I want to be outside instead of locked in a room, wrestling with my guilt. I'd love to sit on the beach all day and stare out at the ocean, but I know that isn't in the plans.

"You ready to go?" Uncle Vic asks as he locks the front door. I want to tell him that I'd rather walk, but I don't want to be rude.

"We could walk, but who knows when a storm might blow in," he says, reading my mind. "That and the fact that I'm a lazy bastard and would rather drive the half-mile than waste my much-needed energy walking."

I laugh and follow him to the old, rusty Ford that sits in the driveway. The passenger door shrieks in protest when I open it.

I prop my left foot on the floor and lift myself up, closing the door behind me. This thing is ancient. I'm surprised it still runs.

We drive across the bridge toward the theatre in silence. I'm a little apprehensive about meeting everyone. They've had time to get to know one another. I feel like I'm the new kid in school. What do they know about me? What has Vic told them? Are they going to look at me weird? Like I'm dangerous or severely messed up? My chest tightens. Shit. I forgot my anxiety meds this morning.

When we get there, Uncle Vic pulls around to the back and parks in front of a door that reads *Theatre Staff Only*. He turns off the truck and sits. I reach for the door, but he stops me.

"I just want you to know that you can talk to me," he begins. The familiar hint of annoyance surfaces. What is it with these people? Always wanting to talk about feelings.

"But I don't expect you to," he continues. "In fact, I'm not going to say another word about why you're really here. As far as I'm concerned, you're here because you love theatre and you wanted to spend your summer helping me out. I have a great group of college kids working here, and my staff is friendly. I think you'll get on just fine with everyone. They know that my nephew is coming, but they don't know why. You don't have to share any more than you want. Okay?"

"Okay." This eases the anxiety quite a bit.

"At the same time, it's up to me to keep you busy and keep you safe. If you feel overwhelmed, or depressed, or anything, you have to tell me. There will also be rules. Before you go anywhere, you need to tell me where you're going and when I can expect you home. If you can do that, we'll have no problems. Deal?"

"Deal," I tell him. I don't see myself going anywhere other than home and to the theatre, so this shouldn't be a problem.

"What are you waiting for? Let's get inside and get to work," he says with a smile.

I open my door and manage to get out without falling. I'm

relieved that he didn't mention my obvious attraction to Cole again. I've not come out to my parents. I honestly don't know how they'd take it. So many of their friends are conservative. I know Vic is gay, and they seem fine with that, but what if it's different when it's their son? I guess if anything Vic would be the right one to confide in.

Maybe another time.

I follow him up to the door and watch as he punches in a code.

"Two-four-nine-nine-seven," he speaks aloud. "In case you need to get in. That's the secret code."

As soon as I walk through the door, orange light flashes through the room, and the strong smell of smoke follows. It's gone as quickly as it appeared. It takes me by surprise and for a moment, my bearings are off. I grab the wall to steady myself.

"You okay?" Vic asks.

"Just lost my footing," I say. "I'm okay."

He passes a worried glance my way before leading me into a large open space. The sound of hammering echoes from somewhere deeper in the building, and I can hear voices. A woman says something and a deep, booming laugh follows.

"This is the scene shop." Sawdust covers the back part of the floor. Boxes of nails and screws sit on shelves above a row of power tools hanging from the wall. To my right is a long rack that contains tall, thick pieces of lumber. A guy with dark hair kneels beside a platform, measuring something with a tape measure. My pulse kicks up when he looks over, and I realize it's Cole.

"Hey, Vic," Cole calls, standing and dusting off his knees. His gray T-shirt clings to his chest, damp with sweat. "Almost finished with this group of flats. I'll be in for rehearsal as soon as I get this placed and can get changed."

"Great. You remember my nephew?"

"Hey." Cole's smile is genuine, and when he walks over to shake my hand, I notice paint smudges on his forearms. "How's it going?"

"Good," I manage, hoping my voice sounds normal.

"Cole is a jack of all trades. He builds sets, acts, directs, and is one hell of a singer and dancer."

"Thanks, Vic." I can't help but smile when I see the way Cole blushes at Vic's compliment. "See you in a bit."

He walks away, and I force myself not to look at his ass.

"This is where the set pieces are built," Vic says, gesturing to the space around us. "These are flats and platforms. Flats are used to construct the set walls, and platforms are used to build floors and set levels." I follow him and try to stay focused, but part of my attention drifts toward Cole as he holds a flat in place while a middle-aged man uses a drill to anchor it to the floor.

Vic takes me past a large sink and then several shelves filled with various paint cans and brushes. I follow him out to the stage. The set is only half-built and unpainted, more framework than scenery, with sheets of plywood propped like ribs waiting for skin. I stare out at the sea of maroon seats, imagining the patrons that will fill them in a few days.

I peer over the edge of the orchestra pit, remembering the girl from my dream. Orange light flashes again, and a scream echoes in my ears. I stumble backward, but manage to catch myself before tumbling into the pit. My pulse hammers. What the hell is going on? My hands go clammy, my forehead beads with sweat. I can't have a panic attack. Not now.

I look around, making sure no one noticed. Cole has left, and the middle-aged guy is back in the scene shop.

"Heath, let me show you the prop room."

I follow Vic's voice offstage and find him at the bottom of a set of stairs.

"The prop and costume rooms are up here," he tells me as he starts up. He moves much faster than I, so he ends up waiting for me at the top. When I get there, I find myself in a huge room lined with shelves filled with everything from books, dishes, and glasses to vases, pictures, and luggage. It's like a resale shop on steroids.

"I could use your help up here the next few days," he tells me. "Since you're not familiar with building set pieces or able to climb a ladder to hang lights, I'm going to have you do inventory. We've had a ton of donations the last several weeks, and I need to have a record of everything. I know it's not very exciting, but it needs to be done."

He hands me two large binders and a laptop, then walks me through the layout of the prop room. "These two boxes need sorted and cataloged," he says, indicating two large storage boxes sitting on the floor.

"I haven't even had a chance to get started on the costumes yet." He flips a light switch and leads me into the next room. For being a new theatre, there sure is a ton of stuff. There are at least ten long rows of clothing in here.

"My rehearsal starts in an hour. We'll be in the rehearsal hall. If you need anything before then, I'll be down in my office." He leaves me standing in the doorway between costumes and props, trying to decide which to tackle first. I decide to sort through the boxes on the prop room floor. It seems like a much less daunting task.

After I've labeled the various plates and cups from the first box, I open the second, which is filled with books. I begin the tedious job of documenting every title and then placing each book on the appropriate shelf. This is so boring.

I reach into the box and pull out a composition book. I'd had to have one of these black-and-white notebooks for my English lit class back in high school. Written on the front in neat, cursive writing is a name. Catherine. The cover is worn, the pages yellowed with age. My curiosity gets the better of me, and I open it to the first page:

October 3
Well, it happened. I have a boyfriend. He's amazing. He's

a senior. I was afraid my mom would totally freak out about it since I'm only a freshman, but I think the fact that he has money made her happy. What's even better than her being happy? I'm happy. For the first time in five months, I can honestly say things are looking up for me. After Daddy died, I wasn't sure how I was going to make it. I think I found my answer.

December 20

I'm so bad about keeping up with this journal. I have a very good reason, though. I'm in love! Yes, it's true. Catherine Whitley is 100% in love. I don't think I've ever been this happy in my whole life. Phillip means the world to me. I know it's love because I would do anything for him, and I hate being away from him. He's out of town this week visiting relatives for Christmas. I can't wait until he's back. I miss him so much.

Part of me feels like I'm invading someone's private life, but the curious part of me—the part that believes Phillip could be my father—decides to read further.

Footsteps echo up the stairs, accompanied by voices. The intrusive whirring of power tools and hammers starts up again from below. I grab the journal and take it into the costume room where it's quieter.

I walk to the far wall and pull my phone from my pocket to check the time. It's only 11:00. I place my phone on the shelf next to the rows of shoes, take a seat on the step stool, and crack open the journal.

January 5

Phillip and I were supposed to see a movie tonight, but he canceled on me to hang out with his friends. I don't understand why I couldn't join them. He said it was a party for seniors. He just got back a week ago, and I've only seen him once. I hate this. Why does it hurt so much? I keep telling myself it's only one night, but I miss him.

March 3
I snuck out tonight and went to Phillip's house. I threw rocks at his window until he finally woke up. At first, he was mad, but I finally convinced him to come down and talk to me. I know it was a stupid thing to do. My mom would've killed me if she'd known. Then again, she's been high or drunk pretty much every day for the last month. The only things she notices anymore are the men she brings home. It's like I don't even exist.

That doesn't matter, though. I have Phillip. The way he held me, protecting me from the cold wind that blew off the ocean will stay with me forever. Everything seems right when I'm in his arms. So long as I have him, everything will be okay.

April 5
Our power is off again. Mom's running around, screaming like a lunatic. She claims she paid the bill. I didn't bother asking with what money. She was fired, again, last week. I hate it here.

Wow. So much teen angst. This is kind of cringe, but I also kind of can't look away. Was I ever this dramatic?

April 12
I started babysitting to bring in a little extra money. I can't get a real job for another year because I'm not sixteen yet. Not many people want the daughter of the town pariah to babysit for them, though. The good news is, Melanie talked to her mom, and they're going to let me come in and help at the diner a couple nights a week and pay me cash. I'll also clean their house once a week. Every little bit helps.

Phillip is busy with swim team. I hate that I don't see him much. He's always at practice or at a meet. I miss him. Why do I feel so empty when he's not around?

May 3

My mom has a new boyfriend. This is the first guy she's had that she's kept around for more than a week. She let him move in, and it sucks. I don't understand how she can do this. My father's been dead for just over a year, and she's already shacked up with more men than I can count on one hand.

She treats me like shit. Last night I woke up to find him watching me sleep, and when I told her, she blamed me. She said I should have locked my door. I shouldn't dress the way I do.

And she's always so angry. When I asked her if she was taking her medication, she said she couldn't afford it anymore. I wanted to tell her she might be able to if she'd lay off the drugs and alcohol, but I didn't want to get smacked again.

Light footsteps echo from a few rows over, pulling my attention away from the journal. I freeze.

"Hello?"

No answer. The footsteps continue, soft and hesitant. I peer around the rack of costumes. "Vic?"

A soft sound drifts from a few aisles over.

"Is someone there?" I edge down the rows of costumes. Each rack sways as I pass, but no one appears. Four rows down, I catch a glimpse of a foot and a flash of white fabric at the end of the aisle. Someone is walking along the back wall.

"Hello?" Again, no one answers. My skin prickles.

That's it. I need a break.

Just as I move toward the prop room, the tap of small footsteps drifts from the stairs at the far end of the costume room. The racks of clothing stand still, shadows pressed between them. I fix my eyes on the back wall, expecting movement.

Nothing.

Invisible threads tug me toward the door. Each step is careful, reluctant. Every instinct begs me to turn back, to go downstairs where there are people. My body refuses to listen.

I step toward the door and stop. A sound bleeds from behind the walls. I press my ear to the door.

Someone is crying.

It's not a wail or even anger. It's the sound of a heart breaking.

I don't know what comes over me, but I try the doorknob. It's locked. I knock softly, and the crying continues. I knock again, this time a little louder.

"Are you okay?"

Still no answer. I try the door again, thinking maybe it was just stuck, but it still won't budge. I give the door a shake and suddenly the doorknob burns in my hand, sending searing pain through my palm. I jerk away, hissing through my teeth. The crying has stopped, but the silence feels worse.

I back away from the door, palm throbbing, and force myself down the stairs. What the fuck is happening to me?

CHAPTER SIX

I edge down the stairs. The door behind me seems to pulse with malevolent energy, as if something behind it strains against the wood. When I reach the landing of the costume room, I make my way back down to the scene shop. A couple of guys, both about my age, struggle with flats stacked on the top shelf against the far wall. A tall, skinny guy is up on the edge of the top shelf, trying to hand the other guy one of the flats.

I watch them for a moment. The shorter of the two, with blonde surfer dude hair and the build of a gym bro, turns and looks at me.

"Give us a hand," he tells me. I hate when people tell me to do things rather than ask. I trudge down the stairs and over to them.

"Could you maybe move a little faster?" he asks. "Help me hold this so it doesn't fall."

I stand against the shelf and grab the bottom of the flat as the skinny guy lowers it to us. Once it's down, Blondie Bro flips it over and carries it to the stage without even acknowledging me. What a dick.

"Heya. I'm Luke." Skinny guy shimmies down the side of the shelf like a monkey. He's a couple inches taller than me and about fifty pounds lighter with a mop of shaggy chestnut hair. He reminds me of a pencil with a patchy beard and wide-rimmed glasses.

"I'm Heath," I tell him, still pissed at the dick that just snubbed me after I helped them out.

"Vic's nephew? Bruh, I know you. Our dads were high school buddies. We met a long time ago." He offers me his hand, and I study his face, trying to match it with a memory, but it doesn't happen. "You don't remember me, do you?"

"Bad memory," I say as I shake his hand. "Nice to meet you… again."

"The guy who just snubbed you is Ryan. He's kind of a dick, but we're stuck with him for the summer. He's an architecture student from the University of Oregon. He's in charge of the set design for the musical. He likes to boss the younger people around. Makes him feel important." He says this with a shrug, as if that's an excuse for acting like an asshole. "His dad grew up around here. He owns a bunch of hotels along the coast or something. I guess he's like a multimillionaire. Totally loaded. And he's sponsoring the summer shows, so we kind of have to play nice. Come on, I'll introduce you to everyone."

I follow him through the scene shop, dodging sawdust piles and paint cans along the way.

"So Seattle, huh? Cool city. I'm from Salem originally, but I visit here every summer. You been to Rock Harbor much before this?"

He barely takes a breath. The questions come rapid-fire, making it impossible to answer any of them.

"I'm actually north of Seattle, and no—"

"What college do you go to? Oregon State, here. You go to UW?"

"No, I did two years of community college and—"

"Your Uncle Vic's been talking nonstop about you coming to help for the last couple of weeks. Are you hurt?" He finally notices my limp.

"No, I'm fine."

"But you're limping. Do you need some ice? Did you fall?"

"I'm fine." My jaw clenches. His constant yakking is like listening to my parents. I can't get a word in edgewise.

"It's cool, man. I just wanted to make sure you were all right."

My irritation must have shown. Now I feel guilty. He was just trying to be friendly.

"I was in an accident back in March. I have a pin in my hip. I've only been able to walk again for a few weeks now."

"Oh, shit. That really sucks. What happened?"

I start to shrug him off, but stop myself when I notice the genuine look of concern on his face. "Car accident."

"That sucks."

He has no idea how much it sucks.

"Hey, everyone, I'd like to introduce you to Heath. He's Vic's nephew."

Every head swivels my way, a wall of eyes pinning me in place. I'm suddenly on display. Heat creeps up my neck.

"That's Ray," he says, pointing to the middle-aged man I saw earlier. He's a stocky, fireplug of a man, and he waves from atop a very tall ladder. "Ray is our technical director."

He points to a woman in the distance. "That's Jenny, Ray's wife and our resident faux painting expert."

Jenny is a plump woman with stringy blonde hair pulled back in a headband. She looks like a hugger—the aunt that insists on pinching your cheeks and smothering you with kisses at family reunions. She waves at me, ignoring the splatters of paint that fall from her brush onto the floor.

"You've met Ryan." He indicates the guy from earlier, who still doesn't acknowledge me.

"And this little lump of love is my best friend and partner in crime, Josie," Luke says, tugging the pigtail of the girl standing next to him. She's short, and standing next to Luke, she looks like a gothic garden gnome, but radiates a jagged kind of cool. Her jet-black hair teases blonde roots. A pink stripe runs across the front like a neon beacon. She wears a black T-shirt, cutoff jean shorts over fishnets, and clunky boots. She's a whole vibe.

She smiles and gives a small wave that's almost a salute. "Hi, Heath. I vaguely remember you from when we were younger. How are you?"

"Fine, thanks." I study her face, but she doesn't look familiar either.

"Josie's our costume goddess. She's here for an internship as well. We both attend Oregon State."

"Are you guys…?" I ask, assuming they're dating.

"Oh, God. Eww. No," Josie says. "We're just really close friends. No relation and definitely not dating. We've known each other for years."

"Josie's girlfriend is playing the lead in Chicago."

"Correction, she's the understudy to one of the leads," Josie says.

Girlfriend. Wow. I majorly screwed that one up. "Oh, okay," I stammer. "Sorry for assuming—"

"That I'm straight? It's cool. It happens. Heteronormativity, am I right?" She shrugs like she gets this all the time.

"Yeah, we're just a couple of jolly homos," Luke says. "Welcome to the family."

I can't help but laugh. I could probably be friends with these two. In school, I'd always thought theatre geeks were beneath me. I didn't venture far outside of my clique of jocks and cheerleaders. It was a good way for Jake and me to hide our feelings for one another. We stayed far away from anyone or anything that might place suspicion on us. I feel a twinge of guilt as I realize that had Josie and Luke gone to my school, I probably would've made fun of them.

"Heads!" Ray shouts just as his tool belt hits the ground.

Screwdrivers and wrenches scatter across the floor.

"Shit, man. Are you trying to kill me?" Ryan yells.

"Everyone all right?" Ray calls as he descends the ladder.

Ryan glares at the older man. "Barely. I was almost impaled by your screwdriver."

I move to help Ray pick up the tools. Ryan storms by, purposely knocking into me.

I stumble, barely catching my balance before falling. "What the fuck, dude?"

"Stay out of my way," he says, chest puffed and shoulders back as if he's trying to intimidate me.

"Calm down, CrossFit. I wasn't in your way." I step closer, matching his aggressive stance. He might try to intimidate the new kids, but I'm not going to be one of them. I don't care how much money his dad has.

"Keep poking at me, bro. I dare you." His nostrils flare, and he glares at me. Some people work extra hard at being assholes. Ryan makes it look effortless.

Luke steps between us, arms outstretched. "Relax, you two. We're not auditioning for America's Next Top Alpha Male."

I step around him and get in Ryan's face. "You dare me, huh? You might start shit, but I guarantee I'll end it."

He shoves me, and I stumble. Luke reaches out with his wiry arms and grabs me before I can hit the floor. Heat pours over me. Not just anger, but something deeper. It's a dark rage that's been simmering since the accident. I want to hurt something. Someone. Ryan's just given me permission.

I break free and shove Ryan hard. He goes down.

He's up in a flash, coming at me. He swings and I duck, but instead of tackling him, I step back. The pain in my hip flares, reminding me of my limitations. I'm not the same person who could once throw down without consequences.

"Break it up!" Vic storms onto the stage and steps between us. "What the hell's wrong with you two?"

"You'd better tell your nephew to stay out of my way," Ryan huffs and storms off toward the scene shop.

"What happened?" Vic asks me. I watch Ryan retreat, my fists still clenched.

"It wasn't his fault," Luke says. "Ryan was being a dick and pushed him for no reason. Heath was just sticking up for himself."

"I'd appreciate it if you don't pick fights with him."

"I didn't pick a fight with him."

"Heath, Ryan's a cocky little shit. He likes to think he's in charge. I know it's frustrating, but his dad is sponsoring the season. If we lose Ryan, we lose our funding. If you can't get along with him, then stay out of his way. Okay?"

I don't answer. I'm still burning holes into Ryan's skull as I glare at him across the way.

"Heath? Can you do that for me?" Vic asks as he turns me toward him.

"Yeah," I tell him, though I'm not thoroughly convinced I can.

"Why don't you call it a day? Go grab some lunch or something. I'll be finished with my rehearsal in a few hours, then I have some paperwork to finish up. You can take the truck if you want. Just come back and pick me up around 6:00."

"We can take him, Vic," Luke says. "Josie and I were going to go grab a bite now anyway. You want to join us, Heath?"

The fire settles in my soul, rage retreating. I want to disappear, but maybe I need allies more than solitude. "Sure."

I follow them down a long hallway to the rehearsal hall. The actors are all on break and fill the hallway. Josie stops to speak to a girl who is a few inches taller than she is. She has dark skin and eyes, the complete opposite of Josie.

"That's Patrice, Josie's girlfriend," Luke tells me. "And that's Molly." He points to the girl I met yesterday. She turns and catches us looking at her. When she sees me, her face lights up.

"Heath!" She practically bounces over to us, like she's known me for years. "How was your first day? Are you surviving the manual labor?"

She steps into my personal space, her hand resting on my arm as she talks. Luke notices and wiggles his eyebrows at me.

"It's fine," I manage, stepping back slightly.

"Well, I'm glad to see you're settling in. A bunch of us from the cast are meeting up later to grab drinks and play pool. You should come." Her smile is bright and expectant.

"Um, maybe." The words taste like chalk in my mouth. "We were just heading to lunch…"

"Oh, fun! Where?"

"The diner," Luke says.

She barely glances at him. "I love that place. Their milkshakes are amazing. Try the salted caramel one. It's my fave."

"Sounds good." Why is she standing so close?

"Well, you all enjoy." She squeezes my arm before heading back to the other actors.

Luke immediately starts to laugh. "Dude, she is thirsty for you."

"Whatever." I play dumb.

"You can't tell me you didn't notice. Several guys in the cast and on the crew have been trying to get her to notice them for the past three weeks, and then you walk in and she's all over you. And on your first day."

Cole walks by and taps me on the shoulder, and I completely stop listening to Luke. He winks, and my face flushes. I struggle to find something to say, but words fail me. Again. This is not lost on Luke.

"Oh, shit. Oh, man, I would not have clocked that."

"What?" I ask.

"You're one of us?" A smile spreads across his face.

I look away, not ready for this conversation right now.

"But for the record, Cole and I are kind of seeing each other.

It's not super serious."

"Really?" I ask. For some reason Luke doesn't look like Cole's type.

"I mean, we have been flirting a lot, and Josie says he's into me, so…"

I nod. "Cool." Not like I had any intention of hooking up with him anyway. I'm not here for that.

"But there are lots of guys here. We can find you someone to have a summer fling with. You're fresh meat, and you know how horny gay guys can be. And straight guys if they get enough beers in them, amiright?"

"Could you not…" I say, glancing around.

"Oh." Understanding clouds his face. "You're not out?"

I don't reply. I don't know what to say.

"It's totally cool, dude. theatre people are built different. This is a safe space. Trust me. You have nothing to worry about."

"Can we just… Who's that?" I ask, pointing at a tall girl with bleached-out hair.

He follows my gaze. "Oh, that's Julia Fischer." While the other girls wear sweats and T-shirts with ponytails, Julia sports matching workout gear. Her hair is perfectly done, and her face is all made up. She looks like one of those girls who doll themselves up to go to the gym and hit on guys. "She's Ryan's girlfriend—100% drama. We do our best to stay out of her way. Everyone hates her. She's one of the leads, and she thinks she's much better than she actually is."

I can see that. She has an air of importance about her. She stands away from the rest of the cast, her back to them while she types on her phone, as if they're all beneath her.

"All right, everyone, lunch is over. Let's run it again," Vic calls as he enters the room.

I watch the girls as they take their places. Julia and Molly begin tap dancing. At one point, Julia stumbles, knocking into Molly. She stops the music, glaring at Molly as if it were all her fault. She and her boyfriend are obviously made for each other. The tension hangs for a beat before everyone resets. I take that as my cue to follow Luke and Josie out to the parking lot, where we climb into Josie's Volkswagen Bug.

"So, what brings you to good old Rock Harbor?" Josie asks as she buckles her seatbelt.

Nope. Not having that conversation. Not yet. Maybe not ever. "I just needed a change of pace."

"My mom said she met you yesterday. Dr. Plummer?"

Great. I'm going to lunch with my shrink's daughter. "Oh, yeah. She's cool."

"She's a pain in the ass, but she's good at what she does." Josie pops the car into reverse, glancing behind her as she pulls out of the parking lot. "But seriously. Why are you really here? No one just comes to Rock Harbor to hang out. What did you do? I need the tea."

"Yeah, mama loves her drama," Luke chimes in.

My hands start to shake as the anxiety settles over me. I'd agreed to go to lunch, not be interrogated. I know I'll need to tell them eventually if I'm going to hang out with them, but I don't know them well enough to talk about this right now.

"It's not that exciting."

"Damn, I was hoping for some good drama. You sure you didn't escape from juvie? Witness an attempted assassination, and now you're in witness protection?" She glances into the rearview mirror and smiles.

"No."

"I'm surprised your uncle decided to do *Our Town*," Luke says, changing the subject after sensing my discomfort. "That's the show they were doing when the theatre caught fire."

"My grandmother's having a fit because of it," Josie says. "She says it's bad luck. That Vic isn't being respectful."

"Why does she think that?" I ask, happy to steer the conversation in a different direction.

"Superstition. She was there when the fire happened. She directed the show. She knew the girl who died. My mom was friends with her."

My stomach drops. The girl who died. "Josie's grandmother claims the ghost of Catherine Whitley still haunts the theatre. A lot of people do. My dad says she was unstable," Luke says.

"Leave it to a straight man to call a young girl unstable. Troubled is probably a better word. Or maybe misunderstood?" Josie corrects.

Catherine. The same name from the journal. I grip the door handle. "Did you say Catherine?"

"Yeah, why?" Josie asks.

"It's weird. I found something today while I was putting away props that had the name Catherine written on it."

"What was it?" She seems a little too excited about this.

"A journal."

"What did it say?" She stops at a stoplight and turns to look at me.

"I don't know," I lie. "I didn't read it."

"Is it still there?" Josie asks.

"Yeah, it's upstairs in the costume room."

The car behind us honks when the light turns green. Josie gives them the finger and pops the car in gear.

"Do you guys think the theatre is really haunted?" I ask, thinking back to what I heard earlier.

"I've never seen anything. Then again, I don't really believe in ghosts," Luke says.

"Every theatre has a ghost," Josie says with a smile. "You can't have a theatre without one."

"Have you ever seen her?" I ask Josie.

"Her?"

"The ghost. At the theatre."

"No, but I've gotten some strong readings the last couple of days." She turns into the parking lot of a very busy diner and opens her door.

"Readings?"

"Josie thinks she's a ghost hunter," Luke tells me as he helps me out of the car. Sometimes it really sucks being in constant pain.

"I *am* a ghost hunter. I've witnessed things. You've been there to witness some of them with me."

"If you say so."

As we walk toward the diner, I can't shake the ghost of Catherine Whitley. She died, and from the way her journal read, she was in love with my dad. I know there's more in those pages, but I'm starting to wonder if I'll like what I find. And if the nightmare from the other night wasn't so much a dream as it was a warning.

CHAPTER SEVEN

After lunch, Josie and Luke drop me off at Uncle Vic's. I check my socials, watch some TV, then go upstairs and pop one of my pills. When I wake up, the room is dark. The clock reads 9:00. I've been out for five hours. I go downstairs to find Vic banging around in the kitchen, singing what sounds like a show tune.

"Hey," I say as I walk in.

"Hey there. Have a good nap?"

"Yeah, I guess I must have needed it." I sit at the table, watching him put away the dishes. "I'm sorry about this afternoon. That Ryan guy just pissed me off."

"Ryan's good at that."

"It won't happen again," I promise him.

"Good," he says with a smile. "Did you talk to your mom? There was a message from her when I got home. She said she's been trying to get in touch with you all afternoon. I guess you must have slept through it."

That's weird. I always wake up when I hear my phone ring.

"Shit."

"What is it?"

"I left my phone in the costume room."

"Wanna take the truck and go get it?" Vic asks, pointing to the keys on the counter.

"I can walk. Do you have a theatre key I can borrow?"

"Just use the code to the back door. Two-four-nine-nine-seven," he reminds me.

I head upstairs to grab a sweatshirt. When I come back, Vic sits in the recliner watching reruns of a medical drama on the television. "You sure you don't want to take the truck?"

"It's cool. I need some fresh air, and my PT at home told me I need to try and walk as much as possible."

I step outside, and, apparently, the late June evening forgot it was supposed to be summer. It's much cooler out than I expected. The breeze blowing across the bay cuts like ice, making it feel more like early spring.

It takes me a lot longer than expected to reach the theatre. As I cross the bridge, I think about Cole's wink and my heart stutters. Then I remember Molly's eager smile and the way she touched my arm, and my stomach knots with guilt. She's nice. She doesn't deserve me leading her on when I know I can't give her what she wants. I don't want to use her like I used Amy.

I always had my pick of girls growing up, and honestly, I loved the attention. I never really knew I was gay; I just knew I didn't seem to be as excited by the girls my age as all the other guys were. And it wasn't like I was interested in any of the guys. Most of us had grown up together. We were like brothers. But then one night, my fifteen-year-old boner wouldn't behave. Pictures of naked women and straight porn weren't cutting it anymore. Curiosity struck. I found my way to a gay site, and a whole new world presented itself.

And I was terrified.

I didn't want to be gay. At first, I convinced myself that it was just the excitement of experiencing something different. It was a fetish. Just something I liked to watch, but something I'd never act on.

But the more I watched it, the more paranoid I grew. I immediately started dating Amy. I guess I was afraid the other guys would smell the dude porn on me and figure me out. I needed a cover. And it worked.

But then, one night after a basketball game, Jake stayed over. I went to grab snacks, and when I came back, he was on my laptop. He'd found the porn. I'd forgotten to clear my browser history. I was terrified. A thousand excuses tried to force their way out of my mouth at once, but then I noticed his hand in his pants.

He told me to close and lock the door. And then everything fell into place and I knew exactly who and what I was. From that moment on, Jake was my everything.

Until he wasn't anymore.

I snap myself back to reality as I walk up the side street to the staff door. There's very little light, so I do my best to punch in the numbers on the keypad. When the door unlocks, I take small steps inside the building, holding my hands out in front of me. I feel around for a light switch, but can't find it. The door slams shut, plunging me into total darkness.

I bump into the shelf that holds the flats and steady myself. Where the hell is the light switch? I feel along the shelf, shuffling to avoid stubbing my toe.

A light, smoky scent teases my nose. The smell is waxy, similar to the scent left in the air after blowing out a candle. Why would someone be burning candles in here?

My toe knocks into an object at the end of the shelf, sending it rattling across the floor. I step forward and slip in a wet, sticky puddle, its sour smell turning my stomach.

What the fuck is that?

I keep walking, hands outstretched so I don't run face-first into a wall. The darkness presses against my chest. I've lost all sense of direction. The light switch could be anywhere.

"Where are the damn lights?" I pause for a moment, almost as if I expect someone to answer. I edge forward until I bump into a wall, then drag my hand along it until I find the switch. Light floods the room, revealing a spilled can of red paint and a trail of footprints marking my path.

"Shit." I move to the sink and grab a rag. It takes me a good thirty minutes to clean up the mess on the floor. I hope they don't need that paint for anything. As I rinse the rag, I hear a scuffle across the floor, then a soft thump from the stage. I squint into the darkness, searching, but the stage is empty.

When the sound doesn't return, I move toward the stairs, turning on the light before I climb. Reaching the top, I let my eyes adjust. The prop room looks untouched, but hesitation grips me as I inch toward the costume loft, Josie's ghost stories whispering through my head.

"It's bullshit." I say it aloud to calm myself. I push the fear aside and march into the costume room, flipping on the light before starting back to the far wall where I left my phone.

Three missed calls from Mom flash on my screen, along with a text from Molly:

Hope your first day went well!

How did she even get my number? The cheerful tone makes my stomach knot with guilt. I should text her back, but I don't know what to say.

Thump.

I freeze, listening.

Thump. Thump.

My pulse hammers in my throat. The air won't come right. I force myself to breathe slowly. In. Out. "Come on, man. Ghosts aren't real."

As soon as the words leave my lips, the lights go out, throwing me into darkness.

Fuck.

"Hello?" My mind races, keeping time with my frantic breathing. "Is someone there?"

Afraid to move, I close my eyes and count to ten. When I open them, the dark hasn't changed. I switch on my phone, its glow casting eerie shadows across the costumes. Slowly, I creep down the row. With every step, I brace for a hand to grab my ankle or someone to lunge from the racks. My pace quickens. The floor betrays me with a loud creak each time I place a foot down.

At the end of the row, I stop. I wait for another thump, a whisper, anything. But the quiet stretches on, and somehow that's worse. It's almost like something is waiting.

Something stirs in the costumes behind me, fabric whispering against fabric. I freeze, straining to listen, my breath caught in my throat. Nothing follows. Just silence. My pulse hammers so hard I can feel it in my ears. I force one step forward, then another, every creak of the floorboards echoing like a gunshot.

Fabric whispers behind me. Not the random shift of hanging clothes, but like someone stepping through the racks, pushing aside hangers one by one.

The air suddenly feels thicker. Colder. Like the room itself is holding its breath. Then it touches me. Cold against the back of my neck. So faint I almost convince myself it was nothing. Almost. The second burst comes sharper, deliberate.

A breath. On my skin. My body locks, every nerve screaming, every hair on end, waiting for what comes next.

The faint smell of smoke curls around my nose, bitter and sharp. It's followed by another icy breath on the back of my neck.

Someone's there.

Close. Too close.

Every hair on my scalp lifts, my skin prickling with awareness.

I don't move. I don't breathe. Every second stretches like it might snap under its own weight.

Nothing comes. Just silence, thick and pressing, the kind of silence that makes your own pulse sound like a percussion band.

My knees tremble. My jaw locks.

Maybe I imagined it. Maybe it's just nerves.

Then, another burst of air, colder this time, like icy wind kissing bare skin. My throat tightens. Whoever's behind me hasn't moved. They're still there. Watching. Waiting.

And then I feel it. Fingers, glacial and deliberate, sliding up the back of my neck. The touch moves slowly, unbearably slow, threading through my hair like it belongs there.

Every nerve in my body screams. I spasm so violently my teeth clack together. Instinct explodes through me.

I run.

I stumble through the door, somehow not smashing into the wall. My foot snags on something in the dark, and I pitch forward, hitting the floor hard. Pain shoots through my hip. My phone skids away, clattering out of reach.

Stay down. Don't move. Don't breathe. Maybe it'll pass by. Maybe it didn't follow.

Seconds stretch. Silence presses on my ears.

Too still. Too empty.

I need my phone.

My hands scrape the floor, frantic, searching. Splinters stab my skin. Dust clogs my throat.

Nothing.

I crawl faster, palms smacking wood, sliding over grit. My breath comes in shallow bursts. My heart slams so hard I think it'll shake me apart.

My fingers hit a wall.

I freeze.

Where's the door?

Where am I?

I inch to the right, one hand sliding forward before I drag the other to follow. My breath is shallow, ragged in my ears. Then—there. My phone. Just out of reach. Relief sparks, but it dies instantly as the cold returns, threading across my skin like invisible fingers.

Something soft brushes over my hand. Fabric. I recoil, pulling back too quickly, my heart battering against my ribs. Sliding sideways, my palm hits something solid. A shelf. I cling to the edge, forcing myself upright, careful not to make a sound.

My fingers trail along until they knock something that rattles faintly. A box. I snatch it and feel the weight. Matches.

The scrape of wood against sulfur echoes too loudly, but then a fragile flame blossoms to life, burning bright enough to show the stairs less than ten feet away. Salvation. I decide that I don't care about the phone. I just want out.

The crying starts again. Softer now. Not the desperate wail from this afternoon, but a low, broken sobbing that seeps into the room. My chest tightens until I can barely breathe.

The match gutters against my skin. I blow it out, hands shaking, and strike another.

The crying stops.

I creep down the steps, the flame trembling with each breath I take. My heartbeat thunders, louder than the hush of the flame. Then, with no warning, it dies, as though lips pressed against it and snuffed it out.

Cold surges through the air, wrapping me in frost. My skin prickles, muscles locking. I squeeze my eyes shut, bracing for whatever comes. Then, just as quickly, the cold recedes.

The smell of smoke follows. Sharp. Thick. It coils down my throat with every step.

I light another match. Orange light spills across the paint shelf, and in the corner of my eye, something pale moves. White fabric. A figure crawling out of the orchestra pit.

I stagger backward, eyes fixed on the stage, but when I blink, it's gone. Darkness swallows me again as the flame dies.

Another strike. Another flare.

She's standing right in front of me.

Ash-streaked blonde hair hides her face, a white dress hanging in tatters. Ash stains the hem, her arms dangling at her sides, her hands blackened with soot and blood.

I take a step back, choking on my own breath. The flame dies.

One match left. My last chance. I strike it, the light bursting too bright for a heartbeat before settling. The girl has vanished.

My teeth unclench, tension releasing. And then I turn.

She's there. Inches away.

"Why are you leaving me?" she shrieks, her voice ripping through me like glass.

The crying rises again, filling the room, pressing into every corner, every crack.

"Phillip?" she sobs, voice trembling with heartbreak. "I thought you loved me."

The flame burns into my fingers. I should drop it. I can't.

"Answer me!" Her head jerks back, hair falling away. Her face is ruined. Charred flesh hangs in strips. Her skull gleams white through the gaps, and her eye sockets are caked with ash. Her mouth opens too wide, revealing teeth stained black with soot.

The scream that tears from her rattles my bones—

—and the lights snap on.

Blinding. White.

She's gone.

Thought shuts off.

My body takes over.

And I move like my life depends on it.

Lungs heaving, heart breaking itself against my ribs, I don't stop moving until I reach the bridge.

I limp up the front steps of Uncle Vic's house, my hip screaming in pain. The house is dark, meaning Vic must be asleep. I lock the door behind me and quietly make my way through the kitchen, making sure the back door is locked and the windows closed.

When I get upstairs to my room, I check all the windows and then lock my door. I don't know what I just witnessed, but

I know it was real. I just don't know how to put it into words. And I don't think anyone would believe me even if I could.

CHAPTER EIGHT

Someone pounds on my door, jolting me awake. It takes a second to remember where I am.

"Heath? You up?" Uncle Vic calls from the other side.

Sleep clings to my eyes. "Yeah."

"Get showered. We need to get going."

Last night's events flood back as I sit up. I'm still wearing yesterday's clothes, wrinkled and stale against my skin. Proof that none of it was just a dream.

I shower quickly and then get dressed. Vic's irritated voice carries up the stairs as I head down. He's speaking to someone on the phone.

He hangs up and snatches his keys. "Grab a bagel or something. We need to go."

"What's wrong?"

"That was Ryan." He strides toward the door. "He's pissed off. Something about paint and the set. He was talking so fast and yelling so loud I could barely understand him."

We climb into the truck. I barely get my door closed before he's backing out and flying toward the theatre.

When we get there and walk inside, everyone stands around staring at the set. I push to the front and see what everyone is staring at. Red paint covers the floor and spatters the flats. It looks like a slaughterhouse. It's like something bled out on the stage overnight. Written across the flats and platforms that line the back wall are the words:

I warned you

Silence fills the space. They just stand and stare at the set, as if expecting the paint to clean itself up. Tears fall from Jenny's eyes as Ray comforts her. She'd painted all day yesterday.

I climb the stairs and stand by Luke, who nudges me with his elbow.

"I'll kill whoever did this." Ryan's voice cuts through the quiet. "I worked too hard on this set, and we open in a week." Steam practically rises from his head.

"I don't understand who would do this." Jenny's voice breaks with defeat.

Ryan's glare burns into me. He stares at my shoes.

Red paint.

"You motherfucker." Before the words hit my ears, he's storming toward me.

Luke jumps between us, holding Ryan back. Ryan shoves against him as I stumble, trying to move away.

"Ryan!" Vic bellows. "Back off."

"You warned me, huh?" Ryan struggles against Luke's grip.

Vic grabs my elbow. "Come to my office. Now." His breath is hot against my ear. My shame burns hotter. I keep my head down as I follow him, the weight of everyone's eyes following until we disappear down the hall.

"I need you to explain to me why you did this," Vic says from behind his desk. He's deliberately calm, but I can tell he's holding back his anger. It's taking every bit of self-control he has.

"I didn't do it." My voice cracks. "I swear I didn't."

He leans back in his chair and runs his hands over his face, causing his beard to stand out straight. He doesn't believe me.

"You were up here last night, correct?"

"Yes, I came to get my phone."

"When I went to bed, you'd been gone for more than an hour. It should have taken you no longer than that to get here, grab your phone, and walk back home." He leans forward on his desk, staring at me. "There's something you're not telling me."

I stare back, refusing to break. Why would I? I didn't do anything, but how do I explain what happened without sounding insane?

"I got up here last night and couldn't find the lights. I felt my way along the scene shop and my foot hit something." I choose my words carefully, staying calm. "I finally managed to get to the wall switch. When I turned the lights on, I realized I'd kicked over a paint can and stepped in it. I spent twenty minutes cleaning up after myself. I salvaged what paint I could and cleaned up the rest. I went upstairs to grab my phone, and while I was in the costume room, I heard noises, then the lights went out."

I stop there. Do I tell him about the figure I saw? The breath on my neck? The feeling of someone running their hand through my hair? Or do I admit that sometimes the medication Dr. Reeves prescribed makes me do things I don't remember clearly? But that hasn't happened in a while.

Unless you count the other day when my mom found me standing half-naked outside.

"So, you're saying someone else was in the theatre?" he asks.

"It sounded like it." I can't look him in the face. A sick twist coils low in my gut, guilt curling there even though I've done nothing wrong.

"Did you see anyone else?"

I hesitate, then shake my head. "No."

It's not a total lie. I'm not sure what I saw was even real.

"You think someone else was in here? Hiding, perhaps? And they wrecked the set after you left?"

"That had to be what happened." The explanation sounds weak even to me, but what else could have happened? I know I didn't do it.

Don't I?

"Heath, there are only a handful of people who have the code to get into this building."

He doesn't believe me.

"Uncle Vic, it wasn't me. I swear I had nothing to do with it. I told you what happened." I stop and breathe. I need to stay calm. Letting my temper get the best of me won't help.

"You're trying to tell me that one of my staff came in here and trashed a set they've been working on for weeks? Why would they do that?"

"Why would *I* do that? Are you saying you don't trust me?" My voice shakes. I can't lose my cool. I won't. I've only been here two days. I can't fight with Vic.

"I want to trust you, but I can't believe one of my staff would have done this, and I know damn good and well it wasn't me."

"Ryan probably did it to set me up. You saw how he acted toward me yesterday." I'm grasping at straws, looking for any explanation.

"Ryan can be a hothead, but he wouldn't do something like this."

"But you think I would? Seriously?"

"I don't know what to think, Heath. I know you're going through a lot, and sometimes people act out of character when they're under stress—"

"Don't start with this shit." I slam my hands on his desk. "I don't need to be hounded by you, too."

"I'm not hounding you, Heath. I'm trying to reason with you. You lying to me isn't helping the situation."

"I'm not a liar! I'm not some rando dick who would do

something like this. If I wanted to get back at Ryan, I would have done something to him directly. This affects you and many other people I don't even know."

I'm not a liar.

His face reddens, and I can tell he's doing his best not to scream at me. "I hope you're good with a paintbrush. You'll be staying here tonight and painting the floor."

"I have plans with Luke and Josie."

"Not tonight, you don't. We have a show to open next week, and the set needs to be finished by tomorrow so we can start tech rehearsals. The painting *will* be done tonight, and *you* will be the one to do it."

"Bullshit!" I slam my chair back and storm toward the door, but he stops me before I can leave.

"Your parents sent you here and asked me to watch over you. We agreed that you would abide by my rules." His voice stays level, controlled. "I don't like being a hard-ass, but you need to learn that there are consequences for your actions, regardless of what you're personally going through."

I storm out of his office without another word. He obviously doesn't believe me, and there's no way I can convince him otherwise.

Anger propels me down the hall as fast as my injured leg allows. I slam into the door to the rehearsal hall as it opens.

"Oh my God! I'm so sorry!" Molly covers her mouth. "I totally didn't mean to hit you."

"You're good. I wasn't watching where I was going." I try to act like she didn't just smack me in the head. Like it's totally normal for my eyes to water this way.

"Are you okay?" Her eyes search my face with genuine concern.

"Yeah. Fine." I offer a weak smile and step around her, but she doesn't move much, forcing me to brush past her.

"I'll try to pay more attention next time." She bites her lower lip.

"It's cool."

At the door leading back to the scene shop, I stare at my paint-spattered shoes. Even though I wasn't the one who messed up the set, I'm branded with the guilt. How can I face everyone? If I apologize, I'm admitting to something I didn't do. If I say nothing, then I look like a total asshole. There's no way to win.

"That set isn't going to paint itself." Vic's voice carries from down the hallway.

I swallow the biting comment that threatens to punch its way out of my mouth. The door opens, and I start up the steps as he disappears into the rehearsal space.

"Hey, what's going on?" Luke asks. He has a can of paint in one hand and a roller in the other. Jenny pulls paint cans from the shelf. Some tall guy with dark hair, wearing an old '80s band T-shirt, helps her.

I move toward Jenny without answering Luke.

"Jenny?" My voice comes out quiet.

"Yeah?" She continues to work, refusing to look at me.

"I'm really sorry about what happened, but it wasn't me. I promise. I know you don't know me at all, but I need you to know that I would never do something like this."

"Okay." She places a can of paint on the floor, glances at my shoes, then my face, before looking away again.

"I know it looks like I did it, but I promise I didn't. I was up here last night and couldn't find the lights. I knocked over a can of paint and stepped in it then—"

She walks off, leaving me hanging.

"I didn't do it, Luke."

"All good. We'll help Jenny repaint the flats, and it'll be over and done with." He won't look me in the face. He doesn't believe me either.

"I'm serious, Luke. I need you to believe me. I'm not a dick like that. Yeah, Ryan pissed me off, but I would never trash a set."

"I believe you, bro. Come on, let's fix this mess."

We make our way to the stage where everyone is furiously painting the flats.

"It's going to need at least two, maybe three coats to cover all this." Jenny's frustration colors every word.

Ryan stands with his back to us. I find myself walking toward him, but Luke catches my arm.

"Maybe not the best time," he says quietly, his fingers warm against my skin.

But I ignore the advice. "Hey, Ryan?"

His back tenses at the sound of my voice.

"This really sucks, and I'm sorry it happened. I just need you to understand that it wasn't me. I would never do something like this."

"Fuck off," he growls without turning around.

"Seriously, man. It wasn't me."

"Bullshit." He spins to face me, and I brace for another fight. "The evidence is all over your shoes. Now get the fuck away from me before I stick this roller up your ass."

Every muscle in my body screams to punch him in the face. Instead, I walk away, taking slow, even breaths. Everyone watches from the corners of their eyes as I join Luke and Josie.

The rest of the afternoon passes in tense silence. The only sounds come from the rehearsal hall. Around 6:00, the noise of the cast winding down filters through the theatre. The door to the main stage bangs open and Julia storms in.

"Ryan? I'm ready to go." Her whiny voice breaks the silence.

"I'm almost finished."

"No, we need to go now. I need to get out of this place before my head explodes. I swear to God, if I have to spend one more minute here with these amateurs, I'm going to strangle myself."

She says this loud enough for everyone to hear. I don't even know this girl, but I already hate her as much as I hate her boyfriend. I can't help but smile when I see Patrice and Molly mocking her behind her back.

"Let me wash my hands." Ryan moves backstage.

"Hurry." She crosses her arms with her back to us. When Ryan doesn't return immediately, she storms backstage after him.

"Hey, hot stuff." Patrice gives Josie a smack on the butt. "Having fun?"

"Tons." It's one of the few words I've heard Josie speak all day.

"Sounds like little Miss Perfect is at it again."

"She's special." Patrice rolls her eyes.

"She thinks she is, anyway." Molly laughs.

Cole walks in, pulling a sweatshirt over his wide shoulders, and I feel myself getting all antsy again.

"You guys about done?" Patrice checks out the set as she pulls her tight curls into a ponytail.

We've managed to finish all of the flats, and Jenny has textured almost everything.

"Yeah, I just need to wash up. I'm starving." Josie starts backstage.

Patrice checks her phone. "Some of the cast is going to your grandma's diner. I said we'd join them if that's okay."

"Can I come with you guys?" Luke asks.

"What about you?" Cole steps onto the stage toward me. "You should come."

His invitation sounds genuine, not just out of politeness. The way he looks at me—like he actually wants me there—makes something warm unfurl in my chest. But then Jake's face flashes in my mind, and the warmth turns to ash.

"Grab your shit and let's go." Patrice picks up her bag.

"We need to wash up first." Luke moves to pick up the used paint trays and rollers, but I stop him.

"I'll get it. You guys go ahead."

Josie looks surprised. "No way, bruh, you're coming with."

"No, I still need to do the floor."

"You're not coming?" Cole steps closer, and I catch a hint

of sandalwood and patchouli. His face falls in disappointment, and for a minute, I want to say fuck it and go with them. But I can't do that to Vic.

"No."

"Bummer." He nudges my arm lightly. "Maybe next time?"

I nod and look away. "Maybe next time."

"Come with us, and then we'll come back and help you with the floor," Luke calls after me as I carry the used rollers to the sink.

"I got it. You guys get out of here."

"You sure?" Cole asks, his voice softer than the others.

"Yes. Go."

I listen to their hushed voices as they leave the theatre. Why am I like this? I lean against the sink, shoulders sagging as I wallow in self-pity.

Water circles the drain with traces of black paint. I'm completely spaced out and don't hear Vic walk up behind me. He grabs my shoulder, and I let out a scream, spinning around, ready to fight.

"Didn't mean to scare ya. I was calling your name. Didn't you hear me?"

"No, I didn't." I lean back against the sink, my heart hammering against my ribs.

"Let's go get some dinner."

"No, thanks. I'm not hungry. I still need to paint the floor."

"Come on. Let's go eat, and then I'll come back and help you."

"I got it." I know I'm being a little bitch, but I don't care. He told me I was going to stay up here and paint the floor tonight, so that's what I'm going to do.

"Want me to bring you back something?"

I grab a can of black paint and head to the stage. "I'm not hungry." The truth is I'm starving, but too proud to admit it. I only had half a sandwich for lunch.

"I'll come back and pick you up in an hour or so."

"It's okay. I'll walk." I don't look at him. "Unless you think you need to come up and make sure I didn't mess up the set again."

"Heath—" he begins, but I keep walking.

"I'm gonna lock up," he says. "Use the back door when you leave, and make sure it's shut all the way."

His footsteps echo down the hall, and I wait to hear the front doors close. The silence presses against my ears. Every shadow seems deeper, every corner darker. I suddenly realize I'm alone with whatever pursued me last night.

I immediately go backstage and grab one of the flashlights off the stage manager's desk. I test it twice, making sure it works before sticking it in my pocket. Last night proved the darkness here has teeth.

And I don't want to get bitten.

CHAPTER NINE

I pat my pocket one more time, confirming the flashlight hasn't sprouted legs and wandered off. Obsessive? Maybe. But I'm not risking a repeat of last night. I tune the old-school radio to a local classic rock station and crank up the volume. I need the music loud enough to drown out any stray noises that might mess with my head.

I dip the roller into the paint tray and get to work on the stage floor. The repetitive motion steadies me while the beat of the music pounds around me. Sweat drips down my back. Before I know it, I'm already three-quarters finished. I grab the paint bucket and refill the tray as a burst of static crackles through the radio. Quick. Almost undetectable.

When I stand, the crackling returns, but this time it doesn't go away. I drop the roller and adjust the dials. Gotta love these relics. Am I even doing this right? Words fade in and out through the music and static, like two stations bleeding together. I unplug the radio, but the crackling dialogue continues.

"What took you so long?" The young woman's voice is barely discernible through the faint crackling. At first, I'm not sure I actually heard it.

"I have things to do, Cathy. What do you need?" The man's voice is perfectly clear. The crackling is completely gone now. It's almost as if I've tuned into a phone conversation, or some sort of old-time soap opera.

"I wish you'd take me seriously." The girl's voice trembles, and I already know who it is. Cathy is Catherine. I recognize the voice from the beach. "I need to tell you something."

"Why couldn't you just tell me on the phone? I don't have time for dramatics," the man says, annoyed.

"I'm pregnant."

The silence is louder than the static. Then, the man laughs, low and ugly. "Well, it's not mine."

"You're the only one I've been with. You were my first," Catherine insists. Her voice steadies, desperate but firm. "I've never been with anyone else."

"Yeah. Right." His voice curdles with contempt. "Everyone knows what your mother's like. You're no different. It's probably Phillip's kid. You're always fucking around with him."

"No!" She's crying now. "Phillip and I never... We never..."

"You dangled yourself in front of me just to make him jealous. You led me on. You teased me. You begged for it just because you wanted Phillip to pay attention to you. And now you want me to take responsibility for your mess?"

"It happened, and now it's done. You have to help me. I need you to take me to have an abortion. I can't afford it, and my mom will kill me—"

"It's not mine. It's not my problem."

"It *is* your problem!" she snaps. "This is *your* child."

There's the sound of movement. Fabric brushing, a sudden scuffle.

"Let go of me!" Catherine cries.

His voice hardens. "You think anyone's going to believe you over me? It's your word against mine. Do you know who my father is? You are no one. You're trash. If you bother me about this again, you'll be sorry."

"You can't just walk away—"

"Watch me." His voice drops to a chilling whisper. "This is your mess. You take care of it."

What the hell is this? I try turning the radio off and on, but no matter what I do, the conversation continues playing through the speakers.

"You're a piece of shit," she yells, followed by a thud.

"You bitch. Throwing shit at me?"

There's a struggle, and her scream cuts through the speakers, raw and terrified. Can I stop this? Is this happening in real time, or is this another vision from the past?

I rush up the stairs, ignoring the pain shooting through my hip, and flip on the light. I search the prop room and costume room, but find nothing. Everything is still.

"Help me!" Her scream pierces my ears. "Help!"

"You want an abortion? Huh?" Whoever this guy is, he sounds unhinged. He's really going to hurt her. "How 'bout I do it for you? A nice little tumble down these stairs should do the trick."

Panic floods my chest. How can I help her if I don't know where she is?

"Hello?" I yell. "Is everything all right?"

No answer. Only the sound of struggling and Catherine screaming.

I scramble toward the stairs, spotting my cell phone beneath a shelf. Dead. Completely dead. Catherine's screams keep pouring from the radio, like the theatre itself is bleeding sound.

I stumble down the stairs, crash into the stage manager's desk, and snatch the landline. I slam it to my ear, punch in 911, then freeze. The same struggle hisses through the earpiece. No dial tone. Just her screams.

"Please, don't!" Catherine's voice sobs through the phone. "Don't do this to me!"

A scream tears through the air. Then the sickening tumble of a body. The phone drops from my hand. A soul-crushing wail echoes through the theatre, and then everything goes still.

My heart hammers against my ribs, pulse thudding in my ears. I freeze, my knees threatening to give out on me. A tear slides down my cheek. What just happened? I force myself to breathe, scrambling for what to do next. A loud, fast tone blares from the phone dangling off the desk, making me jump. I pick it up and press the lever. Now there's a dial tone.

I start to dial Uncle Vic when a loud, fast banging comes at me from the back door.

"Heath? Are you in there?"

It's Luke. I compose myself and head to the door. When I open it, Luke and Josie beam at me. They push their way into the theatre, followed by Patrice, Molly, and Cole.

"I can never remember that damn code. Bruh, you look rough. Did we scare you?" Josie laughs as she stares me down.

"You all right?" Luke asks, pulling the door shut behind them.

"Yeah. Fine."

"Hey." Cole touches my shoulder. "You sure you're okay? You look shaken up."

Something in Cole's voice makes me look up. His hand still rests on my shoulder, warm and steady. For a moment, everything else fades.

"Yeah, I'm fine." The lie comes out shakier than I intended. "I was just in the zone. The banging on the door scared the shit out of me."

"We came to help you finish the floor." Luke closes the door and claps me on the back.

Josie picks up the roller I'd dropped and begins painting the last few feet I hadn't finished.

"How was dinner?" I ask, trying to clear my mind of what I

just heard—or thought I heard.

"It was fine. We got a little rowdy and had to leave. Josie's grandmother was irritable tonight."

"Was everyone in the cast there?" I ask, trying to figure out whose voices I might have heard. I'm not willing to admit it wasn't real.

"Everyone but Julia and Ryan." Molly steps closer to me. "But she never comes out with us. We're too far beneath her." Her perfume drifts toward me, and I take a small step back.

Was it Ryan that I heard? Was he the one attacking the girl?

"Is there a girl named Catherine in the cast?" I know Catherine was the girl who died here, and for some reason, the one I keep seeing, but I'm hoping that maybe there's someone in the cast with that name. Someone who may have been here tonight.

"Nope," Patrice says.

"Are you sure?"

"I don't know anyone by that name," Molly says, tilting her head. "Why?"

I shake my head, still processing what I heard. Cole pretends to scroll on his phone, but I catch him watching me out of the corner of his eye. I'm suddenly very self-conscious. I probably sound out of my mind.

"What's with this whole Catherine thing?" Josie asks, wiping a blob of paint from her fingers.

I'm not sure what to tell her without making her think I'm crazy. "I thought I heard someone calling for Catherine earlier, and I was trying to figure out who she was. I don't quite know everyone's name yet." It's a bad lie, and I can tell by the look on her face that she doesn't believe me.

"Are you being haunted by the ghost of Catherine Whitley?" She smiles, but when I don't smile back, concern crosses her face. "Are you sure you're okay?"

"Yeah, I'll be fine."

"I don't believe you." She leads me to the stage manager's

desk, away from prying ears. "Something spooked you."

"I just…" I scrub my face with both hands. "Thought I heard something."

"What did you hear?" She sits on the desk and faces me, her ice-blue eyes searching my face.

My mouth opens, then closes. I glance at the radio, then back at her expectant face. "You'll think I'm crazy if I tell you."

"I like crazy. Tell me."

She waits expectantly, and I look around to make sure no one else is listening before I continue. "I heard voices. A guy and a girl."

"What were they saying?"

"They were talking. They were in the theatre." The words are hard to form. Saying it all aloud makes it seem even crazier than when it was happening.

"But what were they saying?"

"They were arguing, and then he must have grabbed her because she told him to get his hands off of her, and she hit him or something. I couldn't tell. He got angry, and I'm pretty sure he slapped her. She was crying, and then she was screaming for help and begging him to stop. I think he pushed her down the stairs."

"Oh my God." Her mouth gapes, and her face turns white. "Where were they? Did you stop him? Did you scare him off?"

"I don't know where they were. I just heard them."

"Where were the sounds coming from?"

I stare at her, knowing that the truth is too insane. "I'm not sure."

"Was it coming from upstairs? Did you look for them?"

"Yes, I looked for them, but I couldn't find anyone. I looked upstairs, in the lobby, the rehearsal hall, but no one was around."

"Did you call the police?"

"I tried, but the phone… wasn't working."

She grabs the phone off the stage manager's desk and lifts the receiver. "It's working now."

"I know, but it wasn't at the time."

"What's going on?" Cole appears beside us. He must have noticed the look of shock and confusion on Josie's face. Luke joins us a moment later.

"Heath thought he heard someone being attacked before we got here," Josie tells them.

"What do you mean attacked?" Luke asks.

"A girl was being assaulted," Josie says.

"Where?" Cole's voice sharpens.

"I don't know."

They ask all the same questions that Josie asked, and suddenly, I find myself getting irritated with the whole situation. I'm irritated by their questions and at myself for even bringing it up. The whole thing doesn't make sense. I don't have the answers they're looking for.

"Where were the sounds coming from?" Luke asks again.

"Look, it was probably nothing. Just my imagination. Since the accident, everything freaks me out. It was probably just my mind playing tricks on me."

Josie places a hand on my arm, and I flinch. "Heath, this is serious. We need to report this."

"Seriously." Luke nods. "This isn't something we can just forget about. Where did you hear this happening?"

I take a deep breath. "It was coming through the radio."

"Like a radio program?" Luke looks at me with a raised eyebrow.

"That's what I thought it was at first, but… it sounded real."

They both look at me like I've lost it, just as I expected.

"Maybe it was some kind of satellite interference," Luke says.

"Yeah, it had to be." I force conviction into my voice. "It doesn't make sense otherwise."

"Why were you asking about Catherine?" Josie asks.

"What do you mean?"

"You asked if there was a girl named Catherine in the cast."

"Yeah, the guy called her Catherine. Or, actually, he called her Cathy. Look, I'm sure Luke is right. The radio was probably picking up interference or something, and I let my mind get the best of me." I try to convince myself that Luke is right, but what about the phone?

"Either that or the ghost of Catherine Whitley is trying to contact you." Josie's face is serious.

"Oh, geez, Josie. Not that again. You sound like your grandma," Luke says.

"Gran won't set foot in this place because she swears Catherine's ghost is still here, waiting for revenge." She crosses her arms and stares at him.

"Wait, this place is haunted?" Cole asks, eyes lighting up.

"Yep." Josie grins.

"No," Luke says at the same time. "It's stupid to think it could be. Why now? People have been in this building since it burned, and nothing has happened."

"That's not true." Josie shakes her head. "Gran says when they first tried to reopen the theatre, all sorts of things went wrong." She pauses, glancing at Cole, who nods for her to continue. "When this place was a movie theatre, people were always saying they could smell smoke. The guy who managed the place said he would sometimes hear a woman crying when he was alone. It scared the crap out of him."

"But that still doesn't prove there's a ghost here. It's just a rumor. Just like how everyone says the Seasider Hotel in Seaside is haunted. Or the ghost ship that people claim to see on Siletz Bay. They're just stories people tell to add to the charm of the coast. They're not real."

My head tells me I need to listen to Luke because that's the rational thing to do, but at the same time, it's hard to rationalize what I've witnessed up here the last two nights. Maybe my brain doc in Seattle was right about the medication affecting my perceptions.

"So then you're saying that Heath's crazy?" Josie challenges him, mirroring my own thoughts.

"No, I told you what I think. He heard some sort of interference on the radio from someone's television, or something. That's the only logical explanation. Now, are we going to sit around and talk about ghosts all night, or are we going to go do something fun?"

"I need to get going." I wave them off. "Thanks for the help."

"We're heading down to Lincoln City to catch a movie. You want to join us?" Luke asks.

"Come with us," Molly says, stepping closer again. "It'll be fun. You shouldn't be alone after… whatever that was."

The genuine concern in her voice makes me feel guilty for being uncomfortable around her. She's trying to be nice.

"No, thanks, I'm beat. I need to get home. Thanks for the offer, though." A movie would be a good distraction, but I don't want to be a tag-along.

"You sure?" Cole asks quietly. "I could stay if you want some company."

The offer sends warmth through my chest, followed by Jake's face in my mind. Three months. Is that enough time to feel attracted to someone new? To wonder what it would be like to kiss someone else?

"No, I'm good. You guys go have fun."

"You ready to go, ladies?" Luke calls as he walks out on stage.

"Actually, I think I'm going to pass on the movie. My back is killing me." Cole smiles at me. "I can give Heath a ride. If you want."

His offer catches me off guard.

"He wants one," Josie answers for me.

Luke looks at both of us, a strange look on his face. "But are you sure you don't want to see the movie? It's supposed to be great."

"You can tell me all about it tomorrow," Cole says with a wink.

Josie motions to me to hang back as the others walk ahead. Once they're out of earshot, she whispers, "Why don't you come over to my house for dinner tomorrow night? I think we need to do some digging on Catherine."

"Maybe Luke's right. It was probably nothing."

"Heath, whatever you heard tonight obviously has you shaken up. Has anything like this ever happened to you before?"

"Just last night. But not before that." Unless you count the dreams I have about my dead friends.

"What happened last night?"

I see Luke, Molly, Patrice, and Cole turn to see what's keeping us, and I shake my head. "I'll tell you another time." I don't need everyone here thinking I've snapped.

"Ready to go, ghost hunters?" Luke asks us.

"Yeah, let's go."

As we move toward the door, I realize I still have the flashlight in my pocket. I turn back and place it on the stage manager's desk. I glance up and freeze. Catherine, burned and broken, stands center stage, watching me with hollow eyes.

In a blink, she vanishes into darkness.

CHAPTER TEN

Cole's convertible smells like fresh leather. I pull the door closed and suddenly have no idea what to do. It's like I've never been in a car before. My hands don't know where to go. Lap? Armrest? I settle for crossing my arms over my chest. The engine purrs when he turns the key. Neither of us speaks.

I should say something, but what?

Wind whips through my hair. Cole keeps his eyes on the road, his profile sharp against the darkening sky. Strong jaw. Straight nose. I look away when he glances over.

"What do you want to listen to?" he asks.

"Whatever you want."

He clicks on the radio. Some pop song I don't recognize fills the space between us. It's not really my vibe, but better than silence.

I sneak another look at him. His fingers tap the steering wheel in rhythm with the song. They're nice hands. Strong. Tan. A silver ring on his right thumb catches a glint of twilight.

Jake had nice hands, too.

My chest tightens. I stare out the window at the passing trees. Green blurs against the dusk.

"You good?" Cole asks.

"Yeah. Just tired."

It's not a total lie. I am tired. Bone tired. Soul tired. The kind of tired sleep can't fix.

Cole nods and turns to cross the bridge leading toward the harbor.

"Thanks for the ride," I say, just to say something.

"No problem."

His voice is deep and smooth. Like honey poured over gravel. I wonder if he's gay. The way he looks at me sometimes makes me think so. The small touches. The winks. Luke said he was, but Luke also said they were kind of together. I can't help but wonder if that was just wishful thinking on Luke's part.

But it's not that it matters. I'm not looking. Jake's been dead less than three months.

We pull into the driveway, Vic's old house looming before us. The convertible stops with a gentle lurch.

"Here we are," Cole says.

I unbuckle my seatbelt. "Thanks again."

"Sure you're okay? You seem…" He trails off, searching for the right word.

"I'm fine."

I'm not fine. I'm the opposite of fine. I'm a walking disaster with a pulse, and I'm seeing things. I'm one haunting shy of being locked away.

"Going straight to bed?" he asks.

I sigh. "Probably."

His eyes are on me. Warm chocolate brown with flecks of gold. I focus on the radio dial, the gear shift, anywhere but his face. They make me feel things I'm not ready to feel.

"Cool. Well, good night then."

I should get out of the car. My hand is on the door handle. But something keeps me in the seat. Maybe it's the way his cologne mixes with the night air. Maybe it's the way loneliness sits on my chest like a brick.

Fuck it.

"Actually," I say, the word stumbling out before I can catch it. "I'm starving."

Cole raises an eyebrow. "Yeah?"

"Yeah. I haven't eaten since breakfast."

It's not a big deal if I just hang out with him. It's not betraying Jake's memory to have a friend. After everything, maybe I deserve some normal human contact. Someone to talk to who doesn't look at me like I'm broken.

"You want to maybe grab food?" I ask.

He runs a hand over the steering wheel. "I just ate before picking you up."

"Oh. Right. Sorry." My face burns. Stupid idea.

"But, I'm happy to take you somewhere," he offers. "Everything in town is probably closed by now. We could drive to Lincoln City if you're up for it. They've got some fast food places that stay open late."

My stomach growls at the mention of food. "Lincoln City's like half an hour away."

He shrugs. "I don't mind the drive if you don't."

"Okay," I say, surprising myself. "Let me just tell Vic I'm home and going back out."

"I'll wait here."

The front door to Vic's house opens with a soft click.

"Vic?" I call out.

"In the kitchen!"

I follow his voice. He stands at the island, chopping vegetables. His sleeves are rolled up, revealing forearms covered in colorful tattoos. He looks up as I enter.

"Hey. How'd it go?"

He seems to have gotten over our argument and my earlier attitude. That's a good sign.

"It went fine." I don't tell him about the attack I thought I overheard. Best to keep that to myself. I already said too much to Josie and Luke.

"You hungry? I'm making stir-fry."

I shake my head. "Actually, I'm going to grab food with Cole if that's okay."

Vic's knife pauses mid-chop. His eyebrows rise slightly. "Cole, huh?"

"Yeah," I say without meeting his eyes. I'm not ready to have this conversation.

Vic smirks. "Don't be too late."

I know he knows. Hell, he's gay. He's the first person I should come out to.

Someday.

"I won't," I tell him.

I head upstairs to my room. I toss my backpack on the bed and pull off my T-shirt.

I dig through my dresser for something clean. I settle on the dark green Henley Jake always said brought out my eyes. My throat tightens as I pull it over my head.

In the bathroom, I splash water on my face. My reflection stares back at me. I look like shit, but I can't do anything about that right now. At least it's dark out.

I grab my deodorant. Swipe it under my arms. Find the cologne Jake gave me for Christmas. Just a tiny spray. Not enough to be obvious. Just enough to smell good.

It's not a date. It's just food.

Back downstairs, I find Vic still chopping.

"See you later," I say.

"Phone charged?"

"Yes, Dad." I roll my eyes. It's not, but I'll see if Cole will let me borrow his.

He points the knife at me. "Don't sass me, young man."

I almost smile. Almost.

Outside, Cole's car idles in the driveway. He's texting someone, face lit by the blue glow of his phone. He looks up as I approach.

"Ready?" he asks.

I slide back into the passenger seat. "Ready."

He puts the car in reverse. "Lincoln City, here we come."

We pull away from Vic's house. The night air feels cool against my skin. The radio plays softly. Cole hums along. I stare at the road ahead, lit by headlights that cut through the darkness like search beams.

For the first time in weeks, I feel something besides grief. It's small. Tiny. Just a flicker. But it's there.

Peace.

The turn signal clicks in rhythm with the music as Cole turns into the Burger Barn drive-thru. My stomach growls, a reminder that I've barely eaten all day. The smell of grease and salt fills the car when he passes me the paper bag, warm against my fingers. I dig through it and pull out a fry, shoving it into my mouth before we even leave the parking lot.

"You want to eat here, or should we go somewhere quiet so we can talk?" Cole asks, drumming his fingers on the steering wheel.

My heart gallops. I clutch the bag to my chest like someone might try to steal it. "Whatever's easiest."

He nods and pulls back onto the main road. "I know just the place."

Bugs splatter against the windshield in random patterns. I count them while stuffing my face with fries, focusing on anything except Cole's profile in the dashboard light. The curve of his jaw. The way his fingers tap the steering wheel. The way I want them to touch me.

"Hungry much?" Cole laughs as I stuff the burger into my mouth. It's greasy and perfect.

I nod, unable to speak around the food. My stomach growls in appreciation. I hadn't realized how hungry I was. Now I can't stop eating.

"Sorry," I say after swallowing. "Not very attractive."

"It's fine. I'm just giving you shit."

Thirty minutes later, we're parked at a scenic overlook outside of Rock Harbor. The dashboard lights cast shadows across his face. His eyes look almost black in the darkness. The windows are down, and salt air mixes with the smell of greasy food. The ocean stretches before us, gray and angry, waves crashing against the rocks below.

Cole cuts the engine but leaves the radio on low. Some indie band I don't recognize fills the silence between us.

"So," Cole says after I finish demolishing my burger, "you're staying with your uncle for the whole summer?"

I wipe my hands on a napkin. "Yeah. My parents thought it would be good for me."

"And what do you think?"

I shrug. "Better than being at home."

He nods like he gets it. Maybe he does.

"What about college?" he asks. "You going anywhere in the fall?"

The question stings more than it should. I crumple my burger wrapper into a tight ball.

"I've been at a community college on scholarship playing baseball for the last two years. I just wanted to get some basics out of the way first."

It's what Jake wanted to do. I always did what Jake wanted.

"Nice. What are you studying?"

"Just the basics for now, but I was thinking about environmental engineering. Boring, I know."

"It's not boring if you like it."

I don't, actually. It was my dad's idea. Something practical. Something with a future. I went along with it because it was easier than fighting with him.

"I was supposed to transfer to Oregon State this fall," I admit.

Cole perks up. "No way. That's where I go. Molly too. Josie, Patrice, and Luke go there as well. How fun would that be?"

My mouth speaks before I give it permission. "I'm not sure I'll be there."

"You're not going anymore? To Oregon State?" Disappointment colors the edges of the words.

I stare into the darkness where I know the ocean churns. I can hear it. Smell it. But I can't see it. Kind of like my future. I know it's out there, but I can't make out the shape of it.

"I don't know," I say finally. "Probably not."

"How come?"

The question hovers between us. Simple words. Complicated answer.

I take a deep breath. The air fills my lungs with salt and night and unknown futures. "Something… happened."

Cole waits. Doesn't push. Just lets the silence stretch until I'm ready to fill it.

"I was in an accident," I continue. "I was driving. My friends died."

The words fall flat. They don't capture the horror of that night.

Screeching tires.

Losing control.

Rolling.

Strapped in the front seat, my body bounces off the steering wheel, trying to break free of the restraints. When the rolling stops, I'm upside down with blood dripping from my head. Jake's body hangs motionless to my right, his seatbelt twisted around his crooked neck. Above the music still blaring from the speakers, Amy screams, "Get it off. Get it off!" My seatbelt clicks free, and I drag myself through the open window. My right leg buckles when I try to stand. Pain rips across my hip. The Jeep lies on top of Amy, the roll bar resting on her pelvis, crushing her. She's shaking. Blood runs from her nose and mouth. No sign of Meredith. No sound from her either.

"Help… Me…" Amy reaches for me, her eyes pleading. "Please."

Blood trickles from the side of her mouth.

"It's okay," I tell her. "Everything is going to be okay."

But it wasn't. And I can't get any of it out of my head. The screams. The blood. The way Amy looked at me as she cried. The way Jake hung from the seatbelt. The way it felt when I realized he was gone.

"Shit," Cole breathes. "I'm sorry."

I nod. My throat feels tight. "Jake was my best friend…" No, he was more to me than that. "He, uh… He was in the car. He died. He and I were going to go to Oregon State together. Now I don't know if I can go there without him."

I don't say Jake had been my boyfriend. Don't explain that we'd been planning this for years. Our escape. Our chance to be ourselves without hiding. But something about Cole makes me want to tell him more.

"I recently broke up with my boyfriend," Cole says. "Well, it was six months ago. He was the love of my life. I thought that was traumatizing, but nothing like what you went through."

The word boyfriend hangs in the air between us. It's nice to get the confirmation directly from him.

"I didn't know you were…" I trail off.

"Gay?" He smiles like he doesn't believe me. "Yeah. Since birth. The last time I was near a vagina was when I came out of the birth canal." He shrugs. "Female-free ever since."

An uncontrollable laugh escapes me. It feels strange in my mouth. Unfamiliar. I haven't laughed like this in a long time.

"Me too, I guess." I crumple up the bag that held my fast food. "But I… dabbled. With girls. Or… I tried to…"

And just like that, I've come out to Cole. The words that always stuck in my throat around most people slipped out far too easily.

In the dark.

With the ocean roaring its approval.

"Jake was more than your friend, wasn't he?" Cole asks gently.

I nod. My eyes burn. "Five years. Since we were fifteen."

"That's a long time."

"Yeah."

My fingers find the edge of my seat. I grip it tight.

"We kept it secret," I continue. "From everyone. My parents don't know. Jake's parents didn't know. No one. We were going to finally be out at college." The words tumble out now. "We were both star athletes, and our town wasn't exactly… open-minded. But Oregon State was going to be our fresh start. No more hiding."

Unconsciously, I run my finger along the scars on my wrists. "Now it's just me, and I don't know if I can do it alone."

I pause to take a breath. I didn't realize how badly I needed to say all this.

"I'm still… I don't know. Weird about it, I guess." I pick at a loose thread on my shorts. "This is the first time I ever talked about it to anyone other than Jake. I'm not out to anyone."

"Well, now you're out to me," Cole says.

"And now you." I take a deep breath. "Sometimes I feel guilty for still being so… quiet about it. I mean, I know there are people out there who still hate gay people, but I feel like I should be showing myself and standing up to them. It's hard, though."

Cole reaches over and takes my hand. His skin is warm and soft against mine, different from Jake's calloused fingers. "Hey. There's no one way to be gay, you know? Some people are loud and proud. Some people are quiet about it. Both are okay. There's no rule book. It'll get easier for you."

His hand feels solid around mine. Real. The first real thing I've felt in months.

"You're not letting anyone down by doing it your way," he continues. "And I bet Jake would tell you the same thing."

Tears sting my eyes, and I blink them back. "Thanks."

We sit there for a long time, listening to the ocean pound against the shore. Cole's hand stays in mine, and I don't pull away. The weight of it anchors me. For the first time in months, the crushing guilt in my chest loosens just a fraction. Just enough to let me take a full breath.

The moon breaks through the clouds, turning the water from gray to silver. Something like hope flickers in my chest.

Faint. Fragile. But there.

CHAPTER ELEVEN

When Vic and I get to the theatre the next day, I hope the set survived the night. As I walk down the hall, upbeat music and the sharp rhythm of tapping spill from the rehearsal space. The door is open, and inside, several dancers move in perfect sync—Molly at the front, with Cole and two others backing her up.

The dancers nail every beat, sharp and precise. They're mesmerizing, but my eyes keep drifting to Cole. The way he moves is fluid, confident. His T-shirt clings to his chest, damp with sweat. When he spins and catches me staring, heat rushes to my face.

My mind drifts to last night. The warmth of his hand in mine. The time we spent side by side, saying nothing, and how right it all felt. How it felt to be seen and accepted by someone other than Jake.

And the way I really wanted him to kiss me.

When the music ends, I'm still lost in thought.

"Hi there." Molly's voice startles me. She's noticed me in the doorway.

Heat burns my cheeks as I turn away. "Hey, sorry, I was just walking by. You guys are really talented."

"Thanks. We came in early to work on the dance numbers before everyone else gets here." She grabs her water bottle, taking a long drink. "We missed you last night."

"How was the movie?" I force myself to look at her instead of Cole, who's toweling off his face nearby.

"Kind of dumb, actually." She rolls her eyes. "Some horror movie that Luke picked. I wouldn't recommend it."

"I'll keep that in mind."

We stare at each other for a moment. She smiles, and I can tell she's waiting for something more from me. The problem is, I don't have anything more to give her. Not the way she wants.

"So what's your deal? Like, what brings you here?" She sits on the floor and begins to stretch.

This is so awkward.

"My story?"

"Yeah, what brings you to Rock Harbor?"

"I'm just helping my uncle out." I shrug, acutely aware that Cole is looking my way.

"Do you come here every summer?"

"No, I haven't been here in a few years."

"So, why this year?"

"Why not?" That came out harsher than intended.

"Just curious. Where do you go to school?"

"Up north. Washington. A community college. You've probably never heard of it. I'm supposed to start at Oregon State in the fall, but…" I trail off.

"But?"

"I was in an accident." Why can't I just say it? "The limp—you probably noticed—it's my hip—"

"I never noticed a limp." Her smile is kind. "I'm sorry about the accident."

"Thanks."

"I go to Oregon State, too. Several of us here do."

"Yeah, Cole told me last night. That's cool."

She takes another drink from her water bottle, and I notice Cole gathering his things to leave. Disappointment twists in my chest. I don't want him to go before I can say hi.

She reaches out a hand, expecting me to help her up. "Maybe we could grab lunch later? Just the two of us?"

I help her to her feet and then come clean. "I need to be honest with you."

Her face shifts, and she cocks her head.

"I'm not in the right headspace to date anyone right now. I'm still figuring some things out."

Her eyes search my face, then follow my eyes toward the door where Cole disappeared. When she looks back at me, understanding dawns in her expression. A small smile crosses her face.

"The nice, hot boys are always more interested in other boys." She says it with a head shake and a chuckle. "I should have known."

My stomach drops. Heat floods my face. She knows. I open my mouth to deny it, but no words come.

She brushes dust off her leggings. "It's okay, Heath. Really. I should have seen it. I probably came across as really thirsty, huh?" She laughs. "I'm so horrible at flirting. But, hey. I'm a great ally."

I want to disappear into the floor. "I don't know what you mean."

"You don't have to explain anything to me." Her voice is gentle now, understanding. "But if you ever need someone to talk to, I'm here. Cole is pretty great, by the way."

"Good morning, Molly!" Uncle Vic's voice saves me from having to respond as he walks in. "There are bagels backstage."

"Thank you. I ate already."

"Are you auditioning for me next weekend?"

"I'm thinking about it." She takes a swig from her water bottle.

"Thinking about it? Why wouldn't you?"

"I hate leaving my grandmother alone. This is the first time I've been away from her for so long. My aunt and her family are out of town for the next few weeks, and she's all alone."

"I'll understand if you decide to go back to Portland, but I'd love for you to stay and do the next show."

"I'll audition if Heath will." She winks, but it's playful now instead of flirtatious.

I stare at her in surprise. "I don't act." The thought of being on stage, trying to remember lines and where to walk while hundreds of people stare at you is terrifying to me.

"Come on, it'll be fun. We can play George and Emily. Right, Vic?"

"Sure. You'd make a great couple on stage."

"See, he's already cast us." She nudges me with her elbow, and I manage a small smile.

Vic laughs. "Now don't be announcing that. I'll get a reputation for playing favorites."

I steer the conversation away from acting. "Is there anything you need me to work on today, Uncle Vic?"

"You can keep working on the inventory. Josie's going to come up and help you in the costume room today."

That's a relief. I don't want to be up there alone.

The rest of the cast begins to file in, and I make my way toward the door with my head down.

"Heath." Molly's voice stops me. "You know where to find me if you want to talk, okay? About anything."

"Thanks." This time, I mean it.

I step into the theatre and spot Jenny sponging paint onto some flats, turning them into convincing brickwork.

"It looks good." I'm still trying to get on her good side.

"Thank you." She gives me a small smile.

Ryan strolls past, nail gun in hand. "Yeah, until you come in and fuck it up again."

I can't help but glare at him.

He smirks. "Ooo, someone's cocky." He lifts the nail gun, aiming it at my face. A sharp pop cracks the air when he pulls the trigger. I duck instinctively.

"Relax, it's not even loaded." He laughs and walks away.

My heart slams against my ribs. It takes everything not to launch myself at him. If I start swinging, I know I won't stop. I force myself to breathe, to settle, then head upstairs toward the costume room.

Halfway down the rows, I hear rustling. Not this again. I don't freeze this time. Still burning from Ryan's shit, I storm toward the sound, ready to fight whatever's been fucking with me the last few days, only to stop dead when I see Josie.

"Hello, oh haunted one," she greets me with a slight curtsy. Today she looks like a deranged ballerina in a frayed, pink tutu over her standard fishnets and hiking boots, paired with tattered, layered tank tops.

"Hey." I join her.

"So, I did some digging around at my grandma's house last night. I found a ton of old photo albums stuffed full of pictures and articles about the theatre."

This reminds me of the journal I hid in here. I search the shelf, but can't find it.

"What are you looking for?"

I push several pairs of shoes aside and run my hand along the shelf. "That journal I was telling you about. I put it right here. I know I did."

"Maybe Catherine grabbed it. Since she's back, maybe she has a few more things she'd like for us to know."

"About that. It all just seems too weird. I'm thinking that everything I thought I saw and heard might just be a residual effect of my accident and the medications I'm taking. It messed me up pretty bad, and I've had recurring nightmares ever since it happened."

She sits on the step stool. "Look, I don't know what went

down at home, and I'm not gonna push you to tell me. I've been thinking about this, though, and it's possible that what happened left you susceptible to a haunting. I've read where people who have experienced emotional trauma sometimes open themselves up to the paranormal. I don't mean to pry, but did someone die in the accident?"

"Yeah." My voice comes out hesitant. "What does that have to do with anything?"

"Maybe it put you in tune with the dead somehow."

I want to think she's joking, but her face is serious.

I roll my eyes. "Oh, what, so now I'm a ghost whisperer? Call the networks. Maybe I can get a reality show out of this."

"I really think we should look into everything that's happened since you got here. Maybe you're right, and all of this is just a figment of your imagination, but what could it hurt? Besides, I need some excitement. How cool would it be to do a little ghost hunting? It'll break up the monotony of working on theatre stuff day and night. Lord knows there's nothing else to do around here."

I shrug and nod reluctantly. What do I have to lose?

"Awesome. We'll start by digging through Gran's old stuff. We're going to have to ditch Luke, though. He'll treat it all as a joke. I'll see if I can get Patrice to keep him busy."

"Sounds good."

She places a hand on my shoulder. "You know, you can talk to me about what happened if you need to. Sometimes having a friend to listen helps."

I open the laptop and pull up the inventory spreadsheet. Maybe she'll get the hint that I'd rather work than talk about the accident.

She closes the laptop. "Come on. Don't shut down on me."

"Did your mother put you up to this?"

"No, my mother would never talk to me about one of her patients. I don't know anything about you other than what you've told me. Look, I'm not trying to force it out of you. I'm just saying. It's obvious whatever happened messed you up."

Messed up. Yep. That's me.

"Josie?" Molly's voice comes from the doorway. "Vic sent me up to ask you if we might be able to do a costume parade this afternoon. I think he's feeling a little anxious."

"Sure. Most everything's done. I'll go check with the stitch-bitches and see if they're ready to go."

"Stitch-bitches?" I ask.

"That's how we lovingly refer to ourselves in wardrobe. Are you guys on a break?"

Molly leans against the door. "Yeah, Julia had another diva fit, and Vic's dealing with her. He gave the rest of us a break."

Josie sighs and rolls her eyes. "She's such a bitch."

"No comment." Molly flashes her sweet smile.

Josie grabs her knapsack and leaves the two of us alone. Molly lingers in the doorway.

"So, you get the honorable job of cataloging all of these, huh?"

"Yes, it's very exciting. Best job I've ever had." I pretend to type something in the spreadsheet.

"Wow, you must have had some crap jobs." She moves down the aisle of clothing, running her hand over the fabric of a long, black cape.

"I've never really had a job. Unless you count mowing our lawn."

"Oh, so you're one of those privileged boys, huh? Mommy and Daddy pay your way while you play?" She's joking, but something about it rubs me the wrong way.

"I'm not privileged. I'm just an only child, and I was always busy with sports. I never had time for a job."

"Relax." She walks back toward me. "I was just messing with you."

"Sorry. I guess I'm a little sensitive."

"It's okay." She places a hand on my arm.

"I overheard you and Josie talking before I came in. I don't mean to pry, but…" She cuts herself off.

"But what?"

"You mentioned an accident earlier, and I heard Josie say something about it just now. What happened?"

I look into her blue eyes, searching for what she might already know. Is she testing me? Did Cole tell her already?

"My dad died eight years ago. He had a drinking problem. He ran his car off the road and died instantly." She twists the ring on her finger. "My mom couldn't deal with the grief and everything else that came after. She'd never worked a day in her life. When he left us with nothing, we lost the house. Then Mom took her own life."

The ease with which she unloads something so heavy knocks me off balance.

"I'm sorry to hear that."

"It's okay. I've learned to move on. The pain never really goes away, but you figure out how to live with it. You'll get there." She flashes me another smile and turns to go.

"Molly?"

She turns back. "Yeah?"

"Thanks."

"For what?"

"For understanding. Maybe one day we can talk or something."

"I'd like that." She turns and walks out the door.

I stand there feeling lighter somehow. My therapists have always said that talking about it helps. I guess maybe they're right.

Since I'm supposed to be helping Josie, I head back downstairs to find her. Patrice points me toward the dressing rooms. I hear Josie's voice behind one of the doors and step inside. Three guys, including Cole, are in various states of undress. Josie is crouched down, stitching the hem of one guy's pants. I notice her just as Cole slips his off.

My breath catches. His legs are solid muscle, dusted with dark hair. All those years in locker rooms, surrounded by half-dressed teammates, and I felt nothing. But Cole in boxer briefs has my blood flowing to places it shouldn't. He's not even naked, but you'd never know that by the way my body reacts. I can't look away from him.

Then I realize he's still. Just standing there. Watching me. Our eyes lock, and a smirk tugs at his lips. He winks. Heat surges straight south, my dick responding before I can think.

I want to smile back. Flirt. Something. But panic wins. I blurt out to Josie that I'll meet her in the theatre, then bolt, forcing myself to think about dead fish and fresh roadkill. Anything to get the vision of a very sexy half-naked Cole out of my mind. I need to calm down. I can't walk into a crowd of people with a boner.

I duck into the nearest restroom and splash cold water on my face until I feel halfway human again. By the time I make it back to the theatre, the costume parade is already gearing up.

It drags on for nearly three hours. I'm not sure what's worse, doing inventory or sitting in the house while twenty cast members parade across the stage, modeling costumes as Uncle Vic gives feedback to Josie and the other stitch-bitches.

At some point, I nod off. Luke jabs me in the ribs, and I jerk awake, praying I wasn't snoring. I definitely drooled, though. I wipe my chin and sit up straighter.

"Ready to go?" Josie asks once she's finished taking notes.

"Where are we going?" Luke asks.

Josie shoots me a sideways glance. "Heath is coming over for dinner. Gran wants to meet him."

"You're gonna brainwash him with ghost stories, aren't you?"

Josie was right; he'll be no help with any of this.

While Josie gathers her things, Cole strolls up—thankfully fully clothed. I'm not ready for a public repeat of what I saw earlier. "Hey. Got plans tonight?"

"Uh, yeah. Josie invited me to her grandma's for dinner. I

guess she knew my dad, and now she wants to meet me." I shrug. Why did I feel the need to say all that?

"Ah, cool. I was gonna see if you wanted to grab food or catch a movie. Maybe next time?"

My heart stutters. "I'd really like that."

"You'd *really* like it, huh?" His grin curves into a wink, casual but lingering just long enough to stir the heat in my body again.

I want to throw something back at him, playful or bold. Anything. Instead, I trip over the safer option. "It'd be fun. To hang out, I mean. Last night really helped. A lot."

His hand finds my shoulder, and he gives it a squeeze. "Glad to hear it. Can I get your number? Maybe I'll text you later."

My heart ricochets off my ribs. "Yeah, cool." I give it to him, and seconds later, a text buzzes through.

Add me.

I bite back a smile as I reply: **Done.**

"Catch you later." He heads off, and my eyes stay locked on his ass. Maybe this is a sign that I'm healing?

"Ready?" Josie asks, tossing her keys into the air and catching them.

"Yep." Not really. I'd rather be with Cole, but this has to be done. I'm ready to figure out what's been haunting me.

We climb into her car and head north along the coast, pulling up to a small beach house a few miles outside town. Weathered but cared for, it sits behind an arbor crawling with white blossoms. Wind chimes greet us with an offbeat tune as we step onto the creaky porch.

"Hey, Gran, we're home," Josie calls, closing the door behind us.

"I'm back here." A voice calls from what must be the kitchen.

Josie kicks off her shoes by the door and puts her bag down on a stool by the stairs. I remove my shoes as I look around.

The inside of the house isn't what I expected. The light tan walls and white window trim make the room feel fresh and calm. The decor is simple, reminiscent of most houses on the coast. Family portraits hang on the walls, and the occasional lighthouse, starfish, and ship in a bottle sit on the shelves. Sheer curtains flicker in the breeze that blows through the open window, mixing the salty scent of the air with the smell of pasta sauce simmering on the stove.

"Hey, Gran." Josie walks up and kisses her on the cheek.

"Hi, honey. How was the theatre today?"

"Fine, we had the costume parade this afternoon. Vic loved everything, but we've got a lot of adjustments to make before we open." Josie sits at the table and kicks a chair out for me with her toe. "Oh, this is Heath."

Mrs. Plummer is a pretty woman with kind green eyes and a welcoming smile. Her gray hair is pulled back in a headband, her flower-print shirt speckled with tomato sauce. She reminds me of my grandmother when she was alive—kind, generous, and always baking something.

"Hello, Heath." She stops stirring and stares at me. "My gosh, you look just like your father."

"So I hear."

"It's lovely to meet you."

I smile and nod. "Nice to meet you, too, Mrs. Plummer."

"Please, call me Marilyn." She pulls two glasses from the cupboard and fills them with lemonade.

After gorging ourselves on lasagna and garlic bread, Josie and I offer to help Marilyn with the dishes, but she refuses, so we go to the living room while she cleans up. Josie offers me a seat on the couch and goes to a closet to pull out some old photo albums.

"I found these last night. Gran has tons of old photographs from before the theatre burned. I thought maybe you would like to see them." She places three large albums on the coffee table and sits next to me.

We thumb through the first album. Inside are pictures of the grand opening of the opera house in June 1945, pictures of set builds, performances, and opening night parties. The pictures are old, and everyone looks extremely stiff and uncomfortable. We flip through two more albums, eventually finding the one from the late '90s. The years just before the theatre burned.

"Oh my God. It's you." Josie points to a picture of my father. If I were into '90s grunge fashion, I might think the picture is of me. "The resemblance is frightening. You seriously look *just* like him."

"Well, we *are* related."

Marilyn joins us, and as they discuss the similarities between my father and me, I notice another picture of him and a pretty, young girl with shoulder-length blonde hair.

It's her.

I stare at the photo. It's a publicity shot for *Our Town*. Below it are the actors' names: Phillip Ingram as George and Catherine Whitley as Emily. I didn't know my dad ever did theatre. I guess it makes sense, though.

"Can I get you kids anything else?"

"No, thanks, Gran." Josie's voice sounds distant. I'm still stuck staring at the photograph.

"Heath?" Marilyn's voice snaps me out of my thoughts.

"Um, no, thank you, though."

"I'm going to go read for a while. You kids have a good night." She starts for the stairs.

"Thank you for dinner," I say, remembering my manners.

"You okay?" Josie asks after Marilyn is out of earshot. "You're all kinds of pale."

"Yeah. I'm fine." The lie comes out flat.

"No, you're not. You look like you're going to be sick. What's up?"

"I saw her. This girl. Catherine. I saw her."

"Where?" Josie takes the album from me and stares at the girl.

"The theatre. And I think maybe outside my window at Uncle Vic's house."

"You didn't tell me you'd actually seen her. I thought you'd only heard her."

"I was going to, I just never got the chance."

"See! I told you. You're totally being haunted. This is awesome."

I wish I could show as much enthusiasm as she does, but I can't.

"Would you mind if I borrow these albums? I want to study them more closely."

"Go for it. Gran was planning to send them home with you anyway. She said she wanted Vic to have them."

The front door opens, and Dr. Plummer walks in. Josie grabs the album and slams it shut as if we've been caught doing something we shouldn't.

"Hi, guys. How are you, Heath?"

"Good, thanks." It's awkward being in my shrink's house. Seeing her outside the office is weird.

"What are you guys up to?"

"I was just about to drive Heath home." Josie stands and gathers the albums.

"I guess I'll see you on Monday, Heath?"

Right. My appointment.

"See you then." I nod and wave awkwardly before closing the door behind me.

Josie talks constantly the whole way to my house, but I barely hear her. My mind keeps going back to that photograph and the way Catherine looked at my father. I'm pretty sure it's the same way I looked at Cole this morning. She adored him.

When we reach Uncle Vic's house, I climb out of the car, eager to dig a little more.

Walking inside, I find Vic crashed out in the recliner, the TV blaring an infomercial. I flip off the television, hoping the ghost of Catherine doesn't climb out and attack me. That's about the only ghost trick she hasn't pulled. I go up to my room and place the albums in the closet on the top shelf next to some old shoeboxes. I need to sleep. I've had too many nights without much of it. The albums can wait.

After my shower, I hear Vic stumbling around downstairs. I consider going down to say hi, but change my mind. I throw on a pair of pajama bottoms and climb into bed, willing myself to fall asleep, but I can't stop thinking about the photos.

Crawling out of bed, I go to the closet to retrieve the albums, knocking one of the old shoeboxes off the shelf. Contents spill onto the floor—newspaper clippings, some photos, and a watch. I carry it all to the bed, studying the watch. The brushed nickel casing looks brand new. No scratches or smudges. The date reads August 8. The time is 9:47. An inscription on the back reads: *To Phillip with all my love. I'll always be with you.*

I put it on the nightstand. I could use a watch. I'll ask Uncle Vic if I can have it. Obviously, he doesn't have a use for it, or it wouldn't be stuffed in the closet.

Glancing at some of the newspaper clippings, I see they revolve around the theatre. I stuff them back in the box; I'll look at them later. Maybe some of them can be added to the albums Marilyn sent.

Crawling into bed, I take the album we'd been looking through earlier. Flipping back to the page of Catherine and my dad, the resemblance really is crazy. It's kind of creepy. I turn the page and see more publicity shots from the show. There's one of the two of them standing on ladders, facing one another. They're smiling.

There's another picture of Catherine in a wedding gown and my father in a suit. The next picture is of Catherine alone, looking at the camera. She's still wearing the wedding dress. She smiles at the camera, but there's a sadness in her eyes that makes my heart ache for her.

My eyes are heavy, and I know I need to put the album away before I fall asleep, but for some reason, I can't stop looking at her picture.

"I'm sorry." The words escape before I can stop them. "I'm sorry for what happened to you."

I close the album, but stop when I see, or think I see, a tear falling from Catherine's eye.

CHAPTER TWELVE

"Did you have a good night last night?" Vic asks as I join him at the table the next morning.

"Yeah, Marilyn sent some old photo albums she had of the theatre. They're upstairs in my closet." I pour myself a glass of orange juice and join him at the table. I want to ask him about Catherine, but I can't figure out a good way to go about it. "Oh, I found this watch in the closet last night. Mind if I have it? I think it was Dad's. His name is inscribed on the back."

"Let's see it." He holds out his hand. I watch his face as he looks it over. "This was in the closet?"

"Yeah, it was in a shoebox with all these old photos and newspaper clippings. I think the battery's dead."

"It doesn't need a battery. It just needs to be wound up." He winds it, then stops and looks at the face for a moment, an odd look passing over him. "I've never seen this watch before. You can have it."

He hands me the watch, and I stuff it in my pocket as I chug my orange juice and follow him out the door.

"The next few days are going to seem tedious to you." We climb into the truck. "We'll need to get the set changes choreographed and the lights focused today. Luke's going to be in charge of that while I work with the cast. You okay with working the light board?"

"Yeah, it's cool." I hope it's not very difficult.

When we get to the theatre, everyone is running around fixing things. It's like Santa's workshop the night before Christmas, and I feel like I'm in the way.

Luke hands me a clipboard. "I could use your help setting pre-show. Just place these props according to the list."

Twenty minutes later, he shakes his head. "You got it backward. Stage left is actor's left, not audience left." Now I have to switch everything, which seems to take forever.

Vic orders everyone pizza for lunch, so Luke and I go to the green room to grab ourselves a few slices. Cole pulls cheese off his pizza slice, and I can't look away from his fingers. When he glances up and catches me staring, I focus intently on my own slice, cheeks burning. A second later, my phone buzzes in my pocket.

You look cute 2day

My pulse jumps. I catch Cole's eye, and he shrugs.

friend 2 friend ofc

I reply with, **Thx,** and hide my smile as I follow Luke back to the main stage.

Josie rushes around making last-minute costume adjustments, so I don't see her much. After lunch, Luke announces that we will be doing something called paper tech, where we go through all the sound and light cues and the set changes that need to happen. It sounded simple enough when he explained it, but it's a long and tedious process. Ryan loses it on some of the high school kids helping with the set changes. He makes one girl cry, and another kid storms out.

"Hey, Ryan." Luke's voice cuts across the stage. "Are you going to replace the two kids on my crew I just lost? This show isn't going to run itself."

It's kind of funny to see Luke irritated. He's been so laid-back since I met him, I didn't know he was capable.

"Those kids are idiots. Someone was bound to get hurt."

"Why don't you let me worry about that? I'm the Stage Manager, not you."

"Well, I'm the set lead, and I don't need them messing up my set. I don't have time to fix things when they break them."

"So then show them how to do it correctly instead of yelling at them and calling them idiots."

"I'm out of here. You tell them. And if they break anything, you're fixing it, not me." Ryan rolls his eyes and storms off.

"Such a fucking drama queen," Luke mutters as the door closes behind Ryan. "Okay, everyone, let's call it a day. I appreciate your help, and I'm sorry about Ryan's behavior. I'll do my best to keep him away from you the next few days. Go home and get some rest. I'll see you all at 9:00 AM. Oh, and if anyone knows the two kids who quit, please call them and beg them to come back. I'll buy you all ice cream, or something."

They all file out, leaving Luke to gather up his things.

"Well, that was fun."

He shakes his head. "I hate tech more than anything. I just wish things could go right the first time. This is the only part of stage managing that I hate. Want me to show you how to operate the light board? It'll save us time tomorrow. If I can get that off my plate, I can concentrate on working with the kids on the set changes before the cue-to-cue starts in the afternoon."

"Sure." I follow him down the hall and up a set of stairs I've never seen before to a little room that overlooks the stage. He flips a few switches, and a computer monitor lights up.

"This is your headset." He hands me a set of headphones with a microphone attached. "You need to wear it at all times.

This is how I'll communicate with you."

"Why do I need a headset? I thought you were going to be up here with me?"

"I said I would be with you, but not physically here. I'll be backstage. I'll call the show from there. I'll be connected to you and the sound operator via headset."

My stomach drops. "Who will be up here with me?"

"No one."

"Wait, seriously?" That's not what I expected him to say.

"Are you scared?" He jabs me with his elbow. "Has all of Josie's ghost talk freaked you out?"

"Nah, I just… I've never done this before."

"You'll be fine." He walks to the door to my right and unlocks it. "This door leads to the costume room."

It's the same door I heard the crying come from the other day.

"This door leads to the spot loft and the catwalk." He opens another door, and I peek out to see rows of empty theatre seats below us.

"The board is already programmed. All the cues I had you write down earlier correspond to a cue programmed into the board. To go to the next cue, just hit this button." He punches a black button that has the word *Go* written across it.

"If you mess up—and please don't mess up—hit this button, and it will take you back to the previous cue." He indicates another button that has the word *Back* written across it. "Easy enough?"

"Yeah, it seems pretty straightforward."

"Like I said, I'll be on headset backstage, calling the cues. All you have to do is hit the button when I say so." He pauses, studying my face. "I would suggest you walk through all the cues, just to get an idea of how everything is supposed to look. Vic is very particular about his cues. The lights are timed with the staging and the lyrics. It sounds simple enough, but the lights are what set the mood for the whole show. If they're messed up, it throws everything off for the actors and the audience."

"Got it. I think maybe I'll run through them tonight before I go home. That cool?" Nerves twist in my stomach. I don't want to mess up Vic's show.

"Sure thing." He hands me the light cue script. "I'll let Vic know you're up here."

"Tell him I'll just go out the back when I'm finished. I can walk home."

"See you tomorrow." He walks out the door and closes it behind him.

Opening the script, I look at the first cue labeled "pre-show." I hit the button that takes me to the next cue labeled "house out." The lights slowly fade to complete darkness. I jump when I see my face reflected back at me behind the soundproof glass overlooking the stage. The light from the board glows across my face, giving me a hollowed-out look.

I punch the button, walking through the cues. I can't help but feel like I'm running some sort of concert. The lights flash and fade, bouncing around in different shades of warm white, red, purple, and blue. I make it through all of Act One, and when I bring up the lights for intermission, I jump when I see someone on stage.

"Heath, is that you?" Vic shields his eyes from the harsh stage lights shining down on him.

"Yeah." I dim the lights a bit and then step out to the spot loft.

"I'm about ready to head home. You need a ride?"

"Is anyone else here?"

"A few of the girls are here finishing their costume fittings."

"I'm going to walk through the rest of these cues. You go ahead." Knowing I won't be in the theatre alone makes me feel better.

I wait for him to walk off the stage before I move to the next cue. I get about halfway through Act Two when I hear light footsteps and a shuffling sound coming from the costume room. The hair on my arms rises. I reach for my phone to text Josie, then remember I left it downstairs. I seriously need to staple that thing to my leg. I never have it when I need it.

Standing slowly, I move toward the door that leads to the costume room, doing my best to control my breathing. Someone is definitely on the other side of the door. I will myself to be brave and face whatever it is that's about to happen.

Something brushes against the door. My stomach plummets. The sound stops. Silence stretches. I back toward the other exit, but the door handle turns with a metallic click. The door creaks open, inch by torturous inch.

"Boo!"

I jump as Molly walks into the room. Patrice and Josie are right behind her, laughing hysterically.

"Very funny." I press my hand to my chest, heart still stuttering. For a minute, I want to go off on Josie. She knows what I've been dealing with.

"I'm sorry," Molly says. "Josie put me up to it. It's all her fault."

Josie pushes her way in like she owns the place. Kind of like she always does. "I'm sorry, I couldn't resist. When Vic said you were up here, I had to do it. What are you doing anyway?"

"Just going through the cues." I take a deep breath and stuff my hands in my pockets so they can't see how badly they're shaking. "I've never run a light board before. I'm trying to get familiar with it."

"It's not rocket science. You hit a button every now and then."

"Yeah, I know. I just don't want to screw up the show. Luke's stressed out enough as it is. He doesn't need me adding to it."

"We're finished with the costumes. Are you staying here or what?"

I close the binder containing my script. "Nah, I'm finished."

"Let's go then." She switches off the light board, casting the stage into darkness.

I follow the girls out the door toward the costume room, closing the door behind me.

Don't go.

I freeze. The voice was barely a whisper, but I heard it. Every instinct screams at me to get the fuck out, but something else makes me want to turn back.

"You coming?" Josie asks.

"Yeah." I take one last look at the door.

"Are you okay?" She takes a step toward me, and I start to tell her what I heard, or thought I heard, but Molly and Patrice are here, and I don't want them to think I'm psycho.

"I thought I forgot something." The lie slips out as I limp down the steps and follow them through the costume room.

Josie checks to make sure the front doors are locked and all the lights are out before guiding us to the back door. "Is Vic coming back for you, or do you need a ride home?" It's raining out, and we all stand huddled under the awning.

"That would be great if you don't mind. I don't feel like getting soaked."

"I'll unlock the car." Josie gives Patrice a quick kiss and then dashes off to her car.

"Have a good night. Sorry about scaring you tonight." Molly waves before following Patrice to her car.

"Bye." Josie honks her horn to grab my attention, and I dart off toward her car.

"Gotta love Oregon rain." She pulls out of the lot. "So did you see or hear anything today? I never got a free minute to come and talk to you."

"Nothing at all. It was very quiet and normal."

"What about when we were leaving the light booth? Did you really think you left something?"

It's then that I remember that I did forget something. I left my phone. Again. Seriously?

"Oh shit, I did leave something. My phone is there."

"Do you need it?" She stops the car.

I want to say yes. What if Cole texts? But then I remember

what happened the last time I went back to get my phone.

"No, I'll just get it tomorrow."

She turns her car down the bridge toward Vic's house, the rain glinting off her headlights. "So, I've been thinking. We should do a séance. See if we can contact Catherine."

"You mean with candles and voodoo chants and stuff?" I can't help but laugh. She can't be serious.

"It's not voodoo, but yeah. There will be candles involved."

"Have you ever done a séance before?"

"I've done a few. Nothing like this, though, but it's worth a shot, huh?" Her excitement is infectious. Besides, I've gotten myself in this far, so why not see what else happens?

"When?"

"Tomorrow night, after everyone leaves. I already have it figured out. I'll say I need to stay and finish a few costumes, and you'll offer to help me out. Once everyone leaves, we'll do it."

The theatre fades behind us, and my stomach knots. We're really going to attempt to contact Catherine. Part of me wants to know what she has to say. The other part is terrified we might get more than we bargained for.

"Help... me..."

The words I've heard a hundred times before echo around me. I'm on the ground, paralyzed. My body feels like it's made of lead, every muscle refusing to work. It takes everything I have just to lift my head.

Amy lies across from me, eyes wide, blood spilling from her nose and mouth. Above her, Jake dangles from his seatbelt, neck twisted at an impossible angle.

His eyes snap open. His mouth moves.

"You... killed... me..."

I try to reach for him, but I can't move. My lips part, but no sound comes.

"You... killed... me..." he says again, voice jagged and broken. "I... loved... you."

The words slice through me, my chest caving. Then, from behind the Jeep, comes the sound.

Drag... thump.

Drag... thump.

Meredith staggers into view, lurching forward like something torn from a nightmare. Her head hangs at a grotesque angle, her left arm hanging by a thread of tendon, her right leg dragging behind her. A black stream of blood pours down her face, her body broken from the crash.

Her mouth opens. Her good arm rises, trembling, a finger pointing straight at me.

"Die..."

"Help... me..."

"You... killed... us..."

"I... loved... you..."

The voices overlap, echoing until the words blur into one suffocating chorus. Meredith limps closer.

Closer.

She screams. The sound explodes inside my skull. Hot blood splatters across my face.

I scramble backward—

And bolt awake.

The surface under me is cold, hard. Not my bed. I sit up, heart hammering. Darkness wraps around me, broken only by the howl of wind and the relentless lash of rain against the building.

Where am I?

Crying echoes faintly behind me. My hands fumble across the floor, finding only cold wood and shadow. Then a pulse of orange light flickers ahead, low and sickly, and I realize I'm at the theatre. I'm sitting on the stage, inches from the orchestra pit.

Someone sits a few feet away from me to my right.

"Catherine?" My voice is a whisper, trembling. It has to be her. Who else could it be?

"Yes." One word. Soft. Fragile.

My chest tightens. She's actually answering me. "Are you okay?"

"Help me. Please." Her voice cracks. She sounds terrified, helpless. Her silhouette shimmers in the glow seeping from the pit.

"What's wrong? Tell me how to help."

"Help… me…"

She weeps, the sound swelling from soft sobs to full, broken wails. The grief in her voice digs into me. I inch toward her using tiny steps, not wanting to spook her. When I'm close enough, I reach out and touch her shoulder.

The world erupts.

Flames roar from the pit, engulfing her. Her scream shreds the air, shrill and inhuman. I jerk my hand back as fire races up around her body—

Then everything is gone. Darkness crashes down. The flames vanish.

A beat later, the stage lights snap on, flooding the theatre in blinding white. The air smells faintly of smoke, but the stage is bare. No scorch marks. No sign of her.

Nothing.

I stagger backward, throat tight. A dream. It has to be a dream. Except I feel awake. Too awake.

I turn for the exit, desperate to leave—

"You didn't help me."

The voice is right behind me.

I whirl. Catherine stands a few feet away, eyes red with fury.

"I tried."

"You didn't help me." She sobs, her voice splitting. "Why didn't you help me?"

"Tell me how, and I will." I fumble for the door, palm slick with sweat.

"You were supposed to come back for me." Her voice drops, low and ragged. She jerks forward, each stuttering step punctuating the words:

"You. Let. Me. Die."

I rip the door open and stumble into the storm. Rain slams down in sheets, soaking me instantly. My hair clings to my face, water stings my eyes. My hip screams with every step, but I force myself toward the bridge.

"You. Let. Me. Die."

Her voice is everywhere. Inside me. Around me.

I hear splashing footsteps. To my left. Then my right. Spinning, I find nothing. Just darkness and rain.

Then I turn forward—

And she's there.

Catherine. Skin blackened, peeling from her face in jagged sheets. Eyes burning. Mouth gaping. Throat full of ash and flame.

She lunges.

I jolt awake on my bedroom floor. I'm soaked. Pajamas drenched, feet numb.

What the hell is happening to me?

The house is silent. Too silent. The only sound is the steady beat of rain against the window.

Then—squeaking.

Like a finger dragging down wet glass. Over and over. Faster. Louder.

I force myself to look.

Words bleed through the rain on the window:

You Let Me Die

Sleep won't come. My mind races, twisting through everything that's happened. Shit like this only happens in the movies. It's not real. It can't be. But the wet pajamas on my floor suggest otherwise.

When Uncle Vic knocks on my door, I've only managed to squeeze in about three hours of sleep.

I'm a complete zombie as I follow Vic into the theatre. It takes me a full ten seconds to register that the stage lights are at full blaze.

"Did you leave these on all night?" Vic's eyes burn into me. "Do you have any idea what the electricity at this place costs? Running the stage lights for just a couple of hours practically doubles the bill."

"Josie turned them off before we left, I swear."

He storms across the stage, investigating the damage. "There are three bulbs burned out. Now Ray is going to have to climb up there and fix them, and that's going to put us behind. Damn it." He pushes past me, and I hear the door hit the wall as he storms down the hallway.

I decide to stay out of his way for the time being. Grabbing my phone from where I'd left it the day before, I'm happy to see it still holds a charge. Cole texted three times last night. Shit.

What u up to? *9:48 pm*

U ignorin me now? *10:12 pm*

Sleep tight *11:08 pm*

I start to text him back and explain, but then a text comes in from Josie:

Where R U?

theatre

Walking in now

"What's going on?" She walks in a few seconds later, handing me a bagel and cream cheese. "Vic is pissed about something."

"You turned the lights off before we left last night, right?"

"Yes, you saw me do it." She sits on the floor next to me and spreads her breakfast out in front of her.

"You turned them off. Not standby? Off."

"Yes, Heath. I flipped the switch and turned them off. Why?"

"They were on when we walked in this morning. No one else was here. Vic thinks I left them on all night."

She shrugs. "So, maybe Ray was up here working on them this morning, went to get something to eat, and forgot to turn them off before he left."

I stare at the spot on the stage where I'd seen Catherine. "That's probably it."

She studies my face, trying to read my expression. "Something's wrong."

"I just had a crazy dream last night, and I thought for a second..."

"Thought what?"

"That maybe it wasn't a dream, but it had to be."

"What are you talking about? You always talk in circles.

Spit it out."

I tell her about seeing Catherine last night. I don't mention anything about the message written on my window or the wet clothes piled on my floor this morning.

"Do you remember walking up here?"

"No. I'm not even sure it was real."

Luke walks in, and we stop talking, concentrating instead on our breakfast.

"What's going on?" He joins us.

"Nothing," we say in unison.

"Didn't sound like nothing when I walked in. What's going on?"

"We're just talking, Luke. Calm down. We were trying to figure out who left the lights on. We turned them off when we left last night, and when Heath and Vic came in this morning, they were on. Heath asked if I was sure I turned them off. That's all."

"Okay." He turns and walks off. The way he's acting, you'd think he was her boyfriend or something.

"I think Luke's feeling left out. I need to go make sure everyone's costumes are where they're supposed to be. Do you want me to come up and sit with you while we do the cue-to-cue?"

"Nah, it's cool."

"We still on for tonight?" I'd almost forgotten about our plans.

"Sure. Why not?"

The rest of the morning is complete chaos. Luke sprints between crises, and Ryan terrorizes the crew. I stay out of the way until Luke waves me up to the light booth. I take a seat, put my headset on, and open my script to the first cue.

"Heath. Heath… I love you." The voice crackles over the headset.

My body tenses. "Hello?"

"I want to touch your booty, Heath. You hot piece of man candy," the voice whispers, followed by Luke's unmistakable laugh.

"Do you two need to get a room and work this out?" Sam,

the sound guy, asks.

I laugh. "He's not my type."

"Gee thanks." Luke's tone shifts. "Okay, guys and gals and gays, actors are in place. At this point, I would cue the orchestra, but since they're not here today, we'll just go with the lights. Heath, get ready for the first light cue."

I place my finger over the go button, waiting for his word. This is more nerve-wracking than I thought it would be. The further along we go, the easier it becomes. I relax and go on Luke's command. I only mess up a couple of times when he tells me to stand by for a cue, and I mistake it as go ahead with the cue.

Uncle Vic gives everyone a fifteen-minute break after we finish the act. I go downstairs to talk to Luke, passing Julia and Ryan in the hall.

"Hey, light guy." Julia gets in my face. "Why don't you try not fucking up my cues, huh? Do you have any idea how stressful it is being up there? I shouldn't have to worry about you getting your cues right with everything else I have going on."

"So, then don't worry about me getting my cues right." I brush past them.

"Don't let him get to you. He's a dick." Ryan's voice follows me down the hall.

I shoot him a glance over my shoulder and blow a kiss. That'll get him good and riled up.

I feel like I'm just in the way down here, so I grab a soda from the vending machine and then go back up to the booth.

I put the headset on and wait for Luke to tell me to go. The headset crackles a few moments later, and I wait, expecting to hear him. It sounds as if something is rubbing against the microphone, but then it stops. A few seconds later, it happens again.

"Luke?" No answer. "Sam?"

Again, no answer.

"Phillip?" Catherine's voice comes through the headset. Barely audible above the crackling, but it's there.

"Let's start Act Two, fellas." Luke's voice cuts through the static. The crackling is gone. "Go cue forty-nine."

I push the button. The act begins, and heavy breathing fills my ears over the headset.

"Which one of you is panting in my ear?"

"Not me," Sam says.

"I don't hear any panting." Luke's voice comes through clearly. "Stop talking or you're going to make me miss my cues."

The headset starts to hiss again. I jiggle the wire, thinking maybe there's a short in it.

"Please don't." Catherine's voice cuts through the static, raw and desperate. The sound makes my skin crawl. How can no one else hear this?

"Go cue fifty-two." Luke's voice. The crackling and ragged breathing are louder now. I can barely hear him. I go to cue fifty-two and watch as Julia welcomes the audience, then breaks into a song.

"…cue…fifty—" Luke's voice is breaking up. Was that a cue or a standby? I decide to hit the button anyway.

"Luke, I can barely hear you over the crackling."

"…Fifty-four…" Shit. Sweat beads on my forehead. Was that a standby? It had to be. I'm trying to follow along with the actors in my script, but it's difficult. They aren't wearing their microphones yet, so all I hear is mumbling.

"Stop, please. Get away from me. No. No. No, please." Catherine's screams tear through the headset. Luke's voice disappears under her panic. I hit the go button without thinking. The stage dies to black.

A crash echoes through the theatre.

A loud scream.

I hit the back button and bring the lights up on the stage. Everyone rushes to the orchestra pit. Someone is crying.

"Someone call 911!" Vic shouts.

Luke is in the booth so quickly it's like he teleported. "I told you to go back one cue."

He's trying to stay calm, but the fact that he's pissed is written all over his face. "Now we're down an actor."

"Who?"

"Julia. She fell into the pit. Like you needed Ryan to hate you even more than he already does."

Shit.

"I couldn't hear you. There was all kinds of static over the headset. You were breaking up. I panicked. I was trying to follow along in the script, but I couldn't hear the actors because they weren't wearing their microphones. I'm really sorry. Seriously."

Luke puts the headset on and listens. "The line is fine. I don't hear any static at all. We'd better go talk to Vic. I'm going to let you explain this one."

When we get to the hallway, the EMS is wheeling Julia out on a stretcher. Ryan walks alongside her, holding her hand, telling her everything is going to be all right.

"You'd better hope she's okay, or I'll be coming after you. Watch your back, bitch." He points a finger in my face.

I could apologize, but I know it won't do any good, so I turn and follow Luke to the stage.

"Go get changed. It looks like you'll be going on as Velma," Vic says to Patrice.

She bites her lip, fighting a smile. She squeezes my hand as she passes. Like we had a pact, and I just carried through on my end of the deal.

"Uncle Vic, I am so sorry. The headset was breaking up, and I couldn't hear Luke—"

"It's all right. It wasn't entirely your fault. It was your first time working the light board. If that damned girl had followed the blocking I gave her, instead of insisting on walking downstage for dramatic effect, she wouldn't have walked into the pit."

"Is she going to be okay?"

He shrugs. "They're taking her to the hospital. They think

she may have cracked her ankle. She won't be on stage anytime soon. Thankfully, I have Patrice as her understudy. She'll be fine. It's all going to be fine." It sounds as if he's trying to reassure himself as much as the rest of us. "I'm glad I have insurance on this place. She's the type that'll sue. All right, everyone go back to places. We'll start at the top of Act Two with Patrice filling in for Julia."

I go back to the light booth and prepare the light board for the top of Act Two. The door opens, and I jump.

"Bruh, what happened? Did you do that on purpose?" Josie can't keep herself from giggling.

"No, I swear. How could I have known she wouldn't stick to her blocking and fall into the pit? The headset was full of static, and I couldn't hear Luke."

"Static? Like what you heard the other night?"

"Yeah, and I heard her again. Catherine."

Josie looks around, as if she expects to see Catherine hanging out in the booth with me. "I heard Julia chewed you out for messing up her cues."

"Yeah, she said something to me on break."

"Ryan thinks you were getting back at her. Trying to prove a point." She pulls up a chair next to me.

"I wasn't. I swear."

"Well, you're a hero to the rest of the cast. Julia probably won't be able to perform since we only run for two weeks. Patrice is beyond excited. She gets to play Velma, and Cole said he's so happy to have her gone, he wants to kiss you."

Heat floods my face. I know it's a joke, but I can't help but imagine his lips on mine. For once, guilt doesn't immediately follow.

"Go cue forty-nine." Luke's voice interrupts my daydream. "Let me know if the static comes back. You may want to open the door, so you can hear the actors until I can get Ray up there to check out the connection."

"Will do." I motion to Josie to prop the door open.

Act two goes smoothly. Patrice is ten times better in the role than Julia ever was. When we're finished, Vic showers the entire cast and crew with words of praise. By the time we're finished with our notes, it's going on 3:30. Vic releases everyone for a late lunch, and then tells the actors he needs them back for a sing-through with the orchestra by 5:00. I join some of the cast and crew for lunch at the diner and then have Josie drop me by the house.

The chirping of my phone wakes me. I have a text message.

Bruh, get yr ass down here

It's Josie. She must be waiting for me outside. I glance at the clock and see that it's only 8:45. She's early.

Be right there

I stand and grab a fresh shirt from the dresser. The sun is setting and casts an eerie pink glow in my room. I grab a sweatshirt from the closet, grab my house key, and join her in the car.

"What the hell were you doing up there? Jerking off?"

"I was sleeping. You're early." I yawn.

"They'll be finished soon. I asked Vic if I could work on some costumes, and he gave me the okay to be up there. I told him you'd be with me."

"I'm sure that made him feel better since every time I've been the last one out of the theatre, something's happened to piss him off."

"Not every time. Nothing happened after we painted the floor."

We stop and grab coffee, then drive to the theatre. We park in the back and enter through the backstage door. As we enter the theatre, the orchestra swells around us, and the cast erupts in applause.

"Beautiful! Absolutely gorgeous. You all sound wonderful. I couldn't be happier." Vic wipes a tear from his eye and smiles when he sees us walking across the stage. "Did you hear that?

Didn't they sound amazing?"

I nod. "We just caught the tail end, but it sounded great."

"The whole attitude of the cast has changed. There's no tension. They're committing to the show 100%. They've all done a one-eighty. I hate to say it, but Julia falling in that pit was the best thing that could have happened to this show. I know. It's awful. I hate to wish harm on anyone, but that little hussy was a thorn in my side."

Josie and I crack up at his honesty. He walks back toward the green room, yelling at his cast that he loves them.

"Damn, bruh. You look like somebody ran you over, dusted you off, and then backed up over you just for the hell of it. You are wrecked."

Luke walks out on stage, ignoring Josie's comment. "I seriously don't think it's possible to be any more tired than I am right now. What are you guys doing?"

"I have some costume adjustments to make for Patrice. I asked Heath to keep me company, so the scary ghosts don't get me."

He rolls his eyes. "So, I see I've been replaced."

"You haven't been replaced, lover boy. You are more than welcome to stay up here with us if you want. I didn't ask you because I figured you'd be exhausted."

"You're right. I am exhausted, and as much as I love you, I'd rather be sleeping than watching you sew costumes. You two have fun." He turns off the lights on the stage manager's desk and heads down the stairs.

I follow Josie back to the green room, where she grabs a few costumes to make it look like we actually plan to work. I stand to the side as the cast trickles out. I feel someone grab me around the waist and turn to find Cole smiling at me.

"Hey, you." His hand settles on my back, warm through my shirt. "Let me be the first to thank you for taking out the wicked witch." His thumb brushes against my ribs, casual but deliberate. "You've made all our lives so much better."

The warmth of his touch spreads through my chest.

When I look up, Luke is standing in the doorway, staring at us. His jaw tightens before he turns away. The longing in his expression is painful. I should talk to him.

Molly steps around Cole and throws her arms around my neck. "You are my new best friend. Thank you for accidentally taking out that evil woman."

I laugh and hug her back.

"So I hear we're having a séance tonight to flush out the ghost."

This catches me off guard, and the only thing I can think to do is feign ignorance. "We are?" I thought Josie and I were going to do this alone.

"Patrice said that Josie mentioned something about it. Sounds cool and creepy. I'd heard rumors this theatre is haunted."

"Yeah, me too." I wonder how much she knows. I suddenly feel like an idiot.

"I want to play." Cole moves closer, his shoulder brushing mine. "Count me in."

My pulse quickens at the contact, and I find myself wanting him to stay close.

"Heath? I love you." Patrice runs up and wraps her arms around my neck. "This is seriously the best present anyone has ever given me."

I hold my hands up. "I didn't do it on purpose. I swear."

"It doesn't matter. I still love you." She kisses me on the cheek.

"Careful now. Don't be trying to steal my girlfriend." Josie whacks me on the butt.

The green room slowly empties, exhausted actors heading home for the night, until it's just the five of us left standing.

"You guys need to pretend you're leaving," Josie whispers as we walk down the hall. "If Vic knows all of us are going to be up here, he's going to get suspicious. Drive down the street and wait until you see him leave. Wait five minutes and then text me. I'll meet you at the back door."

"You guys have fun sewing." Patrice waves when she sees Vic locking up his office. "We're out of here. See you tomorrow, Vic."

"Bye, baby. You were wonderful up there. I should have cast you in that role in the first place."

"I know." She winks.

Vic offers us a small wave before heading toward the lobby. "You two stay out of trouble. I'm locking up. This old man needs some rest."

"Good night, Vic. Sleep tight." Josie watches him walk out the front door, locking it behind him.

We stand in the lobby, peeking through the window. We watch him climb into the old Ford, start it up, and drive away. When it seems safe, we walk backstage. I hold the back door open as Josie goes out to her car for the "supplies". She returns with a huge duffel bag.

"Jesus, what's in there? I thought we just needed a few candles."

"I brought all the necessities. I did my research. This is very involved." She lets the door close behind her. Walking to the stage, she places the bag in the center of the floor. She takes four large candles and places them strategically around the stage. She pulls a box from her bag and removes the lid. It's a Ouija board.

"Whoa." My heart slams against my ribs. The board looks innocent enough. It's just letters and numbers on cardboard. But after everything I've experienced...

"It's a Ouija board."

"I know, but why do we need it? Those things are dangerous. What if we make things worse?"

"They're only dangerous if you don't use them correctly. Trust me. I know what I'm doing."

"I don't know if I'm comfortable with this."

"Bruh, chill. It's not that deep. Do you want to get rid of Catherine or not? This is a surefire way of communicating with her. I use this all the time. I know what I am doing." She places the board on a large purple piece of fabric that lies on the floor in the middle of the candles. Her phone beeps, and I jump.

"They're on their way back. Are you ready for this?"

CHAPTER FOURTEEN

"Holy shit, is that a Ouija board?" Molly asks as she walks onto the stage carrying a plastic grocery bag filled with snacks.

"Yeah. Josie thinks this will help us contact Catherine." I stare at the board. "I've never seen one of these before. It's kind of creepy."

She pulls an Oreo apart and licks the icing from one of the cookies.

Patrice sits next to her and rips open a bag of Doritos. Cole appears behind them, looking around at the candle setup with raised eyebrows.

"What are you two doing?" Josie asks. "This isn't a movie."

"Sorry. We have serious munchies. It's been a long day." Patrice licks the cheesy powder from her fingers.

"Get the food out of the circle. The working area has to be clean." Josie grabs the junk food and carries it off to the side, obviously annoyed.

"Geez, grumpy much?" Patrice asks when Josie takes the

bag of chips from her. "Come on Molly and Cole. We'll eat over here and watch the ghost hunters do their thing."

They position themselves outside the candles, and Josie instructs me to sit facing her. She seems agitated. She closes her eyes and takes a couple of deep breaths. I sit and watch her, unsure of what I should do.

"Oh, crap. I forgot to light the candles. Hold on." She grabs a large lighter and walks around in a clockwise motion, lighting each candle and mumbling something under her breath. The house lights die, leaving us in flickering amber light. Shadows dance across the set like living things.

"Vic'll totally kick your ass if you start the set on fire," Patrice says.

"I'm not going to set anything on fire." Josie takes her place across from me.

"But didn't ghost girl burn up or something? If you call her out of hiding, she might try to burn us all. Did you ever think of that?"

"Patrice, you know I love you, but if you don't shut up, I'm going to break your leg."

"I love it when you talk all butch." Patrice laughs.

"Okay, shut it. We need to do this."

The room grows quiet. Josie closes her eyes and breathes deep.

"Okay, place your hands on the planchette and try to clear your mind."

I do as I'm told, acutely aware of four pairs of eyes watching me.

Josie closes her eyes and starts. "Catherine? Are you there?"

I stare at the planchette, waiting for it to move, but nothing happens.

"Catherine? We're not here to hurt you. We want to help you."

I stare at our fingers lightly resting on the planchette, relieved that it hasn't moved, afraid of how I'll react if it does.

"You try. Maybe you're the only one she'll talk to."

I hesitate, unsure of what to say. I'm scared to death but afraid to let it show. No one else here seems to think this is a big deal. Why do I?

"Catherine?" My voice cracks, and I clear my throat. "Um, are you there?" I roll my eyes for everyone else's benefit, hoping they can't see my hands trembling.

The planchette moves. Not much, but it moves.

"Did you feel that? It moved."

"Yeah, it may have just been me, though. I shifted." I stare at the board. I know it wasn't me.

"Ask her something else."

"Like what? I have no clue what I'm doing."

"Catherine, dahling," Patrice uses a mock English accent as she scoots closer, abandoning her snacks. "Can you hear us dahling?"

"Yes, Catherine dear, are you there?" Molly chimes in.

The planchette shakes.

"Don't insult her. Be serious or you're leaving. I mean it." Josie takes a deep breath. "Catherine, are you afraid?"

The planchette doesn't move.

"Ask her if she's afraid, Heath," Patrice prods.

I clear my throat. "Catherine? Are you afraid?"

The planchette moves slowly toward the word "no" on the board and then back to the center. Everyone's eyes grow huge.

"Dude, you totally moved that yourself," Patrice says.

"No, I didn't. I swear." My voice shakes. I take a deep breath. I can't freak out in front of everyone.

"Ask her why she's here." Josie whispers.

"Catherine? Why are you here?"

The planchette moves again, this time a little faster. B-A-B-Y

"Baby? Like your baby daddy? You want Heath to be your baby daddy?" Patrice cracks.

D-E-A-D

"Of course you're dead. That's why you're a ghost," Molly

says under her breath.

"Ghosts don't always realize they're dead," Josie explains.

"Tell us what you want." I want to get this over with so we can get out of here.

H-E-L-P

The planchette moves in slow, rhythmic circles around the center of the board. My fingers barely touch it. I wonder if maybe Josie is moving it. I hope so.

L-O-V-E

Patrice says every word aloud, as if we can't form the words ourselves.

"Girl's obsessed with someone. I wonder if she realizes ghosts can't get it on with mortals."

P-A-I-N

B-U-R-N

H-E-L-P

The planchette moves back to the center of the board after spelling out each word.

"Are you in pain?"

The planchette glides to the word Yes.

"How can we help you?"

T-I-C-K-T-O-C-K

"Tick, Tock? I don't understand what that means."

"Maybe she wants you to help her go viral on TikTok." Patrice laughs.

Josie places her hand on Patrice's knee and gives her a look that says "Stop."

S-E-E-M-E

H-E-A-R-M-E

L-O-V-E-M-E

M-Y-B-A-B-Y

"See me, hear me, love me, my baby? What the hell does that mean?" My eyes follow the planchette as it glides quickly across the board, trying to keep up with every letter.

"Guys, this is freaking me out. I don't think we should be doing this." Molly's voice wavers.

T-I-C-K-T-O-C-K-T-I-C-K-T-O-C-K

H-E-L-P-M-E

D-I-E

A-N-G-E-R

B-U-R-N

"She's pissed."

"I would be too if someone burned my ass up," Patrice says.

B-A-B-Y

T-A-K-E-B-A-B-Y

The planchette stops suddenly. Then very slowly, it moves again—

D...A...N...G...E...R

The planchette slows down as if it's lost steam, as if Catherine ran out of energy.

"Danger? Who is in danger? I don't know what you mean." My voice shakes.

M-U-R-D-E-R

The planchette picks up speed again.

"She thinks she was murdered. Maybe the fire wasn't an accident. Or maybe someone purposely let her die."

Y-O-U

You? Who is she talking to? Is she calling me a murderer?

D-A-N-G-E-R

Or is she trying to warn me?

A-L-L

W-I-L-L

D-I-E

Everyone stares at the board with wide eyes. I can tell they're all as scared as I am. The message is clear.

"Guys, we need to stop. Please?" Molly begs.

The planchette moves between letters faster and faster.

B-A-B-Y

M-Y-B-A-B-Y
D-A-N-G-E-R
N-O
B-A-B-Y
D-I-E
B-U-R-N
P-A-I-N
D-I-E-B-U-R-N-P-A-I-N-L-O-V-E-R-E-V-E-N-G-E-B-A-B-Y

My body is tense with fear, my fingers barely touching the planchette. I can't do this anymore. I jerk my hands away like I've been burned. The planchette doesn't stop. Josie lifts her fingers, but it keeps moving, racing over letters in a blur of rage. No hands. No contact. Just Catherine's fury driving it forward.

"Dude, that's fucked up." Patrice watches the planchette move around the board on its own.

Suddenly, it jerks, flips into the air, and skids across the floor. It rests there, still as stone, daring us to move.

No one speaks. My chest heaves, lungs burning. Molly huddles at the edge of the stage, arms wrapped tight around herself, face bone-white. Cole has moved closer to me, his shoulder almost touching mine—whether for comfort or protection, I can't tell.

"Wow. That was intense," he says.

"Yeah. I think intense is an understatement." Molly's eyes are still on the planchette.

"I just don't understand what she was trying to tell us. She was either warning us or threatening us," Josie says.

"All of us?" As soon as the words leave my mouth, the planchette stirs, and then slides across the floor, stopping mere inches from my leg. It points directly at me. Accusing. As if Catherine herself were pointing her blackened finger at me.

A piercing scream fills my ears. My eyes burn. Smoke floods my lungs. I press my palms against my ears, but the sound comes from inside.

Cole places a hand on my back. "Are you okay?"

They're all looking at me with concern. Evidently, they didn't hear or smell what I did.

"Yeah, my hip is acting up." I struggle to my feet, using the pain as cover for my terror. I need to get out of here.

Cole's hand finds my elbow, steadying me. His touch is warm, solid. I lean into the warmth without thinking.

Josie brushes off her pants. "That was pretty friggin' awesome. I've never seen anything like it."

"I say Josie was moving it herself." Patrice stands and walks back to her food. "No way was that real."

A rattling sound comes from above. We all look up in time to see one of the stage lights crash down toward Josie, narrowly missing her. The entire fixture shatters, sending shards of glass and metal scattering across the floor.

"Holy shit." Josie stares at the remains of the light that almost hit her.

"Are you okay?" I rush to her side. Patrice, Molly, and Cole run backstage in the event Catherine decides to send more lights crashing down at us.

"Yeah, I'm fine." Despite being visibly shaken. "We need to get out of here."

Patrice moves to gather the candles while Molly starts packing up the food. Cole helps me grab a broom and sweep up the remains of the shattered light.

"Vic's going to have a fit. We need to replace this light."

"I need to go." Molly's voice is tight with fear. "I don't want to be here any longer."

"Just leave it. Put the remains in here and we'll throw it in the dumpster out back." Josie hands me a trash bag. "Ray will notice it and replace it later. We need to go."

We spill out of the theatre like the building itself might collapse if we stay any longer. Even in Josie's car, with the headlights cutting through the storm and the heat blowing against my legs, I can't stop shivering. The candles, the board, the way the light shattered. It was all too much.

Later, I lie in bed as a merciless wind rattles the house and large drops of rain beat at my windowpane. Unable to sleep, I mull over the words Catherine spelled out on the board. It's all so vague.

Die Burn Pain Help Me Revenge Tick Tock Baby Danger

What is Catherine trying to tell us?

I turn over, again and again, searching for sleep that won't come. The harder I fight to stay awake, the more the words echo in my skull until they twist into something else entirely.

In my dream, I'm with Jake.

We're hanging out at Lake Wenatchee, something we used to do all the time. This was our happy place. We'd often sneak away to his dad's cabin for the weekend. With no one else around, it was a chance for us to be ourselves. To be in love.

It's spring, and the air is crisp; snow covers the tips of the mountains in the distance. The lake is strangely quiet. We're the only two out here. Neither of us speaks; we just sit, staring out at the water.

"I can't believe you're doing this to me." I finally break the silence.

"Look, we both know deep down that this was never a long-term thing. I have to get serious about life now."

"I thought *I* was your life. You always said…" I'm dumbstruck. This wasn't part of the plan.

"Meredith is getting her own place in L.A."

Meredith? What the fuck does she have to do with this?

"So? I thought you were breaking up with her."

He shakes his head. "UCLA offered me a scholarship."

"So did OSU."

He sighs. "I turned it down months ago. I've been planning to go to UCLA since last fall."

My stomach drops and my mouth goes dry. I don't want to believe this. I can't hide the confusion in my voice.

"Where did this come from?"

"Look, Heath, my family has expectations. I'm an only child. They want grand kids. My dad wants me to take over the business when he retires. He really wants me to go to UCLA. That's where he went."

"So, then I'll apply there too. See if I can start in the winter."

He shakes his head. "No."

"What do you mean, no?"

What is he thinking?

"You're not listening. I don't want you there. We need to stop what we've been doing. It's not right."

"It sure seemed right for you anytime I had your dick in my mouth," I blurt out.

He doesn't respond.

"Seriously, dude? It's not right? How many times have you told me you loved me over the years? How many times have you told me that you don't know what you'd do without me? And now this?"

He shakes his head, indignant. "Things change."

"So you're going to go back in the closet to make Daddy happy? It doesn't work that way, Jake. You're gay just as much as I am and you always will be. You're kidding yourself."

For a second, I think he might hit me. He may as well. He's already knocked the wind out of me with his news.

He sits in silence, shaking his head. "It was just a thing, dude. A phase." The words slice through my heart. "Meredith makes me happy. She always has."

"*I* make you happy." My voice cracks.

He won't meet my eyes, and his silence destroys me more than any words could. The cold hard truth settles in and takes the wind out of me. *I* was the side piece all along.

Not Meredith.

Me.

He never planned to build a life with me. It was just a game.

Tears stream down my face. "What the hell happened to you? We were…"

The plan was everything. It was what I'd looked forward to for years.

"It was a childhood fantasy. You and me… We can't. I'm sorry. I need to be realistic. It's time to grow up. I want a family. You can't give me that."

"You really think you're going to spend the rest of your life with Meredith, and a few of her brats and be happy? Seriously?"

"I love her. I want to marry her." His words hit me like a dumbbell to the face. The tears won't stop streaming down my cheeks.

It's really over.

But then again, was it ever real in the first place?

The scene in my dream plays out exactly as it did in real life. One week before the accident, Jake and I had this exact conversation.

"I'm sorry I hurt you. Stay out here as long as you need. Get yourself together, and then we'll head home." He stands and walks toward the woods behind us.

"Where are you going?"

Wait. This isn't how it happened.

"I'm not going to live forever. Everything ends at some point in time. Life happens. Things change."

What is he talking about? I turn to look at him as he walks away. Amy and Meredith stand at the edge of the woods, waiting for him.

"Don't go, Jake. Please?"

"You need to move on. Let it go, Heath. You have to let us go, or it will kill you." He joins Amy and Meredith. They disappear into the woods, and I run after them, calling to them, begging them to come back.

"What do you mean?"

They're gone.

CHAPTER FIFTEEN

Dr. Plummer's voice carries through the door, sharp with frustration. "This is my office, Josie. You can't just come in whenever you want. I have confidential information locked up in here."

Standing outside on the porch, I listen to the conversation unfold. I'm late for my appointment but don't want to barge in on them.

"I wasn't going through your files, Mother. I'm not interested in any of that." Josie's voice rises to a yell.

"Then what were you doing here?"

"What do you think?"

I'm tempted to leave. Walk up the street and call Dr. Plummer. Tell her I'll be late, or maybe ask to reschedule.

"Is this really necessary, Josie?" Dr. Plummer is no longer yelling, but her voice sounds strained.

Before I can turn to go, the front door bursts open, putting me face-to-face with Josie. She's pissed. I've never seen her like this.

I act like I'm surprised to see her. "Hey."

"Have fun with the drama queen." She stomps down the steps to her car.

Dr. Plummer meets me at the door. "Good morning, Heath." She tries to act as if everything is fine, but something's clearly bothering her.

"Is everything okay? I can reschedule if I need to."

"No, it's fine. Josie's just being Josie." She offers a smile and closes the door behind me. "I thought she'd grow out of this when she went to college. I guess it takes some people longer than others. Would you like some water? Coffee?"

"No, thanks." I follow her back to her office.

"So, how are things going for you?" She busies herself with some files on her desk, and I take the same chair as last time.

"Okay, I guess."

"Just okay?"

"Yeah, I mean, I've been pretty busy and stuff."

"Tell me something good that's happened since you were last here." She finally takes a seat.

I realize that despite the crazy events with Catherine, I'm feeling much better than I was a week ago. "Well, I've made some new friends. They're all pretty cool."

Cole especially.

She asks me about my anxiety and whether my depression is better. While it's still there, it doesn't seem to be constantly nagging at me. We talk about the work I'm doing at the theatre, and she asks me about college. I still haven't decided whether or not I'm going.

"Are you still having nightmares about your friends?" She takes the conversation in the direction I knew she eventually would.

"Yes, but not as often. I used to dream about them almost every night, but since I've been here, it's only happened a couple times."

Thanks, Catherine.

"Would you like to tell me about that night?" She settles back in her chair, brushing her hair behind her ears.

"What night?"

"The night of the accident. I've only heard your parents' side of the story. I'd like to hear it from you." She crosses her legs.

"My parents probably told you everything already." I study the carpet pattern, buying time.

"I'd like to hear it from you. I think it's important you tell me."

Exhaling through pursed lips, I fidget in my chair. How do I say no? I wasn't prepared to talk about this today. "I can't do this."

"I know it's difficult, Heath. I do. But I'm afraid not talking about the details of that night is what's causing your anxiety. You're holding it all in, and it's not healthy. You need to get it out."

Let it go, Heath. You have to let us go, or it will kill you.

"I'm here to help you. I'm not asking you to do this to cause you pain. I'm trying to make it better."

Nodding, I stare at my hands. "This is fucked up." Just thinking about that night is difficult enough; talking about it makes it real.

"I know it is. Start at the beginning. Tell me about your friends. What were they like?"

I take a deep breath, my chest tightening. My hands twist in my lap.

"Jake and I were practically brothers. Best friends since kindergarten, always together. He was the calm, levelheaded one, and I was the hothead. We were inseparable." The next words wedge in my throat, heavy and sharp.

Dr. Plummer tilts her head, waiting. "Go on."

My throat goes dry. "By the time we were freshmen…" The words stick. I force them out. "It wasn't just friendship anymore. We… we were… together."

The silence that follows feels endless. My whole body tenses, bracing for judgment, for some kind of shift in her expression. Instead, Dr. Plummer gives a single small nod, her eyes steady and kind. No shock, no disappointment. Just quiet acceptance.

Relief floods through me in a way I didn't expect. A breath rushes out of me, so forceful it almost feels like a sob. She's only the third person I've ever told, and somehow it doesn't crush me this time. It makes me feel stronger.

I rub the back of my neck and force myself to keep going.

"Amy and I started dating that same year. She was sweet, and I cared about her, but she was more of a cover than anything else. I let her think I was interested, and maybe I wanted to believe I was. But I couldn't keep lying. I called it off before junior year because I didn't want to keep leading her on, even though I guess I kind of did. She was always my date to dances and parties, but I wasn't committed to her. I was in love with Jake, and I felt better committing to him like that."

My throat tightens again, but for a different reason. "Jake never broke up with Meredith though. He kept her around, and she hated how much time he and I spent together. She saw me as the problem, and maybe she wasn't wrong. Every plan Jake and I made, she tried to wedge herself into. She did everything she could to keep us apart. I think maybe she knew about us. In the end, she was the reason he broke things off with me."

She pauses, waiting for me to go on. When I don't, she finally asks, "What happened that night? The night of the accident."

My eyes flick to the clock on the wall. Thirty minutes left. I will the hands to move faster, but they don't.

I take a deep breath. The words tumble out slowly, heavy against my lips.

"It was spring break. We hadn't all been together since Christmas. A friend from high school was having a party, so we went. We decided to leave after only being there for a couple of hours. It'd been raining that night, but the clouds had passed while we were at the party, and Amy begged me to take the top down on the Jeep."

"What did you do after you left the party?"

Deep breath.

The office fades. I'm back in the Jeep, wind in our hair, music too loud, everything about to go wrong.

Meredith wanted to go up to Jake's cabin. I didn't want to go. Jake had just broken it off with me in that exact place a few days before. I didn't even want to be with them that evening. It was too painful watching him and Meredith together. I only went because I hoped he'd realize what a mistake he was making. Hoped he'd change his mind.

At first, I told them I wasn't feeling well and I didn't want to go, but Jake pushed. He said he really wanted me to come, which got my hopes up, so I decided to go with them. I hadn't been drinking, so I was the DD. Before we left, Jake grabbed a bottle of vodka, a case of beer, and some hard seltzers for the girls. He'd had his brother buy it for us, and we'd hidden it under his bed.

As we drove the winding roads to the cabin, Meredith popped open the vodka and started drinking straight from the bottle. I was furious.

"Meredith, put that away. If a cop sees us, we're done."

"There aren't any cops out here." She was already tipsy to begin with, and the way she downed the vodka, it was only going to get worse.

"Give it to me." Reaching over the seat, I tried to take the bottle from her.

She leaned back, winking at me in the rearview mirror, holding the bottle just out of reach. Amy laughed. Jake did too. Why was I the only one who could see that this was a bad idea?

"Seriously, Meredith. Put it away."

"Relax, dude, it's fine. She's not hurting anyone. It's not like she's the one driving." Jake always defended her, no matter what she did.

Meredith screwed the cap back on the vodka and placed it back into the bag. When she pulled her hand out, she had two seltzers and handed one to Amy. Amy looked at me in the rearview mirror. She could tell I wasn't happy, so she put the seltzer back in the bag.

"Drink it. Drink it. Drink it." Meredith chanted over the wind that rattled through the Jeep.

Amy shook her head. "I'll wait until we get to the cabin."

"Are you afraid you'll piss off your boyfriend? Or is he even really your boyfriend? I've never been sure. Hey, Heath?" She smacked me on the shoulder. "Is Amy your girlfriend, or do you just like screwing around with her? I think she deserves to know."

"Come on, Mer. Not cool." Jake could tell I was pissed.

"Oh, wait. You don't screw around, do you? Amy had to get some dude at college to take her virginity because you couldn't ever get it up."

I met Amy's eyes in the mirror. Had she really told Meredith about that?

"Mer. Come on." Jake looked back over his shoulder at her. "Let's not do this tonight, okay? Let's have fun."

"I *am* having fun. I just want to know when Heath is going to finally admit that he's gay and in love with you, not Amy."

I stared ahead as my temper flared. Somehow, Meredith knew exactly how to get under my skin. She'd pushed me well past my limit.

"Everybody!" Meredith threw her head back and yelled, "Let it be known that Heath Ingram is a closeted, uptight piece of shit!"

She took off her seatbelt and stood up, holding onto the roll bar.

"Sit your ass down!" I yelled.

"Oh yes, my friends. This fine piece of man ass is actually coming for your boyfriends. Watch out, ladies. He'll capture your heart, kick you to the curb, and then fuck your dad."

Amy pulled on Meredith's leg, trying to get her to sit back down. I glared at Jake. He mouthed the words *I'm sorry*, and then popped his seatbelt.

That's when I saw the deer and swerved.

"Everything that happened after that is still a blur. I only remember bits and pieces. I tried to help them, but I was in so much pain."

I tried. I really did.

"The only clear thing I remember after that is waking up in the hospital." I run the back of my hand over my eyes. "My parents were there, and after I yelled enough, they finally told me my friends were dead. I'd missed their funerals. Everything else I learned about the accident came from the newspaper articles I found online.

"Meredith was thrown forty feet and suffered a broken neck, broken back, and major head and body trauma. The seatbelt snapped Jake's neck. He died instantly. Amy was still alive when the paramedics got there, but died on the way to the hospital.

"There was an investigation. At first, they thought it was alcohol-related because of the empty vodka bottle, but the doctor confirmed I hadn't been drinking. They didn't press charges. It wasn't my fault. At least that's what they said. All I know is my friends are dead, and I'm the one responsible."

I take the tissue she offers and wipe my nose. Thinking about what happened already hurts. Speaking it aloud rips it wide open.

She places a comforting hand on my knee. "I can see why you might think it was entirely your fault, but what could you have done to change the outcome?"

"Lots of things."

"Like what?"

"I could have stopped the car and made Meredith sit down. I could have paid attention to the road instead of fighting with her. I should have stopped the car." I grab another tissue.

"How could you have known that a deer would be in the road?"

"It's not uncommon. I should have thought of that."

"But Heath, when someone gets in their car, they don't expect to have an accident. No one expects to come upon a deer. There was a lot going on in the car that night. You were not solely responsible for everything that happened. Jake bought the alcohol. Meredith was the one drinking it. Meredith was the one who provoked you."

She doesn't get it. "I let her get to me. I should have stayed calm."

"Even I would have been angry with her if she'd said those things to me. If I were in your position, I probably would've done the same thing."

I know she's right, but it still hurts. I never should have agreed to go to the lake that night.

"I want them back." My voice cracks as I fight back the next wave of emotion threatening to pull me under.

"I know you do, but you and I both know that's not possible. They're gone."

"It's not fair." The words break as they come out.

"I know it's not. It's awful. They were young. They had their whole lives ahead of them, but you know what? So do you. You're still here. You're lucky. Had the others been wearing their seatbelts, they might still be here. You didn't kill them, Heath. It was an accident. You didn't choose to kill your friends. That's what you need to remember. You had no control over what happened. You feel guilty because you lived, and you need to keep living. Do you think any of them would want you to give up?"

You need to move on.

"No."

"Then don't. Don't let this hold you back. You have so much going for you. Everything you had before the accident is still here waiting for you. I'm sure every one of them would want you to move forward. Wouldn't they?"

"Yeah." And I know it's true. If Jake were still alive, he'd be kicking me in the ass, pushing me forward. He always did.

"We're out of time for today. Let's meet again on Wednesday morning. You made good progress today."

I nod, pretending to believe her, but the truth is etched into me like scar tissue. I can tell myself it wasn't my fault a thousand times and still know deep down that it was.

Maybe one day I'll figure out how to forgive myself.

CHAPTER SIXTEEN

After the session, I walk to the beach, emotionally drained but somehow lighter. Like something locked inside me finally broke free.

I'd never talked about the accident like that. It felt good to get it all out. I still have some healing to do, but I definitely feel better. I kick off my shoes and walk to the edge of the beach.

The sand is cool between my toes, the cold water of the Pacific Ocean invigorating. I find a spot on the sand free of debris and flop down on my back. It's surprisingly quiet. Not many tourists this morning. The sky above me swirls with puffy gray clouds, teasing me with the possibility of more rain.

I sit up, watching the waves fold over the sand, massaging the beach. It relaxes me. I let my mind wander, thinking of peaceful things rather than the accident or everything that's happened at the theatre.

When the first raindrop hits my face, I decide I'd better find shelter. I stand to go, and my phone vibrates in my pocket. I have three missed calls and two text messages—all from Josie. I call her back without bothering to check the messages.

"Where the hell are you? Are you okay?" Her voice explodes through the phone without even a hello. "I came back by my mom's office, and she said you left over an hour ago."

"I'm fine." I brush sand from my jeans. "I decided to go for a walk. I'm down on the beach, but it's about to rain. I'm going to walk to the diner. Meet me?"

"I'm already here. I was going to grab some lunch."

"Perfect. I'm starved." I hang up and make my way up the beach toward the diner, praying the clouds don't collapse above me. I don't feel like being soaked. I make it to the front door just as the sky opens up.

Josie waves to me from a corner booth at the back of the restaurant. I push my way through the crowd of people waiting to be seated, my stomach growling as the scent of fried food invades my nose, teasing my hunger.

"How'd things go with the psycho she-devil?" Josie grins as I sit across from her.

"Fine." I slide into the booth. "Really well, actually. Your mom's great."

"I guess. She's supposedly really good at her job. She just sucks at being a mother."

"What were you two arguing about this morning?" I know she knows I heard them, so I may as well ask.

"She was just freaking out because I was at the house—I'm sorry—her office this morning when she got there. Like I'm interested in going through the files of her fucked-up patients. I have enough problems of my own; I don't need to read about her psychos." She doesn't look me in the face. I can't tell if it's because she doesn't want to talk about it, or if she's embarrassed that I overheard them. Or that she basically just called me a psycho.

"Gee, thanks."

"I don't mean you. Anyway, I had my reasons for being there,

I just didn't want to tell her what I was doing." She glances over the menu.

"So, what *were* you doing? Or am I not allowed to ask?"

"Yes, you can ask because it has something to do with Catherine." She stops talking when the waitress walks up. We both order shrimp baskets with fries—extra cocktail sauce for Josie and extra tartar sauce for me. We hand her our menus, and Josie continues.

"Catherine and her mother used to live in that house. My grandparents rented it to them. I was looking around in the attic. I thought maybe I could find something."

"But it's been nearly twenty-five years. Don't you think the house has probably been cleaned out by now?"

"Yes and no. After Catherine's mother killed herself, Gran and Gramps decided to rent it out to summer vacationers, but no one's lived there for more than a week or so at a time. When my mom moved back here three years ago, Gran let her use the space as an office. Lucky for us, Gran has a hard time throwing things away."

"You found something?"

"There were a couple of boxes up there that I think belonged to them. Problem is, I didn't get a chance to look through them. My mom found me, and I left when she started yelling at me."

"Are you going to try to get back up there?"

"Hell yeah, I am. I just need to get up there without her knowing. When do you meet with her again?"

"On Wednesday."

"Perfect. I'll drive you. While you're in talking to her, I'll sneak up there."

"What about her receptionist?"

She waves a hand in front of her face and rolls her eyes. "She's useless. I can get past her."

The waitress arrives with our food. After she tops off our drinks, I dive into my shrimp.

"Speaking of Catherine, get this." Josie speaks around a mouthful of fries. "I went into the costume room this morning to finish up what you and I were supposedly working on last night, and every costume had been thrown on the floor. It took me three hours to sort them all and hang them back up."

"Who do you think did it?"

"It was obviously Catherine. We pissed her off last night. I knew I shouldn't have asked anyone else to join in. I knew Patrice would be a smartass. You can't piss off a ghost."

I decide not to point out that Catherine was already pissed off. Whatever we'd planned to accomplish last night had failed. Instead of helping Catherine, I think we made it worse. The light almost falling on Josie was proof of that.

"How's Julia?"

"Alive, unfortunately. Ryan stormed around all morning because Vic won't cancel the show. He had the nerve to tell Vic the show was going to suck without Julia, and he's embarrassed to have his name tied to any part of the production. Can you believe that?"

"Coming from Ryan? Yes, I can."

We settle the check, and the talk shifts from ghosts and drama to light cues and set pieces. By the time we're back at the theatre, the weight of breakfast gossip has given way to rehearsal jitters.

The first dress rehearsal goes smoothly. There are no missed light cues and only a few issues with the set changes.

After rehearsal, Josie, Patrice, Molly, Luke, Cole, and I end up back at the diner for food. I'm here so much, I feel like I need to have a standing reservation.

We're exhausted, but there's a giddy excitement in the air. The show is great, and we all know it. Right now, at this moment, I've managed to push the sadness aside. No moping, no panic attacks, and no thoughts of Catherine or her warnings. I'm thoroughly enjoying myself. I haven't felt this free in who knows how long. It feels good to laugh again, to be a part of something.

Patrice waits exactly three seconds after Cole disappears for the bathroom before she turns on me. "Okay, tea. When are you gonna make a move?"

"On who?" I know who she's talking about, but I decide to play dumb. Does everyone now know I have a thing for Cole?

"The old dude at the register. Who do you think?" Patrice tosses a straw wrapper at me.

"I'd love to take him out. I have a thing for octogenarians. Do you think he'd be into me?"

Molly laughs, and I dodge Patrice's foot as she attempts to kick me under the table. "You know who I mean, smart ass. Cole has been crushing on you since you got here. Quit stringing the poor guy along. What's the holdup?" For a moment, she sounds like Meredith.

"I had no idea." It's a lie. Of course, I know he likes me, and I like him, but Luke is sitting right here.

"Oh please. That's the lamest excuse I've ever heard." Patrice shakes her head. "He's done everything short of throwing his skivvies at you. Ask him out already."

I can see the pain on Luke's face. It's written and highlighted in bright pink. He looks away, jaw working like he's chewing on words that won't come out.

"Maybe." This is uncomfortable. If Luke weren't here, I'd probably handle this differently.

"Maybe? Why wouldn't you? Don't you like him?"

Patrice won't let up, so I look at Josie. I try to signal with my eyes for her to change the subject, anything to quiet Patrice. Evidently, she's not fluent in eye language because she does nothing.

"Sure, I like him. He seems great. He's a cool guy."

"A cool guy?" She laughs. "My God, that's so dry. What are you, Mormon?"

"No." I laugh. "I'm not Mormon. I'm just trying to be respectful."

Luke keeps glancing around the room and running his hands

through his mop of shaggy hair. He looks so uncomfortable that I think he might explode.

"He doesn't want you to be respectful. Get it, Romeo. He ain't gonna wait forever."

"I'm gonna go." Luke throws a twenty on the table. "I'm really tired." He walks out before anyone can stop him.

Once Luke leaves, Josie slaps Patrice on the shoulder and gives her a look.

"Ouch. What?"

"He's got it bad for Cole." Josie glances toward the door Luke just left through. "Like, really bad. And he's been crushing a little on Heath too."

Wait. What?

"Shit. I didn't know. I swear, I didn't know!" Patrice's eyes go wide.

"And Cole isn't into him." Molly glances toward the restroom. "Are you into Luke?"

"Um, not… not like that." I shift in my seat. "I honestly had no idea he was interested."

Josie leans forward. "Look, Luke is really awkward. He struggles to connect with guys. If anyone shows him even the slightest bit of interest, he latches on. He gets frustrated because guys never see him as anything more than a friend. This whole thing is nothing new. I've been through this exact scenario with him countless times. He'll get over it."

"Okay, now that your boy is gone." Patrice turns back to me. "Are you gonna ask him out or what?"

"Honestly, he's been texting me, and I've been thinking about it. I just hate to think I might hurt Luke."

I glance up to see Cole making his way back toward us. Josie nudges me. "Luke's a big boy. He'll get over it."

"What did I miss? Where's Luke?" Cole asks as he sits back down.

"He was tired," I answer before Patrice can open her mouth.

"I am, too. I should probably get to bed." Josie throws some money on the table.

"We're going to ride with Josie." Patrice gives me a look that says, *Don't even argue with me*, before they walk out, leaving Cole and me alone.

"I guess you're riding with me?"

"I can walk," I say, playing coy.

"You're not walking. Come on."

The drive home doesn't last long enough. We talk about music, about stupid movies, about nothing important. Cole laughs at something I say, and the sound fills me with a sense of hope. Being with him is so easy. This is what normal feels like. He pulls his convertible into Uncle Vic's driveway and puts it in park. "We should do this again sometime. It was a lot of fun."

"Definitely." My pulse quickens. "So I never asked. Where do you live while you're here? I know you're from Portland, but you don't drive back and forth every day, do you? That would suck."

Kind of like my conversation skills.

"No, Molly and I are staying with Patrice in her parents' beach house." He turns toward me in his seat. His arm bumps the horn, and we laugh. I watch the windows, expecting the porch light to come on, but it doesn't.

"So you guys have been friends for a while?"

"I know both Molly and Patrice from Oregon State. Molly and I lived in the same dorm her freshman year. I was her RA. We hit it off right away. We met Patrice in one of our theatre classes. Molly encouraged both Patrice and me to audition for the shows this summer. It sounded more fun than spending another summer waiting tables in Portland, so here I am."

"That's cool." I want to say more, but everything that comes to mind seems childish and stupid. "I should probably let you get going. I guess I'll see you tomorrow?"

As soon as the words pass my lips, I immediately want to kick myself. That sounded so final—like I'm ready for him to leave. I'm not. I want him to stay.

"I'll be there." He looks at me with a shy smile. Like he's expecting something. I want to lean across the console and press my lips to his. Taste his smile. But what if that's not what he wants? I don't want to make an ass of myself.

I open the door and crawl out, closing the door behind me. I wave as he pulls out of the drive.

I should've kissed him.

Josie shows up early Wednesday morning, ready to break into the attic at her mother's office. She calls me from the driveway before I've even managed to crawl out of bed. Everything seems to be an emergency with her.

"Why are you always early?" I mumble into the phone.

"Why are you always so last-minute?" she counters.

"I haven't even showered yet. We still have an hour." I stretch, popping my hip. I look out the window, hoping to see a hint of sunlight, but the gray clouds hang in the air, promising more rain.

"You have ten minutes. Get your stanky ass in the shower and then get down here. I need coffee and breakfast, and you're going with me."

"You're literally the bossiest lesbian I've ever met."

"Correction. I'm the coolest lesbian you've ever met. You're lucky you have me around to keep your gay ass in check. Now get in the shower." She hangs up.

We arrive at her mother's office five minutes before my appointment. When we walk in, Heidi prepares a pot of coffee. A morning talk show plays on the television in the waiting room.

"Good morning, Heath. Sorry I'm late." Dr. Plummer walks in a few minutes after us.

She notices Josie and stops. "There you are. I've been looking for you all morning. Did you stay with Patrice last night?"

"Yes." Josie picks up a celebrity gossip magazine.

The tension between them is still obvious.

"You want to come on back?" Dr. Plummer pours herself a cup of coffee.

I follow her down the hallway, and she closes the door behind us, cutting off Josie and Heidi.

"So, how have things been going for you the last couple of days?" She puts her things down, then takes her place in the chair opposite me.

"Great. Really great." If I could just get up the nerve to ask Cole out, things would be almost perfect.

"Any blackouts?"

"No, none. I haven't even had any nightmares. I haven't seen or heard from Catherine either. It's like after our last session, someone flipped a switch that set everything right again. It's weird."

"Who's Catherine?" She squints at me over her coffee cup. It's then that I realize what I've said.

"Oh, um, I guess I forgot to mention that before. We were so caught up talking about the accident last time..." I let my voice trail off.

She cocks her head to the side and studies me. "Mention what?"

I try to figure out how to tell her that I thought I was, or am, being haunted. Things have been so different—so much better—the last couple of days. All of that seems like nothing more than a bad dream.

"The first few days I was here, I had dreams about this girl in a white dress. I thought I saw her a few times at the theatre." I try to act as if it's no big deal.

"And this girl's name was Catherine?" Dr. Plummer studies my face, her coffee cup frozen in her hand. She looks like a mannequin sitting there, stiff and rigid.

"Yeah, but I'm thinking maybe I just imagined it." I try to sound nonchalant. "I overheard Josie and Luke talking about the theatre being haunted. I think maybe it just got to me."

"Why don't you tell me about it?" Her tone is more hesitant than inquisitive. Like she's afraid to hear what I have to say.

"There's just been some weird stuff happening. Josie thinks it's the ghost of some girl who died at the theatre, but…"

"What do you think?"

"I don't know. I thought maybe I was imagining it, but I'm not sure."

"Why don't you tell me what you've witnessed?" She sets her cup down on the table and watches me.

I hesitate, but then realize there's really no point in lying to her. "There have been lots of things, actually."

"Start at the beginning. When did it first happen?" She looks different, her brow creased with worry. Almost as if she herself has seen a ghost.

I tell her about the night I thought I heard the girl calling my father's name from the beach, what happened the night I spilled the paint, and the attack I heard over the radio. When I stop, I can't help but notice her face has paled. "So, these are all pretty vivid experiences, then? You're not only seeing things, but you're also hearing and smelling things as well?"

"Yeah. Oh shit, do you think I have a tumor?" I'd never thought of that before, but it makes total sense.

"Under other circumstances, I might consider that, but after all you've gone through, and the fact that you had extensive brain scans after the accident, I doubt that's a possibility." She leans forward. "When was the last time you, for lack of a better phrase, made contact with Catherine?"

"Sunday night." It seems longer than that. Was it really just three days ago?

"And what happened then?"

"Josie and I tried contacting her with a Ouija board—"

"Josie was there?" She cuts me off. "Did she encourage this? Was the Ouija board her idea?" She sounds pissed. Did I just get Josie in trouble?

"We thought maybe the girl needed help. We thought maybe we could help her cross over or something." Saying it aloud sounds so ridiculous.

"Did you make contact?"

I pause for a minute and then nod my head. "Yes."

"And what did she say?" Her tone says she doesn't really want to know. She doesn't look directly at me. Instead, she stares at a spot just behind my right shoulder.

"Just a bunch of random words. It didn't really make sense. I think the words were fire, death, baby, help me. Something like that." I try to remember the exact words spelled out on the board.

"Wait here." She stands and moves toward the door. I watch as she walks out into the hallway and listen as she opens the door to the reception area. My heart hammers in my chest when I realize she might see that Josie isn't there. What if she catches her snooping around again?

I calm down when they both enter the room. Dr. Plummer is obviously upset, and Josie looks thoroughly confused.

"Sit down." She tells Josie, indicating the seat she'd occupied not a minute earlier. Josie looks at me, silently asking what's going on. I shake my head because I'm not entirely sure.

"I need you two to promise me you won't do any more of these séances or whatever you call them." Dr. Plummer stands before us. I feel like I'm back in grade school being punished by the principal.

"What are you talking about, Mom?"

"I know you like hunting for ghosts and all that paranormal stuff, but you need to stop, Josie. It scares me." She's really upset.

"I told her about the ghost at the theatre."

"Okaaaayyyy..." Josie still tries to figure out what the big deal is.

"I've never been one to believe in the paranormal. At least not entirely." Dr. Plummer paces. "But if what you're telling me is true, I think there may be something going on that is bigger than either of you. Everything Heath told me…"

We sit quietly, waiting for her to finish, but she doesn't. She just stares at the floor. All the color has drained from her face, and her hands shake.

"What about it?" Josie asks. Dr. Plummer doesn't answer her. Josie looks at me and then back at her mother. "Mom?"

"You need to be careful. Both of you. This isn't something to mess around with." Dr. Plummer's eyes are wide. She's really uncomfortable with all this.

"Mom, tell me what you're talking about."

The room is still. The only sound comes from the clock that ticks away the seconds from its place on the wall. We wait for her to speak, but there's only silence. The intercom buzzes, causing all of us to jump.

"Your ten o'clock is here, Dr. Plummer." Heidi's voice crackles through the tiny speaker.

Dr. Plummer's hand trembles on the intercom button. "I'll be right out."

She turns back to us, and I see something I've never seen in her professional demeanor: terror. "Promise me, Josie. No more séances. This is not something you need to dig up. Promise me."

"Okay."

Though Dr. Plummer interprets this as consent, I know better.

"She was really freaked out." I buckle my seatbelt as Josie starts her car. Dr. Plummer didn't bother walking us out. She stood at the window of her office, staring out at nothing, barely whispering goodbye.

"I've never seen her like that." Josie backs out of the parking space. "It has to have something to do with Catherine. Maybe it's because she knew her or something. Something you told her struck a nerve."

"Did you find anything in the attic?"

"No, I didn't have time to get up there. Heidi was watching

me like a hawk. I'll figure out a way. Now I have to."

CHAPTER SEVENTEEN

The next twenty-four hours are so busy that Josie and I barely have time to speak, let alone plan our next step. We spend all of our time at the theatre prepping for opening night.

Every time I walk through the opera house doors, my stomach clenches. Nothing has happened since the Ouija board incident. Catherine's silence unnerves me more than her presence ever did. I'd like to think she delivered her message and left, but I doubt I'm that lucky.

The final dress rehearsal goes perfectly. When the show opens Thursday night, it's a huge success. All the performances sell out before the weekend is even complete. The stress lifts, and Uncle Vic looks like a new man. Saturday night, the cast and crew plan to hit the beach for 4th of July fireworks—a Rock Harbor tradition. Stepping outside to meet Josie, I freeze. My father stands near the theatre entrance, deep in conversation with Dr. Plummer.

"Dad?" What is he doing here?

"There's my boy." He walks over and pulls me into a tight bear hug. "You're lookin' better already." He studies my face intently, searching for something. What it is he looks for, I don't know.

"Thanks. Is Mom here?" I scan the parking lot for her.

"No, she left yesterday for her book tour."

"What are you doing here?"

"I had some free time and thought I would come down and check on you. Melanie says everything's going well with your sessions. Vic says you're adjusting well."

His eyes dart around the parking lot, never quite meeting mine. He shifts his weight from foot to foot like he's afraid to stand still.

"Yeah, I'm doing fine. I feel good. Did you like the show?"

"Yeah, the show was great. Vic did a great job. I enjoyed it." He stares at the main door of the theatre like he's looking for someone. Or something. "It's so weird seeing this place alive again."

"How long are you here for?"

"A day or two. I have meetings on Tuesday, so I need to be back by then. You all finished here? I thought maybe we could go grab a bite to eat and talk." He avoids eye contact.

"I can't. We're having a cast party down at the beach. I planned to go."

The front door to the theatre pops open, and Josie walks out. "You ready to go get your party on?"

"Dad, this is Josie, Dr. Plummer's daughter."

"Hello, Josie, nice to see you. I haven't seen you since you were just a baby." Dad holds out his hand to Josie. His smile looks forced, his handshake stiff.

"It's on, bitches! Opening weekend was fire!" Patrice bursts through the door with Molly behind her.

"Dad, this is Patrice, Josie's—um—"

"She's my girlfriend." Josie slips her arm around Patrice's waist.

"And this is Molly."

Dad's face goes stoic as he holds out his hand. "Hi, Molly. I thought you looked familiar when I saw you last week. You look just like your mom."

He knew her mom?

"I get that a lot from people who knew her."

He turns back to me. "Can I drive you back to the house?" His voice sounds strained.

"Sure." I scan the theatre for Cole but don't see him. I guess I'll catch him at the party. "I need to change."

I follow him to the car and climb in. We sit in awkward silence until we pull out of the lot.

"Looks like you're fitting in. Are you enjoying yourself?"

"Yeah. I'm great. Really. Why are you here?" I get right to the point. "I've barely been here a week. I didn't expect to see you for at least another month or so."

"The house was quiet with both you and your mom gone. I had some free time, so I figured I'd drive down and surprise you."

He's lying. It's a six-hour drive.

"That's a nice story, Dad. What's the real reason?" I know my dad. If he had downtime, he would have spent it fishing or playing golf, not driving six hours just to say hi when a simple phone call would suffice.

He's quiet. I watch his face, searching for answers in the streetlights that flash over us as we drive across the bridge. His jaw is tight, hands gripping the steering wheel. "Melanie called me the other day. She's worried about you."

"Why is she worried about me?" My chest tightens. She told me I could trust her. If she was worried about me, why hadn't she told me so herself? She said we'd made huge progress after I told her about the accident. I'm feeling better. I'm doing things. I'm getting out of the house, moving forward with my life. Why is she worried?

"She said you were hearing voices. And something about a Ouija board, and trying to contact the girl who died here."

"So you came down here because I played a board game at the theatre?" This is so typical.

"I'm worried about you, son. I want you to come back home with me. I'm not sure this was a good idea."

It never ends.

"Why? I've only been here a week. I'm having a great time."

And I've met someone.

"And Melanie says you made a huge breakthrough the other day. You look great. Hell, you're talking to me, standing up for yourself. You haven't shut me out. You seem to be doing well. Maybe you just needed to reset yourself." He makes it sound like I'm a computer that froze up and needs a reboot.

"I'm not going home with you, Dad. You wasted a trip down here. I have a party to get to." I climb out of the car and head toward the house.

I change out of the black clothing I'm required to wear as part of the stage crew and put on a pair of board shorts and a T-shirt. I grab my Oregon State sweatshirt, spritz a little cologne over myself, and head out the back door. I don't see my father when I leave, and I pray he isn't down at the beach.

When I arrive, most of the cast and crew are already there. Someone has started a small fire that I'm not sure is entirely legal. A few people are roasting marshmallows and hot dogs. Someone plays a guitar, and the people around him sing "Sweet Caroline."

I spot Josie, Luke, Patrice, and Molly sitting apart from the main group and make my way over. Cole is across the way, talking to some of the other dancers. He catches my eye, and I smile and wave.

"Hey, I was wondering if you were going to make it." Cole walks up beside me and bumps my hip with his. He gives me a side hug, and I return the favor. It feels good to touch him. I try not to feel guilty when I notice Luke's uncomfortable reaction.

"Dude, what's your dad doing here?" Josie asks.

"He had some free time, so he drove down to catch the show."

I don't mention that he wants to take me back with him. What's the point? I'm not going.

"Have a seat." Cole pulls me toward him. It takes me a minute to sink down to the log he's sitting on because I'm all kinds of stiff after sitting all night. I stumble and end up sitting in his lap.

"Sorry. This stupid hip."

He wraps his arms around me. "It's all good. You can sit here. I don't mind."

I laugh and sink down to the sand in front of him. He wraps his arms around my shoulders, and my first instinct is to move immediately in case someone sees us. But when nobody bats an eye, I go ahead and lean back between his legs, doing my best to ignore the stiffness against my back.

"What's wrong with your hip?" Patrice asks.

"I was in an accident. Broke my pelvis."

"Damn, boy. What happened?"

"He rolled his Jeep and killed three of his friends." Luke's voice cuts through the conversation before I can respond. How does he even know this?

Josie slaps him on the knee. "Jesus, Luke. Have some tact."

"You can read all about it on the internet. It's not a secret." He shrugs as if it's no big deal. But it *is* a big deal.

Luke takes a long pull from his beer. "Sorry, dude. I was curious, so I Googled it."

Silence falls over our circle. Josie picks at her fingernails, and Patrice studies the label on her beer bottle. My throat fills with cotton.

"I'm gonna go." I stand back up, chest tight. This isn't the relaxing hang with friends I'd been looking forward to.

"Way to go, dipshit." I hear Josie's voice as I stumble through the sand. I don't want to go back to the house. If I do, I'll just have to deal with my dad. I turn and walk down the beach, away from the cast and crew and into the darkness.

"Heath?"

I turn to see Cole's shadow moving toward me, but I don't stop. If anything, I try to move faster, but sand shifts beneath my feet making progress difficult even without my bum hip.

"I'm not going to go away, so you may as well slow down." His voice carries from behind me. I stop with my back to him, breathing deep.

"I'm sorry about that." He catches up to me.

"About what? Luke telling everyone what I did, or that I did it?"

"You didn't *do* anything." He places his hands on my back. His touch makes me want to turn around, but I can't.

"You're wrong. I did do something. I killed my friends."

I feel the tears welling behind my eyes, but I refuse to let them fall. I won't let him see me cry.

"But it wasn't your fault."

"How do you know that? You weren't there."

"Did you drive off knowing that by the end of the night, you would have an accident and your friends would be dead?" He waits for my response.

"It doesn't matter if I planned it or not. I was driving." Maybe my dad needs to be here, so he can hear this. He'll realize I'm not completely over the accident. I need to stay so Dr. Plummer can help me work it all out.

"Heath, I know what you're going through—"

I cut him off. "No, you don't. Why does everyone say that? You have no idea what it's like waking up every morning know-ing you stole everything from three people you'd known your whole life. One of them was the guy I had been in love with my *entire* life. This isn't something you just get over."

I start to walk away, but he grabs my hand, stopping me. He walks up behind me and wraps his arms around my neck, resting his chin on my shoulder. I resist at first, but he doesn't let go, holding me tighter than anyone has ever held me before.

Let it go, Heath. Jake's voice echoes through my head. *Let me go.*

"I realize that I have no idea what you are going through, but I can empathize," he says in my ear. "It's awful, and I'm sorry it happened. It's going to take you a while to get over this, but there are people who will be there for you and help support you." He turns me around to look at him. "I am one of them. I know I just met you. I know we barely know each other, but I'd really like to get to know you. It may not develop past friendship, but if that's the case, so be it."

You have to let it go, or it will kill you…

"It's hard," I admit. "I feel like I'm getting better. Like maybe I'm getting past it, then it comes up again, and the feelings just come right back."

"I know, but it'll get easier. You need to stop pushing people away. Some of us would really like to get to know you."

I want it, too. Suddenly, it doesn't matter what Luke thinks. This is none of his business.

"I'm surprised you don't think I'm totally mental."

"Or maybe I like mental." He pulls me toward him and kisses me firmly on the lips.

I melt into him, one hand tracing up his spine while the other tangles in his hair. I run my tongue over his lips, tasting the tang of the beer he'd been drinking. He pulls away to take a breath and then kisses me on the forehead. "I've been wanting to do that since that first night in my car."

"Me, too." I wrap my arms around him. I bury my face in his hair, breathing in the earthy scent of the bonfire that clings to him. Here in this moment, I finally feel something more than fear or self-loathing. I feel hope, and it feels good. I hold on for what feels like hours, afraid to let him go. I don't want to lose this feeling of being wanted and accepted and needed for exactly who I am.

"It's going to be okay. You'll be okay." He speaks against my neck. "It just takes time."

I nod in response. I can barely breathe, let alone talk.

A loud pop sounds from somewhere down the beach, and the sky lights up in colors of red, white, and blue.

"The fireworks are starting. Let's go back. Let's show Luke he can't get to you." He takes my hand.

"I really don't feel like socializing right now." I plant my feet, refusing to walk back to the group gathered around the fire.

"Want to go somewhere? Maybe we could just go back to your place and talk, or watch a movie or something." My mind lingers on the 'or something.'

"My dad's there. I don't feel like seeing him right now. We had a fight."

"About what?"

"He wants to take me back home with him."

"But you just got here." The disappointment is evident in his voice.

"Don't worry. I'm not going anywhere."

"So, what do you want to do?"

"How about we go back to your place?" He doesn't say a word. He just takes my hand and walks me up the beach toward his car.

CHAPTER EIGHTEEN

"Do you think your dad will let you stay?" Cole asks.

We're lying in his bed, bodies intertwined. His head rests on my chest, both of us groggy and swollen-lipped from thirty minutes of intense making out.

"He has no choice. I'm not going anywhere." It's going to take some convincing, and there may be a lot of shouting involved, but I have to stay.

"I'm so tired." His voice is groggy with sleep. "I have auditions tomorrow."

"So, I guess that means you're not going back to Portland?"

"No. If you're staying, I'm staying."

I smile in the dark as he snuggles closer.

The soft, rhythmic sounds of his breathing put me to sleep. When I wake up, I'm lying on the beach. It's still dark out; stars twinkle at me from behind the swollen clouds moving across the sky. I sit up and notice the figure of a girl sitting a few feet in front of me. She wears a black sweatshirt, and her blonde hair falls across her back. At first, I think it's Catherine, but then I realize that it's Molly. What is she doing out here?

I say her name, but she doesn't turn around. I crawl toward her and realize she's crying; her small shoulders shake as she sobs.

"Molly?"

"I'm so scared," she weeps.

"Why? Molly? Hey, look at me." I reach out and touch her. "It's going to be okay."

"Why are you doing this to me?" She grabs the hand I place on her shoulder.

"Doing what? Do you need help?"

"You can't leave me." She squeezes my hand, holding on for dear life.

"I won't. I'm right here. I'm not going anywhere." It's as if she's in a trance—totally lost in her grief, and I don't know what to say to make it better.

"You have to be careful. Oh my God. What did she do?" She weeps uncontrollably, and I have no idea what to do to console her.

"Who? I don't understand." She squeezes my hand so hard it's starting to hurt. "Molly? Look at me." She turns. Where Molly's left cheek should be, charred flesh peels away in strips, revealing bone. The smell of burned meat fills my nostrils.

"Help me!" She screams, reaching for me.

I scramble backward, dodging her hands as she scuttles toward me like a rabid crab, clawing for my feet. I roll over and try to stand, but her hand grabs my ankle.

"Don't leave me!" I reach back to pry her hand from my leg. She's gone.

I stand, panting, my eyes searching the beach for signs of her, but it's empty.

"Heath?"

I jump, practically pissing my pants at the sound of Josie's voice.

"What the hell are you doing out here?" She walks toward

me, arms wrapped around herself to protect her from the cold wind blowing off the ocean.

"Did you see her? Did you?" I pant, scanning the beach with my eyes, searching for her. The only movement comes from the waves lapping at the sand.

"Who? Did I see who?"

"A woman. I thought it was Molly because she was wearing Molly's sweatshirt… But then she turned around, and she was all burned. She was here." I'm still searching the beach for her.

"Sit down and talk to me. You're freaking me out."

"It was Molly. She was wearing the same OSU sweatshirt she had on last night." I sit next to her on a large piece of driftwood. "She was down there. She was crying."

"Molly's upstairs asleep. I just walked by her room when I went to use the restroom. Cole's door was open and I noticed you weren't there, so I thought that maybe you were in the living room. I looked out the window and saw you out here scrambling around like a madman."

"She was here. I swear. It was Molly. She was sitting on the beach crying about something. She was begging me not to leave her. She turned around, and her face was burned." I shudder as I remember it.

"So it was Catherine you saw?"

"No, it was Molly, but she was burned like Catherine."

"You're not making any sense." Josie's eyebrows draw together as her eyes search the beach.

"It was Molly. She was here."

Josie takes my arm and walks me back to the house. I spend the rest of the morning on the couch. I can't sleep. My mind races. What does this have to do with Molly? Is Catherine after her? I rack my brain trying to remember exactly what the Ouija board spelled out, but it escapes me. Is Molly in danger?

I creep up the stairs, floorboards groaning under my feet. Molly's door stands slightly ajar. I peek inside like a creeper, checking her face for burns that aren't there. Her alarm blares and her hand reaches out from under the blankets, reaching for her phone. I knock on the door and push it the rest of the way open. I'm still rattled. I have to make sure she's okay.

"Hey." She smiles at me. Her face is perfect. No burns. "You okay? What are you doing up?"

"I couldn't sleep."

Cole appears in the doorway. "What are you two doing in here?"

I stammer for an answer. "I woke up early. I saw Molly's door open, and I came in to say hi."

Weak.

"Are you hungry?" he asks. "We've got like… cereal and stale bread. Or we could hit the diner?"

"I should get back to the house. Dad and Vic are probably having a fit." This isn't entirely untrue. I hadn't brought my phone with me. They'd probably waited up all night, wondering what happened to me. I'm bound to get a good, hearty ass-chewing when I get home.

"I'll jump in the shower. Give me a few minutes to get ready." He heads to the bathroom. I hesitate in the hallway, tempted to follow him. After a beat, I decide to return to his room. We're not there yet, and I don't want to rush this. Instead, I prepare the speech I'm going to give to my dad. I can't leave now. I don't want to leave Cole, and if what I'm thinking is correct, Catherine might be after Molly. I can't leave her here alone.

An hour later, Cole has dropped me off, and I'm standing on Vic's porch. I hesitate at the door, not knowing what to expect when I walk inside. The front door is unlocked, and when I walk in, Vic and my father are sitting at the table.

"Late night?" Vic calls from the kitchen.

"I stayed at Cole's."

"I know, Josie told me last night." Awesome. I'm not in trouble.

"Want some breakfast?" He indicates the sausage and pancakes on the table.

"Sure." I join them. My father has yet to say a word to me.

"So, your dad tells me you're heading back home tomorrow. Sick of me already?"

I glare at my dad, but he refuses to look at me. He stares out the window as if I'm not even here.

"I'm not going anywhere." I take a bite from the stack of pancakes Vic places in front of me.

"Well, I'd love for you to stay. We still have four more performances of Chicago, and I'd rather not train another light board operator, but I will if I have to."

"You won't have to."

"Heath…" My father's voice carries a warning.

"I told you last night. I'm staying here." I face him directly. "You brought me here just last week. You insisted that I come. Now that I'm here, and things are going well for me, you want me to go back. It doesn't make sense."

"I'll let the two of you work this out. I need to go get ready for auditions." Vic grabs his keys.

"I'll be up in a little while." I make a point to my dad that I don't intend to negotiate with him.

We sit in silence as my dad sips his coffee and I gorge myself on pancakes and sausage. When I've finished, I rinse my plate and then head toward the stairs.

"We need to talk about this." My father stops me before I can leave the room.

"Talk about what?"

"Heath, I don't want to fight with you."

"So then don't fight with me. I don't get what you're trying to do. Why do you want me to go back home?" I sit directly across from him, forcing him to look at me.

"I'm worried about you."

"You were worried about me back home. That's why you brought me here. Tell me what's really going on."

He stares at me, but says nothing. I take a chance. "It has to do with Catherine, doesn't it?" He looks away when I say her name, giving me the answer I was looking for. "You really think I'm going to leave here without any answers? What has you so worried?"

"Where did you get that watch?" He grabs my wrist and pulls it toward him.

"Upstairs. It's an old one of yours." His face is pale. "Catherine gave it to you, didn't she? How did you know her?"

He runs a hand over his face. Dark crescents shadow his bloodshot eyes, his shoulders sagging under invisible weight. He pauses, looking at me as if he expects to find his explanation written on my face.

"I dated her in high school." The words come out slowly. "She was a freshman, and I was a senior. It was a stupid mistake on my part. She was young and in love, and I wasn't. In all honesty, I only dated her because she was pretty. I wanted a girlfriend, but I didn't want to get too involved since I knew I'd be leaving for college the next year.

"She was young and naive, and we had fun, but she thought I was more serious about her than I was. When I left for college, I broke things off with her. She didn't take it too well. I knew she was fragile, but I didn't realize just how fragile she was until it was too late."

I lean in closer. "How do you mean?"

"She called my dorm room incessantly. Anytime I came home for visits, she would show up at the house. She would stand outside my window at night and beg me to come down and talk to her. Then, one night, she appeared at my dorm at 2 AM, suitcase in hand, claiming her mother kicked her out. I was a wreck. This went on for two years. I just wanted her to leave me alone. I finally decided to transfer to Washington State just so I could be far enough away from her that she couldn't bother me anymore."

"Damn." This sounds intense. I had no idea he'd gone through this.

"I came home the summer before my senior year at WSU. They were doing *Our Town* at the theatre, and Marilyn didn't have anyone who read young enough for the role of George. She begged me to do the show and I agreed, but then when I found out Catherine had been cast as Emily, I almost quit. She was especially fragile then because…" He takes a deep breath. "She wasn't in a good place. Things were still tense between us and I didn't think I could bear doing the show with her."

"But you did." I think back to the photos in the album.

"Somehow, Marilyn managed to talk me into staying, and it ended up not being as bad as I thought it was going to—at least not at first. Catherine seemed fine—better than I expected. She'd just graduated from high school and talked incessantly about finally moving away and leaving all of her troubles behind. I thought that maybe she had matured. That maybe she had finally moved on, but then she started talking about moving to Seattle with me after the show…" He takes a long drink from his coffee cup, staring past me with a distant look in his eyes.

"I didn't know what to do. I had been seeing your mother for almost a year by then and was seriously considering asking her to marry me. I was afraid that if I told Catherine it would send her over the edge. But I knew I needed to have a firm talk with her. One night before a performance, she told me she'd bought a one-way bus ticket to Seattle. When I told her I was in a serious relationship with someone, she lost it. She was out of control. She raged around the dressing room, scaring the entire cast. I finally managed to calm her down by telling her we could talk more about it after the show. That never happened, though. Later that night, the theatre caught fire, and she was killed."

"How did the fire start?"

"It was an electrical problem. The building was over fifty years old and in desperate need of rewiring. I just remember smoke billowing onto the stage. The cast started to panic, and that carried over to the audience. Everyone scrambled to get off the stage and out of the theatre." His face contorts in fear as he relives the scene from that night.

"The only thing I could think about was getting out of the building. I made it off the stage and to the hallway before I heard her screaming for me. I wanted to go back and save her, but I knew it was dangerous. The entire building had filled with smoke. I called for her, but I got pulled away. I didn't want her to die. I can't begin to imagine how awful it must have been for her."

Tears fill his eyes. I know exactly how helpless he feels. He feels responsible for her death, just as I feel responsible for the loss of my friends.

"It's not your fault, Dad." I reach out to grab his hand. "I know it's not, son." He presses his fingers to his eyes. "I don't want to believe the ghost of the girl that used to stalk me has come back from the dead to take my son. It sounds like a plot straight out of one of your mother's books, but when Melanie called me, I got scared. None of this makes sense. I just figured the best thing to do would be to take you back home."

"You said that Catherine was especially fragile. Why?"

He pauses, and for a moment I think he may not answer. "I don't really remember. I just know she started dating someone when I left, and there were accusations of assault…"

"Like rape?"

"No, just… she claimed he got her pregnant. He denied it, and there was an accident at the theatre. She and her mother claimed he pushed her down the stairs to make her lose the baby. There was a lawsuit. It was a mess."

A baby? It's starting to make sense now. The struggle I heard. Why Catherine keeps crying for her baby.

The mystery of Catherine Whitley is slowly coming to light. I have more answers after this thirty-minute conversation than I've gotten all week. There's no way I can leave now. I don't like lying, but it's the only way I can persuade him to let me stay.

"I think Dr. Plummer blew the Ouija board thing out of proportion. I had one nightmare about some girl in white. It was right after Josie told me about Catherine. The board thing was likely a prank. Someone was probably moving the piece around to mess with us." I only give him as many details as he needs, every lie and half-truth vibrating against my lips. "There's no ghost, Dad."

I wait for him to respond. I search his face, looking for a hint of something that tells me he believes me. When he doesn't speak, I continue.

"I know you're worried about me, but I like it here. I feel good. If I go back, I'm afraid I'll start feeling the way I was, and I don't want that. I need this. I've made some great friends, and I've met a guy that I really like."

I watch his face after my admission. I don't know where that came from, but I'm glad it's out.

He cocks his head. "A guy?"

"I'm gay, Dad." The words scrape my throat. "Please don't tell anyone, but Jake… he was my… more than my best friend."

Tears stream down my face. "I loved him, Dad. And he died. And my heart shattered."

Sobs rack my body. There's so much trying to come out of me at one time.

He stands and walks over to me. He wraps his arms around my neck and kisses the top of my head. "Shh. It's okay, buddy. It's okay."

We sit like this for what feels like hours. Once I can breathe again, I pull back. "Please don't tell Mom. I want to be the one to tell her."

"We already know. We were just waiting for you to tell us when you were ready."

What the hell?

He must notice the puzzled look on my face. "You're not very good about clearing out your browser history. And you leave your phone without a password. Someone's bound to find something."

"Well, that wasn't what I was expecting to hear."

"Heath, we don't care who you love. We just want you to be happy. We want you to be okay."

"I will be, Dad. Just, please let me stay here. It's been really good for me to be away."

He nods and sits back down. "So, you're telling me that Melanie just blew this all out of proportion?"

"Sounds like it. Look, I don't know what kind of secret the two of you are hiding, or why it caused both of you to act this way. Honestly, I don't even want to know." This isn't entirely true. I do want to know, but I'm afraid that if I press him, he's going to get suspicious and make me go back. "I just want to stay here. Please?"

We stare at each other, both of us waiting for the other to look away or say something.

"I'll let you stay." His shoulders relax. "But you have to promise me you won't try to do any more exorcisms or whatever it was you were trying to do. That whole Ouija board thing gives me the creeps."

"I promise not to attempt any more exorcisms." Which is true. I don't intend to attempt any sort of exorcism.

CHAPTER NINETEEN

I spend the next hour talking to my dad about the theatre, his job, Mom's tour, and what I'm going to major in. I still haven't decided about OSU, but I don't tell him that. By the time I go upstairs to shower, the earlier tension between us is gone. I've managed to convince him that everything is fine. I'm staying.

He decides to leave that afternoon. This is good news. I won't have to worry about him changing his mind. I'll just need to be careful with what I say to Dr. Plummer from now on.

When he drops me off at the theatre, it's already 3:00 and auditions are winding down. I give him a quick hug before pulling the hood of my sweatshirt up and stepping out of the car into the rain.

"Hey, sexy man." Cole walks up and throws his arms around my neck, ignoring the dampness of my clothing. "What's the verdict?"

"I'm staying."

He plants a big kiss on my lips.

"I told you I wasn't going anywhere." I smile and kiss him again.

"I think I'm going to be sick." Luke's voice carries across the lobby. He storms off down the hallway, bumping into Josie as she comes through the door. "Drama queen." Josie shakes her head as she walks over to join us.

"So, you missed all the excitement."

"What excitement?" I immediately wonder if Catherine made an appearance.

"Do you want to tell him, or should I?" She looks at Cole.

"I got cast as the lead in Our Town. I'm playing the Narrator." I have no idea what that means, but it seems like a big deal.

"And I got cast as Emily." Molly gives a little bow.

"That's the good news." Josie's expression darkens. "The bad news? Vic cast Ryan as George, her love interest."

"Oh, you poor thing."

"Well, maybe if you'd auditioned, this wouldn't have happened." She swats me on the arm and grins.

"I told you, I don't act. I would've been laughed off stage."

"Well, it's a good thing I do. It's going to take everything I have not to barf when he kisses me on stage."

"If he slips you the tongue, I'll kick his ass." Cole pulls me closer.

"Trust me, if he slips me the tongue, *I'll* kick his ass."

The week goes by in a blur. I meet with Dr. Plummer on Monday and Wednesday. After my Wednesday session, I meet Josie for lunch. We've been hanging out a lot this week. Cole and Molly are in rehearsals for *Our Town*, and Patrice's parents are in town for the final weekend of *Chicago*. Luke wants nothing to do with either of us. He's convinced Josie betrayed him by encouraging me to go for Cole, essentially ruining his chances. It's all so high school drama, and I want no part of it, so I've been avoiding him.

"So you never told me what your dad said about Catherine."

She bites into her hamburger.

"He didn't really say much other than she was in love with him, and when he broke up with her, she went a little insane."

"That's all he said? That she was crazy?"

"Basically."

"Elaborate, please." She squeezes more ketchup on her fries. The poor things look like they're drowning in blood. Her entire plate is a massacre.

I give her the full story, telling her everything my dad said.

She polishes off her hamburger, nodding as I speak. When I'm done with my story, she says, "Okay, so that explains part of what we know. What about the baby? Was it his?"

"No, he said Catherine dated someone else for a while. Some rich guy." I fill her in on the rest of the story, and she looks very puzzled. "I wonder who it was."

"I wish we could find that journal. There might be answers inside. I can't believe it just up and disappeared. Someone had to have taken it."

I'd searched the costume and prop rooms relentlessly, thinking maybe someone had moved it. I can't imagine what anyone would want with an old journal unless they knew something about Catherine.

"Did you ever make it back to the attic?"

"No." She licks the ketchup from her fingers. "Have you had any more dreams? Been sleepwalking?"

"Not since Saturday." I shudder thinking about what happened on the beach. Seeing Molly, half-burnt and broken still wigs me out whenever I think about it.

"Don't you think it's weird that you thought you saw Molly on the beach, but she was burned like Catherine?" She's thinking the same thing I've been thinking since that morning.

"I can't stop thinking about it. I may be wrong, but I can't help but think that maybe Catherine isn't really after me. Maybe she's after Molly."

"But why? Your father was the one she was in love with."

"What if Catherine thinks I'm my father? Everyone says I look exactly like him. What if she thinks I *am* him, and I've come back for her or something? It still doesn't explain why she would make herself look like Molly in my dream."

"Or," Josie points a bloody fry at me, "what if she wants Molly for a different reason?"

"What other reason?"

"Hmm." Her brow wrinkles, almost as if she just realized something.

"What are you thinking, Sherlock?"

"Nothing." She shakes her head. "Speaking of Molly, her birthday is Saturday. Patrice and I want to surprise her with a party after the show's closing night. We're going to decorate the rehearsal hall and surprise her after the show. You in?"

"Of course I'm in."

We spend the rest of the afternoon searching for the perfect gift for Molly. I use the credit card my dad left me to buy her a heart-shaped necklace. I hope she'll like it.

The last weekend of the show sells out again. I don't think Vic could be any happier. After the show on Saturday, I lead Molly back to the rehearsal hall for her party. We've all pretended that we had no idea it was her birthday, so when she walks in and sees everyone waiting for her, she starts to cry.

"To a great cast, a great show, and to the sweetest girl I've met in a long time." Vic raises his glass. "Happy Birthday, Molly, and congratulations ,cast and crew, on a successful run. I'm so happy to know all of you. I hope to see you back here next summer."

We all have some cake and a few drinks. Vic kicks everyone out at midnight, and a few of us head down to the beach to continue our party. The rain held off today, leaving us with a clear sky, bright stars, and a cool breeze blowing off the ocean.

Patrice pulls Josie's car up to the edge of the sand and cranks the radio. She and a few cast members dance as if their lives depend on it. I'm not much of a dancer, so Cole and I sit off to the side.

"So when's your birthday?" I ask over the loud music.

"October 23. You?"

"March 14th."

"Oh, a Pisces."

"I have no idea what that means, but that's what I've heard. How old are you?"

"I'm twenty-two. You?"

"I'm twenty. Hmm. I'm dating an older man. That's sexy." I kiss him, ignoring the dirty looks I'm still getting from Luke.

"You can call me Daddy." He places another kiss on my lips.

"Or Grandpa." I tease. He swats me and we laugh.

I notice Luke is still glaring daggers. "Come on. Let's go for a walk. This is getting uncomfortable."

I accept Cole's hand, and he pulls me to my feet. He leads me up the beach, away from the music.

"Going to go fuck your boyfriend now?" Luke says from behind us. He's drunk—really drunk, and his speech is slurred. We ignore him and keep walking.

"Careful, Heath, he'll just fuck with your head, too. Like you need anyone else fucking with you."

I take Cole's hand, pretending not to notice Luke's staggering figure as he lurks a few feet away. After a while, it gets to be too awkward. I stop and turn to face him.

"Look, what's your deal, Luke? What is this? I thought we were cool."

"I'm trying to warn you. He's just gonna fuck you over like he did me." He stumbles forward and grabs my shirt to steady himself. The stench of alcohol rolling off his breath almost makes me puke.

"I didn't lead you on, Luke," Cole says.

"Bullshit. You know what you did."

"Luke, you need to stop." I don't know where any of this is

coming from.

He turns on me. "I told you on day one that I was interested in him." He points a drunken finger in Cole's direction. "And you went and fucked him anyway."

I place a hand on his shoulder, trying to reason with him. "This is stupid, Luke. It's all so high school. Let it go."

"You're just like your dad." He grabs the front of my shirt with both hands. "Using people to get what you want. My dad said he was a no-good son-of-a-bitch, and you're just like him."

I push him off me, and he falls to the ground.

"Fuck you, Heath." He adjusts his glasses. "You two deserve each other."

"Leave him, let's go." Cole grabs my hand and pulls me back toward the party. People are watching us. I don't want a scene. This is stupid.

Luke stumbles up behind me and shoves me, knocking both Cole and me to the ground. My face hits the sand, and the coppery taste of blood fills my mouth. I must have bitten my lip. Cole tries to help me up, but Luke grabs my legs. I kick, connecting with his jaw. His head flies back, and I hear a slight crunch. When he looks up, blood gushes from his mouth.

"Uh oh. The gays are fighting!" Patrice yells. I'd laugh if I weren't so pissed off.

"Luke, back off!" Josie rushes toward him and helps him up. "What the hell is your problem?"

A few of the cast members grab their things and start to leave. Evidently, the party is over. And this drama will be all anyone is talking about tomorrow.

"He's a dick!" Luke yells at my back.

"Let's go," Cole whispers, grabbing my hand. Luke lunges toward us again.

"Luke! Stop!" Josie wraps her arms around his waist.

I slowly back away, focusing on Luke, waiting for him to come at me again. He sinks to the ground, defeated.

My heart hammers in my chest as we walk toward Cole's car. I won't lose it in front of him. I won't.

"You okay?" My hands shake, my breathing quick and erratic.

"I'll be fine. What the hell is his deal?" Cole asks as he unlocks his car.

"He obviously thinks I stole you from him."

We sit in the car for a minute. "This is partly my fault," Cole finally admits. "I kissed him at a party last spring. I'd just broken up with my ex. I was drunk. We made out. That's it, though. Nothing else happened, and I told him the next day that I didn't mean to lead him on. I thought that was behind us."

"Evidently not." I stare out the window. The thought of Luke's mouth on Cole's makes my stomach twist. But why? I have no right to obsess over a drunken kiss that happened months ago.

"You're not mad, are you?" He starts the car. I pick at a hangnail as I breathe deep, trying to calm myself. "No. Just… annoyed at all of this. It's so childish. I didn't come here for this."

"Well, you can always count on drama with theatre people." He starts the car. "You want to stay over tonight?"

"No, I think I need to just go home. Sorry." I'm not in the mood to cuddle and make out all night. I need to process. I need to calm down.

Back in my room, I collapse on the bed, thoughts spinning until exhaustion finally drags me under.

When I open my eyes, everything has changed. My clothes are soaked and I'm shivering. A strong wind rushes over me, covering my body in goosebumps. I realize I'm standing on the beach. The ocean tumbles against the shore, sending water toward me, teasing my feet, beckoning me to come closer. Angry waves splash against the rocks to my right, showering me with a fine mist.

"You're too late. It's done." The voice is barely audible over the howling wind and crashing surf.

"He's gone." The words hang in the fog like a death knell.

"Who's gone?" I ask.

"Him." The voice is louder now, more than a whisper. I turn in circles to see where the voice is coming from, but there's no one there. I turn back to the pounding waves, and I see her. A familiar figure, dressed in a white wedding dress, emerges from the ocean near the rocks. The ghostly blue light of the moon reflects off her dress, giving the impression that she's glowing. Despite the fact that she emerges from the water, she is completely dry.

"Your fault." I watch as she moves toward me. Each time I blink, she's closer to me, moving at inhuman speed. I want to run, but I can't. I'm frozen. I squeeze my eyes shut, wishing her away. *Please don't be Molly. Please don't.*

I open my eyes and she's right in front of me, almost touching me. Something is different. Instead of the peeling flesh, her face is completely unblemished. She looks exactly as she did in the pictures: porcelain skin, ice-blue eyes, and light golden hair.

"It happened." She shakes her head. "I warned you."

"Warned me about what?"

"You should have saved us." She grabs my face in her hands. She pulls me in for a kiss.

Her lips are soft and her hands gentle as she caresses the back of my neck, sending shivers through every part of my body. I push back, trying to remove her face from mine, but she's incredibly strong. She pulls herself into me as if she's trying to push her body inside of mine. She runs her hands under my shirt, caressing my chest and back, kissing me harder.

I can't breathe.

The smell of smoke fills the air, and my lungs burn. It's as if she's sucking the air out of me. Her porcelain skin bubbles and peels like paint in a fire. Her fingers burn through my shirt, searing handprints into my skin.

I wake up, gasping. My whole body shakes as I swallow huge amounts of air. My lungs feel as if I've just chain-smoked an entire pack of cigarettes. I'm soaked, body drenched in sweat.

I need a shower.

I stumble to the bathroom, and as soon as the water hits my skin, I cringe. My chest and arms feel as if they've been sunburned. I look down and notice the red marks all over the upper part of my body.

What the hell?

When I get back to my room, the phone chirps, rattling against the nightstand. Two missed calls and three missed text messages from Josie. They all arrived over the course of the last three hours. How did I not hear my phone?

U there?

Worried about Luke. Said he is leaving town

That seems slightly dramatic.

Call me if u r awake

I glance at the time. 5:15 AM. I received the last text two hours ago. It's too early to call. Whatever it is will have to wait.

When my phone rings, I feel as if I've just fallen asleep. I reach my hand out from beneath the covers and fumble around on the nightstand.

"What the hell? Do you not answer your phone after a certain time?" Josie's voice explodes before I can even say hello.

"What's the emergency?" I'm still half asleep.

"Did you not get my texts? I tried calling you like a million times and sent about a hundred texts last night."

"You called twice and only sent three texts. I woke up around five and saw them, but figured it was too early to call, so I went back to bed."

"Luke is missing."

I sit up in bed. "What do you mean missing? We just saw him a few hours ago."

"Something's wrong. I was trying to calm him down last night. He was upset. He felt like we'd all shunned him. He's really sensitive."

That's an understatement.

"He kept saying how he was tired of being walked on and sick of being taken advantage of. He said he was going to leave and go back home to Salem for the rest of the summer. I thought I'd convinced him to stay. I told him to meet me for breakfast at 8:00 so we could talk, but he isn't here." Her voice cracks with worry.

"What time is it now?"

"It's 8:15."

"He's only fifteen minutes late. Not everyone is perpetually early like you. He's probably hungover. He was pretty drunk last night. Give him at least an hour before you start freaking out."

"But, he's not answering his phone. He always answers his phone. Something's wrong. I feel it." I've never heard her like this. Fear and vulnerability are two emotions I never knew Josie possessed.

"Where was he when you last saw him?" I kick off the covers and walk to the window. The morning fog has yet to retreat. I can't tell if it's going to rain again or not.

"He was on the beach. Cole was trying to give Luke a ride home, but Luke refused, so Molly stayed with him. She said she would make sure he made it home safely."

A pang of jealousy stabs at my gut. Cole went back? And he tried driving him home? I breathe deep. Wow. I'm no better than Luke with the dramatic responses. I should take my own advice and calm the fuck down. I'm sure there's an explanation.

"Wait there in case he shows up. I'm going to throw on some clothes. I'll call Cole to come get me. We'll meet you there."

"Okay. I'm at Gran's diner."

"Call me if he shows up." I disconnect and immediately hit the speed dial number for Cole, forcing back the boiling feeling inside my stomach. Is that jealousy? Irritation? A combination of both?

"Hello?" His voice sounds rough and tired.

"Have you heard from Luke?" I ask without giving him a proper greeting.

"Heath?"

"Yeah. Have you heard from Luke this morning?"

"No, why would I? What's wrong? You sound mad."

I decide it would be best if we talk about this in person, so I ask him to come pick me up. When he arrives twenty minutes later, I'm waiting on the porch.

"Hey." He crawls out of his car and walks toward me. He looks like he's barely slept.

"Hey." I look at the ground.

"What's going on? Is everything all right?" He joins me on the porch, standing close but not quite touching me. He wraps his arms around himself to block the breeze blowing off the ocean, the thin T-shirt and gym shorts failing to protect him from the morning chill.

"Josie's freaking out because she can't get in touch with Luke. She said she thought he was okay when she left him last night, but that you and Molly were the last to see him."

He doesn't answer. I can tell by the look on his face there's something he wants to tell me.

"Did you go back there after you dropped me off?"

"Yes." He moves to the porch swing and takes a seat.

"Why?"

"I felt bad about what happened. The tension between you two is because of me. I thought maybe I could go back, talk to him, and make him see things differently. I thought maybe he would stop acting like a child."

"And?"

"He kept telling me he thought there was something between us. That he's been in love with me since we made out, and if I would just give him a chance, I would see that he's a good guy. I told him I already knew he was a good guy, but I didn't like him as anything more than a friend."

He stops and looks over at me. Why am I so annoyed that he went back there?

"And what did he say?"

"He started complaining that everyone always walks all over him and takes advantage of him. He said he was sick of not being noticed and…" He doesn't finish. I can tell there's more to the story.

"Then what?"

"He was really drunk. Like, even more drunk than when we left. He grabbed me and kissed me." He waves a hand in front of his face, as if he's trying to brush the memory away. "I pushed him away, and he started crying. He apologized repeatedly and kept begging me to give him a chance. It was really awkward. Molly saw us, and she came over and intervened. I left, and Molly was still talking to him. She got home about an hour after I did. She said that after he calmed down a bit, he told her he just needed to walk it off, and he headed down the beach."

He pauses, worry etched across his face. "Please don't over-think this. Don't make it something it's not. It was my mistake that started this in the first place. I went back because I wanted to put it all to rest so we can move on."

Before I can respond, sirens scream in the distance. My skin prickles with recognition. Catherine's voice whispers in my memory: *It's done.*

My phone rings.

"Hello?"

"Heath? Oh my God."

"Josie? What's wrong?"

Cole moves toward me, a concerned look on his face.

Josie is crying. It must be bad. "They found him. They found Luke. He's dead."

The words don't register at first. Luke… dead? Dead like Jake, Amy, Meredith. The familiar numbness spreads from my chest outward, that protective shell I know too well. I drop the phone and sink onto the steps behind me.

"Heath? What's going on?" Cole asks. I can't answer him.

I can't speak.
>
> *Too late.*
>
> *It's done.*
>
> *He's gone.*

CHAPTER TWENTY

I don't remember telling Cole what happened or driving to meet Josie, but here I am, standing in the cool, misty air watching police put up barriers around the jagged rocks. The same rocks from last night's dream.

The burns on my torso throb as I stare at the rocks. Catherine's voice echoes in my memory: *It's done.* What if last night wasn't a dream? What if I were here, in this exact spot, while Luke...

The thought sends ice through my veins. I flex my fingers, the smell of smoke still lingering in my memory. What if the dream was real somehow? What if Catherine—

No. That's insane.

Josie finishes speaking with a policeman and then walks over to join us. Her face is red and swollen; she looks miserable.

"They think it's a suicide, but they want to talk to everyone who was at the party." Her voice is small and hesitant, almost a whisper. "I don't get it. It doesn't make sense. Luke would never commit suicide.”

Patrice puts her arm around Josie's shoulders to comfort her. We all stand watching the police do their best to keep the small crowd that has started to gather away from the site.

A thick-mustached officer approaches us and flips open his notepad. “Were any of you with Mr. Fenley last night?”

“Yes, we all were.” Cole's breathing stays even, his voice steady.

“Would you mind answering a few questions for me? I understand there was an altercation between Mr. Fenley and another young man. Do you know who that was?”

“It was me.” I finally break out of my daze. “We had an argument.”

“Name?” The pencil hovers over his notepad.

“Heath Ingram.”

“What was this argument about?”

“He was angry because I've been hanging out with someone he was interested in. It was really kind of stupid.” I pass a sideways look at Cole, but he doesn't look at me.

“Did this argument get heated?”

“A little.” I'm hoping one of the others will back me up, but they remain silent. I hug myself and rub my hands on my arms, weighing my words.

“Did anyone see you leave?”

“I did. I drove him home.” Cole steps slightly closer to me.

“And did you leave again after you got home, Mr. Ingram?”

“No, sir.” At least I don't remember leaving. But the burns on my upper body suggest otherwise. My mouth goes dry.

“Which one of you was the last to see him?”

“I was.” Cole shifts his weight. “After I dropped Heath off, I came back to make sure Luke was okay. After Josie and Patrice left, another girl from the cast and I tried talking to him. He was really drunk.”

Cole recounts the same story he had given me earlier.

“Did Mr. Fenley have a history of depression?” The officer

doesn't even look up from his notepad.

"No." Josie's voice cracks. "I've known him since we were kids, and he was the happiest guy I've ever known. He was always a little dramatic and felt taken advantage of at times, but he was never depressed or suicidal."

"Thank you. You've all been very helpful. I need the name of the female who was last seen with him and a contact number if you have it. May I get your phone numbers in case we have any further questions?"

We take turns rattling off our numbers, and he scribbles our information on his notepad. As he walks back toward the beach, my phone buzzes. It's Vic.

"Where the hell are you?" His irritation comes through clearly.

"I'm at the beach—"

"What are you doing at the beach? Are you with Josie and Luke? I need you here. This set isn't going to take itself down. We need help."

He hasn't heard the news.

"Something's happened. I'll tell you about it when I get there." I hang up before he can ask any questions.

"That was Vic. He's at the theatre striking the set. He was wondering where we are. I'll talk to him. Why don't you take Josie home?"

"No, I can't sit at home. I'll go out of my mind." Josie has stopped crying, but her eyes are still puffy and red. "I need to work. Vic needs our help, and I need to keep myself busy."

Before we can protest, she walks to her car, followed by Patrice. As I climb into Cole's car, I look back at the beach and watch as the paramedics carry the black body bag up to the ambulance.

The theatre echoes with sounds of hammers banging and drills whirring. When we walk inside, I see Vic, Ryan, and Ray sweating as they disassemble the set.

"It's about damn time." Ryan doesn't look up from the flat he's unscrewing.

"What's going on?" Vic notices our solemn faces. Even Ryan stops stomping around and stares at us. "Where's Luke?"

"Something happened." It's still hard for me to speak. My chest tightens as I force the words out against the conflicting emotions: guilt over the way I treated Luke, sorrow that he's gone, and fear that I may have had something to do with it.

"To Luke? Is he okay?" Vic steps closer, reading our expressions.

"No." I choke out, and that's when the tears come.

Grief wins the battle.

"What happened?" Ray sets down his hammer.

"He drowned." Cole puts his arm around my waist. "They're not exactly sure what happened. The police don't expect any foul play, but none of us believe it's suicide."

"It could have been." Ryan's voice cuts through the silence from where he stands. "He was pretty drunk and upset last night. He was really into you, dude. You really hurt him."

"It's not his fault." I glare at him. This isn't the time to be tactless. "He was drunk. He was probably climbing on the rocks and slipped."

"Or he threw himself off the rocks." Ryan disappears backstage just as he always does.

"My God." Vic sits on the edge of the stage, legs dangling over the orchestra pit. He sways, and for a moment, I'm afraid he may topple over the edge. He rights himself by placing a hand on the stage. I feel like I should comfort him, but I'm not sure how. We all stand in silence. So much to say, but none of us have words.

Footsteps come from backstage, and Molly appears, carrying a backpack. She looks freshly showered and completely oblivious to what happened.

She hesitates at the corner of the stage when she sees our faces. "Is everything okay?"

Vic shakes his head. "Luke's dead."

"What?" Her hands fly to her mouth, and she stares in disbelief. "What happened? I just saw him last night."

Patrice and Cole rehash the story, and Molly cries silently. "I shouldn't have left him. He seriously seemed okay when I left. I was so tired and I just wanted to go home and sleep."

"We gave the police your number." I figure she should know to expect a call. Her eyes widen, mouth dropping open.

"Why? What do you think I did?" She looks like she's about to fly into hysterics.

"We don't think you did anything, hon." Patrice reaches out to touch her arm.

"They asked who the last person was to see him. They just want to speak with everyone to get a clear picture." Cole's voice remains calm and reassuring.

Ryan starts up the drill and begins taking down more flats.

"Leave it." Vic's voice cuts through the noise. "We're done for the day. We can do this later this week."

"I'd rather get it done today." Ryan continues with the drill.

Before I know it, Uncle Vic lunges forward, his fist clamping around Ryan's wrist. The drill clatters to the floor.

"I said, leave it." His voice carries a dangerous edge I've never heard before. "Someone we all knew and loved died today. We're going to take some time to remember him."

Ryan stares my uncle in the face. "I understand your grief, Vic, but honestly, Luke and I were never friends. I have a lot of lines to learn for *your* show, and I'd really like to get this set down, so I don't have to worry about it later."

"The rest of us are leaving, and it's not safe for you to do this on your own. Go. Home." Vic's voice is even and deep as it holds back the emotion I can tell is bubbling inside.

Evidently, Ryan gets the hint that Vic is in no mood to deal with his attitude, so he takes his drill and puts it backstage.

"I'm canceling rehearsal for the next couple of days." Vic addresses no one in particular, his voice an even staccato. "We all need to deal with this tragedy, and I'm going to have to find a new stage manager."

"I'll do it." Josie steps forward. "I know what to do. I've done it before."

"But, you're my lead costumer."

"We have plenty of help in the sewing department. I can stage manage and just supervise the costumers."

"I'll help her." I wipe my eyes with the back of my hand. "I've never stage-managed before, but I learned a lot on the last show. I can help pick up the slack, so Josie's not too stressed out."

"Thank you." Vic's eyes still glisten with tears. "That'll help a lot."

"Hey, Molly? Can I talk to you for a minute?" Ryan calls from stage left. I watch with a guarded eye as she joins him. I try to focus on Uncle Vic as he tells Josie and me about schedules, deadlines, and expectations, but my eyes keep drifting toward Ryan and Molly.

She smiles and nods, then says something. He responds, and she laughs. What are they talking about? "It's a date," he says with a wink and then walks off.

"What was that all about?" I ask when she walks back over.

"He wants to get together and work on our lines."

"Are you okay being alone with him?" Cole asks. "I have a shit ton of lines for the show, too. I could stay up here and work with you guys. I don't trust him."

"I know, and neither do I, but like it or not, I'm playing opposite him in this show, and I'm going to have to work with him. It'll be fine."

"We'll start rehearsals again on Wednesday. Would you mind calling everyone?" Vic asks Josie.

"Not at all. I'll do that tonight. I think I'm going to go pull some rehearsal props if you don't mind. I need to keep myself busy. Can you help me out, Heath?"

"Sure." I don't have anything better to do.

Cole kisses me. "I'm going to go work with Molly and Ryan. I'll keep an eye on things and make sure he doesn't try anything. Call me later?" I nod and watch him go.

"It's going to be so weird not having him around." Josie sits on the apron of the stage with her legs dangling over the pit, and I join her.

"I never got the chance to say I'm sorry. Luke was a great guy. I just wish things had been better between us. Maybe this wouldn't have happened."

"It's not your fault." She bumps my shoulder with hers. "Luke always wore his heart on his sleeve and unfortunately for him, people took him for granted. This wasn't the first time he fell for someone who only liked him as a friend. I guess that's what you get when you're too nice."

"Still, I could've approached things differently. I should've talked to him about Cole, instead of just letting him find out."

"But you and Cole just started… whatever it is you're doing." She swings her legs. "He was hurt way before that happened. He knew he liked you, and it killed him. I'm partly to blame. I should have talked to him about it. I should have included him more. He felt left out. He and I have been best friends for years, and he was hurt that I was hanging out without him. I just didn't want him ruining my ghost buzz, ya know?" She stares into the pit, searching for answers neither of us has.

"I know, and unfortunately, we can't change what's already done. It sucks."

"I do know one thing, though." She stands up, offering me a hand. "His death was not a suicide."

"You think someone killed him?" I want to tell her about my dream, but I'm afraid to.

"Not necessarily. Maybe Cole was right. He probably just walked out to the rocks and got knocked off balance by a wave and fell. I just don't see him doing that, though, especially when he was alone. He'd been drinking, but honestly, he wasn't that drunk. I've seen him much worse. I guess we'll never know."

Josie drops me off after we've pulled all the props. Uncle Vic ordered a pizza for dinner. I don't feel much like talking, so I grab a couple of slices and go to my room to think.

With nothing but the sound of the wind and the distant surf crashing in the background, my mind races, trying to make sense of what's happening. What is Catherine doing? Is this the danger she was warning us of? I can't deny that she had something to do with this, but why? What did Luke ever do to her?

I go to the closet and pull out the albums and the shoebox. Maybe I can find some answers here.

After thumbing through the albums a few times, I realize there's nothing of importance in them other than the few photos of Catherine and my father. I take the lid off the shoebox and empty the contents onto my bed. I set aside Dad's medals and report cards. Nothing useful, just further proof he was always an overachiever.

I thumb through some of the old newspaper clippings, handling them carefully so as not to tear the yellowing paper. I find articles on my dad's high school football team, publicity pieces about shows he was involved in, and another featuring my father wearing a medal from his state swim meet win.

No clues here.

I put everything back in the box and take it back to the closet. I notice a few yearbooks and another shoebox on the back corner of the shelf, so I grab them.

I immediately go to the yearbook from my father's senior year. I find Catherine's school photo in the freshman section. She's very pretty, but there's a sadness in her eyes that comes through even in the yearbook picture. I comb through the book, seeing plenty of pictures of my father, but none of Catherine aside from the individual portrait. It's as if she barely existed at school.

I open the shoebox filled with cards and letters. All of the envelopes have my father's name written on the front in the same perfect, feminine handwriting. There must be at least thirty cards in here, some of them unopened. At the bottom of the box are more newspaper clippings.

I thumb through them, reading the headlines:

LOCAL TEEN KILLED IN THEATRE FIRE
TRAGIC ACCIDENT TAKES LIFE OF LOCAL GIRL
HISTORIC OPERA HOUSE BURNS
TRAGEDY IN ROCK HARBOR

All of them have to do with the fire and Catherine's death. This is what I've been looking for. But it's the next article that grabs my attention. It's from a year earlier:

LAWSUIT AGAINST PROMINENT FAMILY DISMISSED

Rock Harbor, OR – A lawsuit brought against the wealthy Hull family by 18-year-old Catherine Whitley and her mother, Alice, has been dismissed in county court after weeks of testimony and cross-examination.

Whitley alleged that Noah Hull, 21, the son of business owners James and Lillian Hull, impregnated her during their relationship and then attempted to force a miscarriage. According to Whitley's testimony, she met Hull at the local theatre to ask for financial assistance for an abortion. She claims he refused, denied paternity, and pushed her down a staircase during the confrontation.

Hull denied the accusation, stating that Whitley threw herself down the stairs in an attempt to retaliate against him. Several of Hull's friends testified on his behalf, saying Whitley was unstable and had a history of volatile behavior.

Whitley was found bloodied and bruised at the bottom of the theatre staircase by a staff member, who called for an ambulance. She was treated for her injuries at Rock Harbor General Hospital.

Despite the fall, the baby survived, and doctors confirmed the child's health at the time of treatment.

Whitley's mother filed suit against the Hull family for damages. During the proceedings, defense attorneys questioned Whitley's credibility, pointing to past incidents with a former boyfriend and describing her actions as obsessive. The jury ultimately sided with the Hull family, and the case was dismissed.

I thumb through the remaining articles, all with similar headings:

MILLIONAIRE FAMILY ROCKED BY ASSAULT ACCUSATIONS

HEARINGS TO BEGIN IN ASSAULT CASE

My hands tremble and my throat constricts as the pieces click together. Catherine crying about her baby, the struggle I heard, her desperate pleas for help. The newspaper crinkles in my shaking grip.

A chill runs down my spine. Catherine had a baby. A baby that survived. I stare at the yellowed newspaper, my vision blurring. That baby would be roughly twenty-four or twenty-five now.

What happened to your baby, Catherine?

CHAPTER TWENTY-ONE

TOWN DIVIDED AFTER COURT CASE BETWEEN LOCAL TEEN AND PROMINENT FAMILY

Rock Harbor, OR – A contentious case involving 18-year-old Catherine Whitley and the prominent Hull family concluded this week with the court dismissing the charges. The proceedings drew significant local attention, highlighting sharp divides in the community.

Whitley testified that she and 21-year-old Noah Hull had been in a casual relationship when she became pregnant. She claimed she confronted Hull at the Rock Harbor theatre to request financial help with an abortion. According to Whitley, Hull not only denied paternity but also became violent, pushing her down a staircase in an attempt to end the pregnancy.

Hull, the son of a wealthy local family, denied the accusations. He told the court Whitley deliberately threw herself down the stairs. Hull's friends, many of whom testified during the trial, described Whitley as unstable, pointing to past relationships in which she allegedly exhibited obsessive behavior.

Emergency responders confirmed Whitley was found at the foot of the staircase with visible injuries. She was treated at Rock Harbor General Hospital, where doctors determined the pregnancy was not lost.

Alice Whitley brought the lawsuit, claiming damages against the Hull family and demanding financial assistance in raising her daughter's child. The defense argued that the accusations were an attempt to exploit the Hulls' financial standing. After days of testimony, the case was dismissed.

Reactions in Rock Harbor remain mixed. Some residents believe Whitley's account and criticize the influence of the Hulls' wealth, while others support the court's ruling, saying the evidence was insufficient to prove wrongdoing.

I finish reading the article to Josie over the phone, and I'm met with silence.

"So Noah Hull assaulted Catherine, and your dad was somehow involved?" Josie yawns on the other end of the line. I called her immediately after I read the articles.

"Not exactly, but according to one of the articles, my dad, your mom, Luke's dad, and some other woman I don't know were all questioned during the trial about Catherine's mental state. According to the papers, my father was 'previously involved with the victim', which we already know. There's all kinds of information here, but I don't know what's true and what isn't. The only thing they all have in common is that Noah Hull was accused of the crime, and charges were dropped when witnesses vouched for him over Catherine."

"So, now what?"

"I don't know exactly, but I think we need to talk to your mom and your grandma. They knew Catherine well, and your mom was questioned. Maybe she can help us fill in the blanks. There has to be more to the story."

"When's your next session?"

"Tomorrow, but I called earlier and canceled after everything that happened today. I figured I should be there for you and Uncle Vic instead. I won't see her again until Wednesday."

"I can do you one better. Why don't you come over for dinner after the memorial? Maybe we can both talk to her. She might not open up to you, but I can play the daughter card."

The memorial service weighs on me before it even begins. Vic sponsors it at the theatre on Tuesday afternoon. The actual funeral will take place later in the week in Salem, but Vic wanted to have something for everyone in Rock Harbor who knew Luke.

When I walk into the packed theatre, guilt hits me in the chest. I still feel partly responsible. Every seat is filled with cast members, crew, and Rock Harbor residents who all loved him.

One by one, people stand to remember him. Jenny's voice cracks talking about how he always asked about her grandkids. Ray tells about Luke staying until midnight to fix a broken set piece. Each memory cuts deeper. A knife-twist of guilt.

I feel like I should go up there and say something. My last words to him were less than kind. My last action toward him was to kick him in the face. I should make it right. But I can't bring myself to do it.

The stories taper off, leaving the theatre hushed. The grief lingers, but so does the love, hanging in the air like a final curtain call.

"Heath? How are you?" Dr. Plummer appears beside me as people file out of the theatre.

"I'm doing okay. This is all so weird." I stand, still shaky from the emotional service.

"Are you holding up okay? Any anxiety?"

"No, not really." I search the lobby for someone to come

rescue me. I really don't want a psychiatric evaluation in the lobby of the theatre. She's looking for trigger signs, wondering if Luke's death will affect me enough to send me spiraling back into my cave of depression.

"Hey." Josie approaches us with Patrice. Patrice's eyes are puffy and streaked with mascara. She looks even worse than Josie does.

"I need to get back to the office." Dr. Plummer gives Josie a hug and walks to her car.

Cole, Molly, and I join Patrice and Josie for lunch. The conversation feels stilted, everyone trying to avoid talking about the obvious. Patrice is leaving this afternoon to go on vacation with her family. They've agreed to let Molly and Cole use their beach house for the next few weeks while they rehearse for *Our Town*.

Cole drops me off at my house afterward. I'd really love some cuddle and make-out time, but he wants to take a nap before running lines with Molly and Ryan.

By the time Josie picks me up around 7:00, my stomach is churning with anxiety. I've been rehearsing questions for Dr. Plummer all afternoon. What if she calls Dad again? What if she thinks I'm losing it?

When we get to Josie's house, the place feels oddly still. Josie goes to her room to change, and I wander into the kitchen, following the scent of something cheesy baking in the oven. I peer through the screen door and see Marilyn sitting on the porch, staring out at the ocean.

"Heath? Is that you? Come join me." She notices me through the door.

"How are you?" I take a seat in the white plastic chair next to her.

"I'm fine. Just enjoying this beautiful evening. It's not often we have a night without clouds. It's nice to just sit out here and watch the ocean. How was the service?"

"It was nice. We missed you." I remember her fear of the

theatre.

"I felt horrible missing it, but I just can't bring myself to go in that place. It hurts too much. Such an awful thing to happen to such a sweet boy." She shakes her head.

"Yeah, it was."

"Hey, Gran." Josie joins us on the porch.

"Hi, honey. Where's your mother?"

"She said she had some work to do after the service. I thought she'd be here by now."

"How you holding up, sugar?" Marilyn pats Josie's hand.

"I'll be okay."

The timer on the oven goes off, and Marilyn stands to go to the kitchen. I hear a car door slam. It must be Dr. Plummer. My leg jackhammers against the porch floor. My heart pounds so hard I'm sure Josie can hear it.

"You okay?" Josie notices my nervousness.

"Yeah, I'm fine." The lie comes out strained.

"Hey, kids, dinner's about ready. How about you set up the picnic table, and we'll eat outside?" Dr. Plummer calls from the door.

As we finish eating, the sun begins to set across the ocean, casting light shades of red and orange across the water, bathing everything in a pinkish hue. Once we've cleared the table, we all return to the porch. I listen to the three women talk, laughing when they laugh, but my throat feels caked with questions I'm too afraid to ask.

"Heath has something he wants to ask you, Mom," Josie says.

Wow. She's not wasting any time tonight.

I shoot her a look and then clear my throat. "I need you to tell me about Catherine. My dad told me part of the story, but there was a lot he left out."

"I thought we were done talking about Catherine." Dr. Plummer hints at my last session when I told her I didn't want to talk about it anymore.

"I've changed my mind. I lied the last time I spoke with you. I've seen her again."

"What are you talking about?" Marilyn leans forward.

Before Dr. Plummer can stop me, I tell Marilyn everything—the voices, the dreams, Catherine's warnings. If anyone can make her daughter talk, it's her. The only piece of information I leave out is what I dreamed, or thought I dreamed, the night Luke died.

"I told him he shouldn't open that theatre back up." Marilyn's tone carries the weight of what happened years ago.

"I'm sure there's an explanation for everything that's taken place. You suffer from anxiety. You said yourself you were probably just imagining things." Dr. Plummer's response sounds rehearsed.

"So then why did you call my father? Why did he feel he needed to come down here and take me home if you think it's just my imagination?"

"Everything he said has some truth to it, Melanie." Marilyn's voice is firm.

"Let me handle this, Mother." Dr. Plummer's agitation is obvious.

"Mom, I know you don't want to believe in ghosts, but something weird is going on. This has obviously upset you. Your reaction in your office the other day was less than typical for you. Please tell us what you know." Josie urges.

Dr. Plummer shakes her head. "It just doesn't make sense. Catherine died."

"And now she's back. I thought at first maybe this was a residual haunting, but what Heath is experiencing is more than just a single event that plays over and over. It's like she's trying to communicate with him. That's why I thought a Ouija board might help."

"What happened to Catherine was a very tragic thing. There are many stories of people dying a tragic death and sticking around to haunt the place where it happened." Marilyn speaks with surprising authority.

"Look at you, Gran. You're a regular Ghostbuster."

"Hey, I know a few things. I watch those shows on TV."

"Dr. Plummer, please just tell us what you know about Catherine. Whether you believe she's still hanging around the theatre or not doesn't matter. You need to tell us. I'm afraid someone might be in danger. I've seen Catherine a few more times. I don't know if they are dreams or not, but she keeps begging for help and crying for her baby."

Dr. Plummer stands from her chair, and I'm afraid she's going to leave us with nothing. She stares down at me, her face a sickly green color as if she's about to throw up. She wraps her arms around her stomach, staring at the ground, breathing deep. Her face crumples like wet paper. Twenty-four years of secrets claw their way to the surface, etching themselves across her face before she even speaks.

She takes a seat on the step between Josie and me, pressing her hands to her stomach like the words physically hurt to release.

"Catherine was a very troubled girl. She had a bad reputation. Her mother wasn't exactly the town's finest citizen. I did my best to befriend her. I was a few years older than she was, and she looked up to me. She spent a lot of time here, especially after the incident with Noah."

"The assault?" Josie asks.

"Yes. It was a very difficult time for her. Her mother wouldn't let her have an abortion because she thought that if the trial went in their favor, she could use the baby to get money from Noah's family. She's the one who pushed Catherine to press charges. When the judge threw out the case, everything spiraled, and her mother kicked her out."

"Why was the case dismissed?" I have to ask even though I'm not sure I want to hear the answer.

"Like I said, lack of evidence. Your father, Jason Fenley, and a few others all vouched for Noah. They said he was with them the night of Catherine's alleged attack. They said there was no way he could have been at the theatre when it happened." Tears fill her eyes.

"So, they lied?"

"We all lied." She wipes a tear away as it slides down her cheek.

"Who is we?" Josie's voice is barely a whisper.

"My friend Marnie and I were with Jason and Phillip that night. It was the night of my wedding reception. Noah was there, but he came much later. He wasn't with us when we said he was."

"So why did you lie?"

"Money. Noah's father paid us off to keep us quiet. It was a nice amount of money, and all we had to do was say that we'd seen Noah at the party when the assault supposedly took place."

"My God, Mom, that's illegal." Josie stares at her mother in shock.

"I'm not proud of it. All sorts of bad things came out during that trial. I felt so guilty afterward. I did everything I could to help Catherine, as did Phillip. She was in so much pain. We'd betrayed her. We'd made her life worse, and we felt horrible. We helped her as much as we could through her pregnancy. We called her, checked up on her. I drove up from Salem and took her to her appointments to make sure she and the baby were safe because I knew her mother wouldn't do that for her."

She pauses, taking a shuddering breath. "Catherine loved the attention she got from your father. I honestly don't think she cared whether I was there or not. Catherine had never fallen out of love with him. He tried to reason with her. He was too kind to completely push her away, though. He didn't have a mean bone in his body. He knew she was mentally and physically fragile. He was afraid of what would happen after everything that she'd been through with the trial. He was even at the hospital when her baby was born.

"After the baby was given away, Catherine was very depressed. From what I understand, she became even more obsessed with

Phillip. Catherine always vacillated between intense feelings of love and extreme rage for your father. One minute she would be very sweet, and the next she would be raging. She would tell your father she loved him, and then she would scream at him for covering for his friend, threatening that one day she would get even with everyone who covered for Noah. She wasn't psychologically well."

"So, she didn't have an abortion?" Josie's voice is small.

Dr. Plummer shakes her head, tears streaming down her face. "No. She was forced to give it up."

The pieces of the story fuse together like broken bones. "That's why she keeps crying for her baby. They took it from her. Someone took her baby."

A chill knife runs down my spine as I realize the implications. Luke's father was one of those who lied. What if Luke's death is only the beginning?

CHAPTER TWENTY-TWO

My phone buzzes in my hand, making me jump. I look at the caller ID. It's Molly. Weird. Why is she calling me? I send her to voicemail. I can't be interrupted now that we're finally getting some answers.

"She wasn't taken. She was adopted." Marilyn's voice comes from behind us. I'd almost forgotten she was there.

"She? It was a girl?"

"Yes. A very nice family who were able to give her a loving home adopted her; something Catherine wouldn't have been able to provide. She was too young, and her home life wasn't ideal. She was in no shape to raise a child."

"Who adopted her?"

"I'm not sure." Dr. Plummer cuts Marilyn off. "A young couple from Portland, I think. I didn't keep track."

Molly calls again, and I decide to take it this time.

"Hey." I stand and walk away from the others for privacy. "What's up?"

"Are you busy?" Her voice sounds soft and wobbly, like she's been crying.

"No, I'm just talking to Josie and her mom. Is everything okay?"

"Not really." She sniffles. "Can you come to the theatre?"

"What are you doing at the theatre?"

"It was Ryan's idea. He said it might be helpful to run through some of our scenes here, and—"

"And?"

My heart hammers in my chest. "He came on to me—"

"Did he hurt you?" I shout before she can say anything more.

"No, he just tried to kiss me, and when I pushed him away, he got angry and started calling me names and yelling. I tried to leave, but my car's battery is dead. I don't know what to do. Cole left early because he wasn't feeling well and he's not answering his phone now. He tried to get me to leave with him. I should have gone."

"We'll be there in ten minutes. Get in your car and lock the door. If he comes near you, call the police."

Josie notices the panicked look on my face. "What's going on?"

"We need to go help Molly. She's at the theatre. She was rehearsing with Ryan, and he came on to her. She tried to leave, but her battery's dead. Do you have jumper cables?"

"Yeah, come on." She grabs her keys.

I follow her to her car, trying to breathe evenly. My whole body shakes with rage. Like father, like son. I can't help but think of what his father did to Catherine. What if Ryan had done the same thing to Molly?

When we get to the theatre, Josie pulls up beside Molly's car and pops her hood. Before she can even park, I'm out of the car, rushing to Molly as she steps out of her Mustang.

I study her face. "Are you okay?"

"I'm fine. He just freaked me out." Her entire body is trembling.

"Is he still here?"

"Yeah, he's inside."

"How did you guys get in?" Josie asks.

"He still has a key." Molly's voice is barely a whisper.

I start toward the theatre.

"Heath? What are you doing?" Josie calls after me, warning clear in her voice.

I ignore her as I walk into the theatre, my hands clenched so tight my nails dig into my palms. Heat floods my vision. I hear the sound of a drill and a flat crashing against the stage. I follow the sounds down the hallway, clenching and unclenching my fists, my anger flaring with every step.

Ryan doesn't even hear me approach. I grab him by the collar and spin him around. The drill crashes to the floor as my fist connects with his face. He didn't even see it coming.

Ryan falls to the floor, blood spraying from his nose. He struggles to stand, and I kick him in the gut. I lunge for him, but Molly grabs me around the waist, her small body pulling against me. I hear the faint sounds of Josie yelling at me, telling me to stop. The words are barely audible over the roaring in my ears caused by the blood pounding through my veins.

"If you ever touch her again, I swear to God I'll fucking kill you. You got that? I'm done with your bullshit." I tower over him as he struggles to stand. I fight back the urge to kick him in the face.

"Heath, stop, please. Let's go. He's not worth it. Come on." Molly pulls me away from Ryan. Josie grabs me by the arm and leads me down the stairs toward the hall.

"You fuckin' dick!" Ryan yells after us. "This isn't over, Ingram. I'll sue your pussy ass."

"Back off, Ryan. Leave it." Molly's voice carries a strength I haven't heard before.

Josie pulls me outside, not letting go of my arm until we reach the cars. I notice Molly isn't with us and turn back toward the theatre. Josie yells at me to let it go. I stop when I see Molly walking out the double glass doors.

"Why did you do that?" She approaches me. "What good did that do anyone?"

"I've had it with his bullshit!"

"I appreciate you protecting me, but that wasn't cool."

My body is still on fire. I shake with adrenaline and rage. "I hate him. I hate that fucker." I kick the front tire of Molly's car.

Josie places a hand on my chest. "Bruh, stop. You're acting like a straight, white man who didn't get his way."

I let out a breath.

Molly takes a step back. "Please, calm down. You're scaring me. Just let it go."

She inches toward me slowly as if she's trying to calm an angry dog. My heartbeat slows, and my breath evens out.

Josie pops Molly's hood. "We should probably get this done and then get out of here. The last thing we need is Mr. CrossFit coming out here with a two-by-four and bashing our skulls in."

She hops into Molly's Mustang and turns the ignition. The engine turns over a couple times before catching and revving to life.

"Let me give you a ride home." Molly looks at me with concerned eyes.

I nod and crawl into the passenger seat without saying a word. Molly gives Josie a hug and thanks her before we leave.

Five minutes later, Molly pulls up to my house. "You should probably put some ice on that hand."

I look down at the scrapes on my swollen knuckles. Now that the adrenaline has worn off, I'm more aware of the throbbing.

"I will." I don't look at her. The anger has subsided, and my conscience has started to eat away at me. I shouldn't have done that. I should have just let it go.

"Are you okay?"

I can feel her staring at me, but I don't look at her. "I'm fine."

"Look at me."

I try, but I can't. Instead, I turn my head and gaze out the window.

"I know you were just trying to protect me, but I hate violence." Her voice carries that careful tone people use with dangerous animals.

"Heath?"

"What?" The word comes out louder than it should.

"Maybe I should just go."

I climb out of the car without saying a word. I don't even acknowledge her. I just walk up the steps and listen as she backs out of the driveway, her headlights waving goodbye as they flash across my back.

I grab some ice from the freezer and put it in a plastic grocery bag before going upstairs to my room. My phone buzzes.

You OK?

It's Josie. I answer her, doing my best to text with one hand. I can barely even close my fist. I hope I didn't break anything more than Ryan's nose.

Fine

U sure?

Yes

Talk 2morrow?

K

I plug my phone in and place it on the nightstand before climbing into bed.

I shoot a quick text to Cole: **Ryan came onto Molly. Scared the shit out of her. I fucked up his face**

As soon as I press send, my phone rings—Cole's name flashes on the screen.

I answer and flop back onto the bed. "Hey. You're on speaker."

"What happened?"

I tell him about Ryan cornering Molly, her dead battery, finding them at the theatre. About my fist connecting with

Ryan's face.

"Why didn't she call me? I could have come up there."

"She said she tried contacting you."

"That's weird. I didn't have a missed call or text."

That is weird.

"Anyway. Are you okay?"

"Yeah." My knuckles throb, but not as much as the sick feeling in my stomach when I consider what I did to Ryan.

"I don't suppose you'd like to come over?" Hope fills his voice.

"Like to? Yes, but I'm not in a good headspace."

"I understand. Can we maybe carve out some time to hang tomorrow? I'm done with rehearsal at 3:00. I'd really like a night where it's just us. No drama. No theatre. I really would like to get to know you better away from all that."

"Yeah, I'd like that."

"Good. Hey, I think Molly just pulled up. I'm going to go make sure she's okay. Sleep tight."

"Thanks, you too."

I end the call.

As I drift off, all I can think about is the shitstorm that will surely hit when Uncle Vic finds out I punched one of his lead actors. Tomorrow's going to suck.

I stumble through the fog as I walk down the street. It's so thick I can barely see where I'm going. My feet carry me forward through the mist, one slow step at a time. I reach out and pull on the front door of the theatre. It swings open, and I step inside. The moon glows through the windows, barely lighting the area around me. The smell of burned wood fills my nose.

I walk toward the hallway and stop when I hear a loud crash come from the stage.

I get the sense that something's wrong, but I'm surprisingly calm. The hallway is pitch dark, but I don't need light. I just follow the scent of her as I walk toward the glint of light coming from the backstage door.

She stands there waiting for me.

"I need to show you something, Phillip." She holds out her hand.

I reach out to her and let her guide me up the stairs. Her hand is small and cold in mine.

"Close your eyes." I do as I'm told.

"Now open."

She holds the curtain aside and gestures for me to walk out onto the dark stage. I hesitate, but she nods, encouraging me to take my first step. As I walk, stage lights turn on. With each step, the stage grows brighter.

I stop when I see it. A body lies in a spreading pool of blood, dark as motor oil. The heavy platform has crushed everything from the chest up. Only legs and arms are visible. My stomach lurches.

I stagger backward, clapping my hand over my mouth, holding back the scream that pushes at my lips.

"It happened again." Her voice is matter-of-fact.

"What did you do?" My voice is soft and ragged.

"You did it." She points an accusatory finger at me. "It's all because of you."

"I didn't… No…" I stammer.

"You could have saved him. It's your fault." She screams the words at me as she circles me, accusing me of her crime. "Your fault. Your fault. It's all your fault."

I feel as if I might pass out.

"Bye-bye, Noah!" she cries, skipping around me like a deranged schoolgirl.

"BYE-BYE!"

"Heath?"

My head jerks at the sound of my uncle's voice. A golden

slant of early morning sun slices through my window. I'm wet. The plastic bag I'd filled with ice the night before has melted, soaking my sheets and clothing.

"Heath?" He calls again with a loud knock.

"Yeah?" I mumble.

"I'm going down to the diner for breakfast. You want to join me?"

If I go with him, I'm going to have to tell him about the fight, and I'm not ready to do that just yet.

"No, thanks. I'm meeting Josie this morning to go over a few things before rehearsal." The lie comes easily.

Right then, as if she knew she needed to cover for me, my phone rings.

"Good morning, Mr. UFC. How's the hand?"

"I'm okay." I rub my eyes.

"I'm headed to the theatre in a few. Want a ride?"

"Sure. Give me ten minutes."

"Yeah, right. See you in twenty." The line goes dead.

In the shower, I trace the fading burn marks on my chest, Catherine's handprints still visible like a brand. My stomach drops as last night's dream crashes back.

Another body. Another death.

On the way to the theatre, Josie rattles on and on about everything her mom told us last night, but I barely hear any of it.

When we get to the theatre, I notice Ryan's truck is parked in the same spot as last night, and Ray is parked beside him. There are no police cars or ambulances. Everything looks normal.

It was just a dream. Everything is fine.

I release an audible sigh of relief that Josie mistakes for nerves.

"I know. I don't want to see Ryan either. My suggestion is for you to stay away from him. I'm not in the mood to play referee today, got it?"

I follow her into the theatre, and we both stop in our tracks. Ray sits on the theatre steps, his head in his hands, and my blood turns to ice.

"Ray?" Josie glances back at me. "What's wrong? What is it?"

"R-Ryan. He's dead."

CHAPTER TWENTY–THREE

"There was no fight last night. Got it?" Josie stares at me while I gaze blankly ahead. This is the second time someone has died after I fought with them.

Catherine's words echo in my head. *Your fault. You did this.*

What the hell is going on? Did I have something to do with this? Did I kill Luke and Ryan?

"Heath?" Josie shakes me out of my thoughts.

"Yeah, I got it." I lean against her car and watch the small crowd that's started to form. The police made us leave while they do their investigation. Uncle Vic is inside talking to them, but everyone else is waiting outside. The road in front of the theatre is filled with cars that have slowed to see what's going on. I watch as Molly's Mustang pulls into the parking lot. Cole is right behind her.

"Sorry. I got here as fast as I could. What's going on?" Cole joins us.

"Ryan's dead." Josie's voice is flat.

"Oh my God, how?" Molly looks directly at me when she says this.

"Why are you looking at me? Did he look dead when you left last night? You were the last one out of the building." She recoils as if I just hit her.

"That's not what she was asking." Cole steps protectively closer to Molly.

"I just thought maybe you hit him too hard, and he died after we left. I'm not calling you a murderer."

"There was no fight." Josie's voice carries a warning. "We didn't even see Ryan. We're doing this to protect Heath. If the police find out that another person died after fighting with him, they're going to start asking questions."

"But I didn't do it."

"I know you didn't." Josie turns to face the three of us, her face hard and determined. "But do you really want a police investigation? We. Didn't. See. Him. He didn't come on to Molly, and you didn't come to her rescue. None of that happened. We weren't even here last night. As it stands now, it looks like an accident. It *was* an accident. Ryan was dismantling a set by himself—never a smart idea. That's all there is to it."

"We're canceling the show." Vic approaches us, his shoulders sagging. "Stupid kid. I told him to leave the set alone. I told him it was too dangerous to tear it down himself."

"Do you really have to cancel the show?" Cole asks.

"I have to. I'm sorry. This is the second death in less than four days, and this one happened on the stage. The place is going to get a bad rep. If I don't cancel, I look heartless. Besides, after Noah Hull sues me, as he undoubtedly will, he'll own the place, and my ass will be on the street."

A black Mercedes SUV tears into the parking lot and comes to a screeching halt at the front door. I watch as an older version of Ryan flies out of the vehicle and pushes past the cops blocking the double doors.

"Christ. Here we go." Vic heads back toward the theatre.

"I'm going to go see if the cops have any more information on what might have happened to Luke." Josie walks toward the same guy who questioned us on the beach.

"Are you okay?" Molly asks after a few seconds of silence.

"What do you think?" I can't look at her. I can't move.

My chest feels hollow, my limbs heavy as lead.

"Do you want to get something to eat?" Cole asks.

"How the hell can you even think about food right now?" The words come out sharper than intended.

"Do you want to talk about it?"

"Talk about what? There's nothing to talk about." I wrap my arms around my chest, closing myself off.

"I'm going to go home and pack." Molly shifts her weight from foot to foot.

"Why?" Cole asks.

"The show is canceled. I don't have any reason to stay here. I may as well go home and enjoy the rest of the summer."

She's right. If the theatre closes, what then? Will Cole leave? My dad will probably demand that I go home, too. Is all of this over?

"Thanks for what you did for me last night." Molly approaches me carefully. "I'm sorry if I implied anything earlier."

"All good." I give her an awkward hug. "It was fun working with you."

"You, too. Maybe this will work itself out, and we can come back and do it again next year."

"Yeah, maybe."

"And I'll see you at school." She punches Cole lightly in the arm.

"Yeah, you will." He gives her a hug. "We'll chat before then."

She gives a small wave and walks to her car. We both remain silent, watching as she drives off.

"So, this is it, huh?" I ask, staring at the theatre.

"What do you mean?" Cole studies my face.

"I didn't think my summer would end up being just as bad as the previous three months of my life. Things were starting to look up for me, and now…"

"Now what?" He searches my expression, and I look away.

My only response is to stare at my feet. If I look at him, I'll crack, and right now I've got too much on my mind.

"You wanna go do something? Get your mind off things?" He tries to take my hand, and I pull away, shaking my head.

"What's the point? The theatre is closing. We'll both be leaving. It's done."

"What's done? We're just getting to know one another. We have phones. We can stay in touch. And I haven't given up hope that I might still convince you to come to OSU with us in the fall."

I shake my head. A week ago, I had decided that yes, I would attend OSU. With Josie, Luke, Cole, and Molly all there, I'd have a built-in friend group. But after everything that's happened…

"Yeah, I don't think that's going to happen. This has all been a lot. I just need…"

"Space." He finishes for me. "Got it. I'll give you that." He turns to leave.

I want to call after him, but I force myself to stay quiet. These deaths are somehow connected to me. I don't want to put him at risk, too. I look up, just as he turns back.

"I'll give you space, but I'm not giving up."

I nod, and despite trying to fight it, my heart flutters just a little bit.

The sound of footsteps behind me pulls me around.

"Where's Molly?" Josie asks.

"She left. Said she was going to go home and pack, and then head out since everything's going to be canceled anyway. What did the cops say?"

"It's all good. No new developments on Luke. They asked about Ryan, and I told them we hadn't seen him since Luke's funeral. Ray discovered the body. They said they have no reason to question us. It's an obvious accident."

"Was it?" The question comes out more for my own benefit than hers.

"What do you mean?"

I don't answer.

"Heath? Do you know something?" She forces me to look at her.

"No, but… I don't know. I saw something—dreamed it. Again."

"Let's get out of here. We'll go someplace and talk, okay?"

I nod and climb into her car. Josie calls her mother to let her know what happened and tells her I won't be able to make my appointment.

We drive to Josie's place and walk down to the beach. There aren't many people here, so it's easy to find a place where we can talk uninterrupted.

"Tell me." She flops down in the sand beside me.

"It's just more weird shit." I'm unsure of where to start.

"I live for weird shit. Spill."

"The night that Luke died, I had a dream that I was on the beach. Catherine was there, and she kept saying, 'It's done. He's gone'. We were near some rocks. I think they were the same rocks where Luke's body was found."

She stares at me, unfazed by what I'm telling her. "Then, last night, I had another dream about Catherine. This time I was at the theatre, and she told me she had something to show me. She walked me to the stage, and there was a body there, smashed under a fallen platform. Just like Ryan."

"That doesn't mean you did it. In either dream, did you kill either of them?"

"No. I just dreamed that Catherine had come to tell me about their deaths."

"It's definitely macabre, but it doesn't sound like you were involved in any way." Her reassurance eases the tension in my chest.

"I just wish it would stop. I don't get it. It's like if people piss me off, then they die."

My head pounds with the weight of it all.

She shifts next to me. "Can I tell you something? And you have to promise not to freak out."

"What?"

She takes a deep breath and picks up a handful of sand, letting it run through her fingers. "What if Catherine's daughter is here? In town? What if this isn't Catherine doing this? What if it's her daughter?"

"You sound like a lunatic." My brain can't take any more. I can't make sense of any of it, let alone this new twist Josie's added to the mix.

"Think about it." She grabs my hand. "If you were adopted, wouldn't you want to know who your birth mother was?"

"Maybe. I don't know."

"Suppose Catherine's daughter got hold of her original birth records? What if she tracked her down and found out what happened to her? All it would take is a few Google hits and a trip to the local library to read all the past articles. Maybe she came looking for her."

"Catherine is dead."

"But the people who hurt her aren't. What if her daughter is just as mental as she was and is getting revenge on those who wronged her?"

I shake my head in disbelief.

"Look at everything that's happened." Josie is hell-bent on making me hear her out. "Luke's father told the cops that he was with Noah that night to cover for him. Now Luke is dead. Ryan's father assaulted Catherine, and was likely the father of her baby, and now Ryan is dead."

She pauses a moment as she lets it sink in.

"If she's going after the families of those who wronged her mother, there are only two people left, Heath: you and me. Your father and my mother lied to help Noah. If you look at this like a true psycho, she would save you for the grand finale, which makes me next."

"But who could it be?"

"Think about it." She speaks as if the answer is sitting right in front of me.

My head swims. "I have no idea."

"Bruh. It's Molly."

I look at her in disbelief. Is she serious?

"It has to be."

"That's crazy. Molly isn't like that. Her parents died…" My voice trails off. Her father died in a car accident, and her mother took her own life. Just like Catherine's parents. Had she taken her birth mother's story and made it her own? The ground seems to open up beneath me. I'm spiraling downward.

"Doesn't it seem a bit odd that she was the last one to see both Luke and Ryan alive?"

"It can't be her." I shake my head. I won't buy into this. I can't. It's not Molly. The math isn't right. "Catherine died twenty-four years ago, and her baby was born a few months before that. Molly just turned twenty a few days ago."

She tilts her head and raises an eyebrow. "So she lied about her age. Have you actually seen her birth certificate or her driver's license?"

"Stop, Josie. Just stop." I start to stand, but she places a hand on my wrist, stopping me.

"I found this in her bag the other day." She hands me a composition book. It's Catherine's journal. The one I'd hidden in the costume room.

"Where did you find this?" I take it from her with shaking hands.

"I told you. Molly had it in her bag. I was looking for something when I was visiting Patrice a few nights ago. I picked up Molly's bag, and this fell out. I saw Catherine's name on the cover, so I opened it and realized it was the journal, so I took it."

I stare at the journal, my head pounding. I can't believe it. I won't.

"I know it sucks, but isn't it obvious? I didn't want to believe it either, but when you told me you saw Molly on the beach that night you stayed over, it started falling into place. Why else would you see a Molly/Catherine hybrid? When I found the journal, it suddenly dawned on me what was going on. Molly is Catherine's daughter."

"This doesn't make sense." But in a way it does.

No. Molly isn't like that. She's not a psychopath. Cole knows her. Vouched for her.

"I'm going to call Cole. See if he knows more about her. Maybe he can talk to her." I dig my phone out of my pocket.

Josie snatches it out of my hand before I can dial.

"No, we can't let her know. We don't have all of our facts straight. There are a few things I need to check out first. Can you meet me around 9:00 tonight?"

"I suppose I could." I'm in shock. Until now, I didn't think anything could feel worse than finding out you'd killed three of your friends. This just may top the list.

"Promise me you won't tell Cole. We can't have him tipping her off."

"Josie, she may already be gone. She said she was going home to pack—"

"That definitely means she's guilty. Just promise you won't say anything to anyone."

"Okay."

Even if Molly is Catherine's daughter, that doesn't explain the dreams I've had, or the voices I've heard at the theatre. There are still far too many questions and no logical answers. I scour the internet, searching for anything on Catherine I didn't already know, but my search yields no new results.

Cole calls around 4:00, but I let it go straight to voicemail. I don't know what to say to him. I don't know what to think anymore. On the surface, everything Josie said seems plausible, but something is nagging at me, and it won't go away.

Three hours later, I'm still scrambling. I've combed the internet, the newspaper articles in the shoebox, and gone over everything my father and Dr. Plummer told us, but I can't find anything about Catherine's daughter. I've hit a wall.

Wait a minute.

There is someone who may be able to give me the information I need.

When I go downstairs, I find Vic sitting at the table with his head in his hands.

"Hey. You okay?"

"How did this all go so wrong, so fast?" He shakes his head. "Everything was going so well. The first show was a hit. Now I have a wrongful death lawsuit on my hands, and the theatre is closed. Maybe Marilyn was right. Maybe the place is cursed."

He leans back in his chair and runs his hand across his face. He seems to have aged about ten years since this afternoon. I hate that he is going through this, but I have something I need to do. I can't be here for him right now.

"Can I borrow your truck for a while?"

He sighs and leans back in his chair. "The keys are on the counter. I don't plan on going anywhere tonight."

"Thanks." I grab the keys and my phone, then rush to the truck.

I grip the steering wheel of the old Ford as I drive toward the diner. I haven't driven since the accident, and the feel of the wheel in my hands is almost foreign to me. Raindrops spatter against the windshield, and I have to search for the wipers. The truck is so old that I have to pull a knob on the dashboard to turn them on.

The diner is packed, and the waitress at the bar tells me Marilyn left an hour ago. I drive out to her house, happy to see that neither Josie nor Dr. Plummer's cars are in the drive. When she answers the door, she looks surprised to see me.

"Heath? Josie's not here."

"Yes, I know. I was wondering if I could talk to you for a minute. Please? It's important."

"Of course you can, come on in. Would you like something to drink?"

"No, thank you."

I follow her into the living room. She picks up the remote and turns off the television, taking a seat on the sofa. I sit on the love seat across from her, questions wrestling in my head as I try to choose the best one to start with. My phone buzzes in my pocket, and I hit the off button without even looking at it.

"What would you like to talk about?"

"I need to know who adopted Catherine's baby." I cut to the chase. I can't waste any more time.

"It was a nice family from Salem."

That's not right.

"Last night, Dr. Plummer said Portland." I don't want to call her a liar, but it's obvious someone is trying to hide something.

"Yes, that's what Melanie said, but that's not true. They were from Salem."

"Why would she lie?"

"She was trying to protect Josie."

The words slam into me. The room tilts sideways, and I grip the chair arm to keep from falling

It isn't Molly.

"Josie is Catherine's daughter?" The words barely make it past my suddenly dry throat.

"Yes."

"Wait. That doesn't make sense. Catherine died twenty-four years ago. I thought Josie was only twenty-two."

Marilyn shakes her head. "She was a couple of years behind her peers…" Her voice trails off.

"Does she know?" My head spins with more questions. My phone buzzes again, and I take it out of my pocket, glancing at the screen. It's a text from Molly.

I'm here. Where are you?

She's where? I ignore it. I have bigger problems that need fixing right now.

"Josie's always known she was adopted. She just didn't know who her mother was. Melanie has done her best to keep it from her."

"Why?"

"Melanie was afraid it might have a negative effect on her. Josie lives with several mental health disorders. Melanie was afraid of what would happen if Josie learned the truth about her birth mother. Catherine's story isn't exactly a happy one."

She has a point. I probably would've done the same thing. "Catherine must have been happy to know that Melanie adopted her baby. Surely she would have wanted her to have a good life with loving parents."

"Quite the opposite, actually. When Catherine learned that Melanie was the one who adopted her baby, it almost pushed her over the edge. Melanie found out she couldn't have children, not long after she was married. When she learned Catherine was pregnant and her mother was forcing her to give up the baby, she paid a lot of money to make sure she was the one to adopt her. She knew Catherine was in no position to raise a child, and Melanie felt that by adopting Josie, she would be doing Catherine a favor. She could give the baby everything Catherine couldn't. She felt so guilty after what she'd done at the trial; she honestly felt that this was what God would want her to do."

"Does Josie know Catherine was her mother?"

"Yes. She figured it out a couple of weeks ago. It's been very tense around here."

"Why didn't any of you say anything about this last night?" I ask.

And more importantly, why was Josie trying to convince me that Molly is Catherine's daughter just this afternoon?

"Josie said she didn't want anyone to know."

"So why are you telling me?" Ice spreads through my veins as I wait for her answer.

"Because I think Josie needs help, Heath. She needs someone her own age she can confide in."

Her voice shakes, and she runs a hand over her mouth. "Everything that's happened the last few weeks is weighing on her, and I think Luke's death may have pushed her over the edge. I'm afraid she may be acting out in an unhealthy way again."

"What do you mean, again?"

She takes a deep breath, and I brace myself for what's coming.

"When Josie was thirteen, Melanie started noticing severe mood swings. We knew mental illness might be genetic, but we ignored the signs. Called it teen angst. Then the bullying started. One day, Josie snuck a kitchen knife to school in her backpack. A girl who frequently bullied her teased her during PE. Afterward, Josie attacked her. Cut her face up pretty bad." Marilyn lets out a deep sigh. "Josie had to spend a couple of years under close observation because of it."

Oh my God. Did Josie kill Luke and Ryan?

My throat constricts, and the room spins around me. Every conversation we've had, every moment she's comforted me, suddenly takes on a sinister new meaning.

No way. She wouldn't do that. She loved Luke. He was her best friend.

"When she was released, she and her mother moved in with me. Melanie and Josie's father had divorced by then. The stress of the situation was too much for him to handle. We've done our best to keep her happy and safe, and she's been an angel for the most part." She shifts in her seat and studies my face. I stare at her blankly, eager to hear what else she has to say.

"Recently, I've noticed a change in Josie's mood. She's easily irritated, she doesn't sleep, and she leaves the house at odd hours of the night. I'm worried about her." She wipes a tear from her cheek. "She's a good girl, Heath."

"I know she is." The words feel hollow as they leave my mouth.

"She's stopped taking her medication again. She's done this before, but we caught it early enough and were able to convince her to go back on them, but this time… she's just being so difficult."

"Where is Josie right now?"

"I don't know." She sinks back into the sofa. "Melanie just called, looking for her. She was supposed to meet her for dinner, but Josie never showed. She won't pick up her phone."

"I'll see if I can find her." I stand on unsteady legs. "Thank you for telling me this."

"Heath?" She stops me before I can leave. "Be careful."

I climb into the truck and head back into town, my mind racing when it suddenly dawns on me that I have no idea what I'm doing. I pull off at a gas station, breathing heavily. I need to think. My phone buzzes again, and I reach for it. I have three text messages from Josie.

Still at the theatre. Meet me here?

Where r u?

It's Molly. I have proof.

My blood turns to ice. She's still trying to convince me it's Molly. She's setting me up.

I want to text her back and tell her that I know the truth, but I don't.

Fell asleep. Still at theatre? I text

I wait less than a minute for her reply.

Yes. Come quick. Molly is here. I need help. I'm scared.

My heart thuds in my chest. She has Molly. My God, what if Molly is already dead?

I put the truck in drive and race back toward the theatre.

My phone rings and I glance at the caller ID. It's Cole.

"Hey. I came by your house, and Vic said you took the truck. Where are you?"

"I'm out with Josie." How much should I tell him?

"Oh." He's annoyed. We were supposed to do something tonight.

"Yeah, she's, uh… having a hard time with everything. I need to be there for her." I decide not to tell him the truth. I can't put him in danger, too. "But I do want to see you. I'm sorry about earlier. Can I call you tomorrow?"

"Yeah, sure." The line goes dead.

I smack my palm on the steering wheel. Why do I fuck everything up?

I'll fix this with him, though. I know I can. I just need to get through tonight.

I park down the street in case Josie is watching. I can't let her know I'm on to her. She thinks I'm at home and would expect me to walk here.

But now that I'm here, what do I do? Is she going to try to kill me? Molly? My hands shake as I climb out of the truck. The night air feels thick and oppressive, like the calm before a storm.

My phone buzzes. It's Josie.

Where r u?

Almost there

When I walk around the corner, I see Molly's car parked in the lot. The building is ominously dark and quiet. I'm about to try the front doors when I hear sirens in the distance. I rush to the side of the building, duck into the shadows and watch as two police cars zoom by, followed by an ambulance and a fire truck. I walk around back, past Josie's Volkswagen, and punch in the code on the door.

The lights are on in the scene shop. Newspaper articles and other pieces of paper litter the floor. I recognize the first article from the shoebox in my dad's room.

LOCAL TEEN KILLED IN THEATRE FIRE

I pick up a few of the scattered pages with trembling hands. They are journal entries, all written in the same handwriting that adorned the cards I'd found addressed to my father. The same handwriting I'd seen in the composition book on my first day here.

My throat closes up as the reality of what I'm walking into hits me like a hammer to the head. I drop the pages, ignoring the others that are scattered around me as I make my way to the stage. Each step feels like walking through quicksand.

Nothing could have prepared me for the scene that awaits me. The stage is empty except for a single ladder in the center. Candles ring the space like a ritual circle, their flames writhing. Shadows crawl across the walls like living things reaching for me. A girl in a white dress stands with her arms wrapped around the ladder. She doesn't move, doesn't breathe. Just holds on as if the ladder is the only thing keeping her from falling.

I slowly make my way toward her, my heart pounding so hard I can feel it in my throat. A massive red pentagram sprawls across the stage floor, its lines thick and wet. The copper tang of fresh blood coats the back of my throat.

"It's about fucking time you got here."

I turn toward the familiar voice and something slams into my skull, knocking me unconscious.

CHAPTER TWENTY-FOUR

Gasoline fumes burn my nose as I come to. A muffled sob echoes across the mostly empty stage. Blinking, I push myself upright and see a girl tied to a ladder, wrists bound tightly.

"Molly?"

She lifts her head, eyes red and wet. Her lips move, but the gag stuffed in her mouth swallows the words.

"Not bad, huh?" Josie sits a few feet away from me, her arms wrapped tightly around her knees. She rocks back and forth, restless energy radiating from her small frame. Her black and pink hair is disheveled, her makeup streaked. She tosses me a photo. It's a picture of Catherine wearing almost the exact dress as Molly, leaning stoically against a ladder. The same shot that I saw in the scrapbook.

"I worked on the dress all afternoon. I don't think I've ever sewn anything so quickly in my life."

"Why are you doing this?" I grab my head, pressing against the dull pain that shoots through my skull. When I pull my hand away, it's covered in blood.

"It's all part of my master plan." She pulls a large hunting knife from behind her back.

She trembles violently, as if electricity runs through her body. Her shoulders curl inward, making her look frail and broken. I inch toward her, doing my best not to startle her.

"Don't touch me! You murdered her!" Josie points the knife at me, scooting backward. "You let her die."

"Look, I know Catherine was your mother," I say carefully. "And I know what happened was awful. But her death was an accident. You know that."

"That's bullshit!" She jumps to her feet. "You're a liar, just like everyone else in this town. She needed help, and they humiliated her. They covered for that asshole for a few measly dollars, and then they left her to die simply because she wanted back what they'd taken from her. She needed help, and they left her to die."

I start to stand, but she kicks me in the face with her combat boot. I hear my nose crack, and a blinding pain stabs at my eyes.

"Don't. Move." Her voice carries a deadly warning.

I sit with my hand covering my face, trying to fight through the pain. Blood streams between my fingers. I can hear her circling me like a predator.

"Is it wrong that she wanted to keep her baby? She carried me for nine months. She loved me and had plans for our future together. They had no right to take me from her. And your asshole father. She would have given him the world, but he wanted nothing to do with her. He pranced around with other women, rubbing it in her face."

I hear Molly's muffled screams from behind the gag as Josie grabs her by the hair, shaking her like a doll, her rage spiraling out of control. "Basically telling my mother that she wasn't good enough." Her voice rises with every word until she shrieks almost incoherently.

"My father didn't love Catherine."

I need to get to Molly. I have to help her.

"He didn't give her a chance!" She bangs Molly's head into the ladder, and I watch as blood trickles from her forehead.

"Let Molly go. She has nothing to do with this. Her family wasn't involved in any way. You're hurting an innocent person."

"You're wrong, buddy boy. My mom's best friend was Molly's mother. She *is* involved, and she needs to die, too." She crouches down in front of me, her eyes filled with blind, burning rage. "I'm going to kill the child of every person who wronged my mother. She deserves that."

"You need help, Josie. I spoke to your grandmother, I know all about your condition—"

"Don't go all brain doc on me, asshole. You're just as messed up as I am. Blacking out, wandering aimlessly in the night. I thought for sure I was going to have to kill you when I saw you on the beach, but you were so blitzed, and focused so intently on the scene playing out in your own fucked up mind, you didn't even see me. The best one, though," she says with a wicked laugh, "was the night you walked in and found Ryan. I love it when a big, strong man screams like a little bitch. I'm almost tempted to let you live just so I can watch you wander around in your pharmaceutical-induced comas. It's quite entertaining."

"That was you I saw? Oh my God. You dressed up like your mother and killed Luke and Ryan?"

"Wrong again, Sherlock. I never dressed up like my mother to kill them. What kind of fucked up, Norman Bates weirdo do you think I am?"

"Why are you hunting us? Why not our parents?"

"Because I want them to feel the pain of losing someone. I want them to know what it's like to have their family ripped apart. You are all as innocent as Catherine. Eye for an eye. Plus, I needed the blood of those who wronged her. It was easier to get it from their children. I had them here at my disposal."

"Why do you need blood?"

"Because that's what the spell calls for, ding-dong." She shakes her head. "Why do you always ask so many fucking questions?"

"A spell for what?"

"A revenge spell. It's my last hope. I've been here almost every night, trying to contact her, yet you are the only one she'll speak with. Then it dawned on me. I wasn't giving her the power she needed to let go. She's trapped. Vengeful spirits can only find peace if their vengeance is carried out. All I have to do is offer up some blood from those who wronged her." She holds up two rags, covered in blood, to illustrate her point.

"I got this from Luke." She tosses a white bandana stained red onto the pentagram. "You kicked him in the mouth so hard he almost bit off his tongue. This is from Ryan." She tosses another rag onto the pentagram. "I got that after I pushed the platforms over on him. Man, those fuckers are heavy."

"What's the point?" Marilyn had said Josie was prone to psychotic episodes, but I had no idea how deeply disturbed she was.

"So she can rest. I owe her that much."

She picks up the knife, twirling it between her fingers like a skilled huntress. She's going to kill me. I try to move, but she kicks me in the gut and grabs my hand. A slicing pain shoots through my palm as she drags the knife slowly across.

"You and Molly are the final piece of the puzzle." She wipes a white rag over the river of blood that flows from my palm. "The only way to lay her soul to rest is to give her the blood of those who wronged her." I watch as she takes the rag and tosses it with the others.

"This isn't going to work. You only have blood from Luke, Ryan, Molly, and me. Melanie was in on it, too. She doesn't have a direct descendant."

"I know that, Heath. I'm not an idiot." She walks backstage to the levers that control the fly system. She releases one of the ropes, and I wait for a flat to come crashing down onto the stage. Instead, Dr. Plummer's body plummets from the rafters. The rope jerks taut with a wet snap that echoes through the theatre. Her head tilts at an impossible angle. If she wasn't dead before, she is now.

"That was kind of anti-climactic, wasn't it?" Josie walks back onto the stage. "It was so much more dramatic in my mind."

I collapse to the floor, swallowing hard, forcing back the acid that rises from my gut.

"This is the last little bit that I needed." She drags her knife across Dr. Plummer's inner thigh and a stream of blood flows down her leg.

"All done." Josie stands up. She turns her back to me and begins fiddling with something on the floor. I have to get out of here. Molly and I are next. It's just a matter of time.

"You didn't really find the journal in Molly's bag, did you?" I drag myself across the floor, inching closer to Molly, wincing at the pain that shoots through my hand. If I can keep Josie talking, maybe she won't turn around.

"Of course, I didn't. But when you told me you thought you saw Molly on the beach, I realized I had a real opportunity to fuck with your head—make you think Molly was the crazy one. It made it easier to set this up."

She still faces away from me. I'm standing now, my hand balled into a tight fist, blood dripping onto the floor. I take a step toward Molly. I hear a soft thud and something whizzes past my head. I turn to see Josie pointing a nail gun at me.

"Almost got ya. Don't move again." She threatens. "We're not finished."

"Josie, put it down, please." I take a step toward her. The nail gun thumps again, and Molly cries out in pain. A red stream of blood stains her dress where the nail hit her thigh.

"I said, don't move, motherfucker. The next one goes into her skull."

I freeze. My mind races as I try to figure out a way that I can get Molly free. Her leg bleeds profusely, her wrists chafed from the rope.

"Josie? Look at what you're doing. Is it really worth it? What do you have to gain?"

"What do I have to lose?"

"You're hurting innocent people. How can you possibly live with yourself? You could go to prison for this." I search for anything I can use to reason with her.

"No, I don't think I will. I've got a plan in place for that, too." She pulls her cell phone out of her pocket and begins to dial, one hand on the phone, the other pointing the nail gun in my direction.

"Hello? 911? I need help. I'm being attacked." She stares me right in the eye as she plays the damsel in distress. "No, I can't wait. Yes, I understand your officers are all dispatched, but I'm in danger. He's already killed my mother and my friend, Molly, and now he's after me." She walks closer, the nail gun trained on Molly's head, daring me to make a move.

"I'm trapped in the Rock Harbor Opera House. Please. Send someone. Yes, I'm safe right now. I'm hiding, but I don't know how long it will be before he finds me." She's face-to-face with me, looking me in the eye, daring me to say something. "Yes. Heath Ingram. His name is Heath Ingram. Hurry. Please."

She powers off her phone and stuffs it in her pocket, flashing a psychotic smile.

"How was that for acting?" The nail gun goes off twice in rapid succession. I scream out as one of the nails goes through the top of my left foot. The other barely grazes my big toe as it fastens my right shoe to the floor.

"I figure I have about fifteen minutes before the police are here. You two will be good and dead by then."

"Josie, stop."

Cole's voice pulls our attention to the stairs leading from the lobby. He runs down the steps toward the stage. My heart drops.

"Cole. Leave. She's got—"

My words are cut off by the thump-thump of the nail gun. Cole grabs his chest, body jerking against the nails that sink into him.

"Cole!"

I watch in horror as he drops to the ground.

"Aw, your hero is dead now, too."

"You fucking psycho bitch!" Tears stream down my cheeks. "He had nothing to do with this. His parents weren't involved."

"Collateral damage." Josie takes the nail gun and sits near the makeshift ritual space.

I sob as I watch her pull a large leather tome from her bag. She opens it to a marked page and begins chanting something in a foreign language. It sounds like it could be Latin, but I'm not sure. As she chants, the flames of the candles grow brighter, completely lighting up the stage.

She finishes her chant, and I watch in horror as she picks up one of the candles and drops it into a small can of rags behind me. As soon as it hits the cloth, it bursts into flames. She kicks it over and idly walks away as the flames dance across the floor. I notice the various rags placed randomly around the stage. That's why I smelled gasoline—the rags are drenched in it. If they all ignite, this place will be gone in no time.

"This is kind of cathartic, ya know?" Josie admires her handiwork. I struggle to pull my feet free, but the nails are deep in the floor. I manage to get my right foot out of the shoe, but when I go to move my left, a searing pain shoots through my foot. The nail went straight through to the floor.

"You can rest now, mama. It's all over."

The flames tease us with their heat as another rag ignites. Smoke begins to fill the air. Molly screams, struggling to get loose, but the ropes are too tight.

I look her in the eye, grit my teeth, and give another pull. The nail head sinks deeper into my foot. Blood squishes in my shoe. The pain is unbearable. Josie watches us from across the stage, her eyes intensely focused, the nail gun trained on me, daring me to break free.

I brace myself to try again when I see a flash of white from the corner of my eye. Lying in the middle of the pentagram is a girl in a white dress. For a moment, I think it's Molly, but it's not. Molly is still struggling to break free of the ropes.

The girl slowly stands, clearly disoriented.

"Help me!" she screams. "Somebody, please. Help me!" She spins in circles, searching for a way out.

"Phillip!" she cries, lifting her skirt to cover her mouth. "Phillip!"

My eyes grow wide in astonishment as I realize that I'm watching Catherine's death played out in front of me. Josie stands across the stage, mouth agape, nail gun at her side.

Maybe I can make this right.

"Catherine. Catherine. I'm right here."

The girl turns, relief flooding her face as she runs toward me. "Phillip, you came back for me." She wraps her arms around my neck, kissing my cheek.

"Yes, I came back." I wrap my arms around her, the blood from my hand staining her dress.

"You came back." She cries.

"I'm sorry for everything." The words my father never got to say pour out of me. "I'm sorry we failed you. I'm sorry you were alone."

Tears stream down her cheeks. "I love you, Phillip." She grabs my face and kisses me. "Thank you for saving me."

A roaring heat blasts me from behind. The grand drape has caught fire. It's only a matter of minutes before the whole place is up in flames.

"We have to get out of here, Catherine." I brace myself for one final tug, praying I'm able to pull my foot free of the nail.

Before I know what's happened, I'm yanked upward and then dropped to the ground. White-hot pain explodes through my foot. The world tilts sideways.

"Come on, we've got to get you out of here." Cole is suddenly beside me, blood covering his shirt. "I'm sorry about your foot. Hold onto me. This place is about to go up, and we can't be in it when it does."

He's not dead.

I nearly pass out and I'm not sure if it's from the pain, or the relief of him being alive.

"We have to help Molly." I forget about Catherine and drag myself toward the ladder, struggling to stand, ignoring the burning pain and the sticky liquid squishing between my toes. I fight to untie the knots that bind Molly's wrists, holding my breath against the influx of smoke. I finally feel the ropes slip, and Molly's hands are free. The rope around her feet is nailed into the floor. I can't get the knots loose.

"Cole! I need help. I can't get these knots free."

No answer.

Where is he?

Josie screams and I hear the sound of the nail gun going off. One shot after another, five, ten, twenty times. I drop to the floor, hands over my head.

"Cole!"

The smoke is so thick, I can't see him. I can't see Josie. She could jump out at any minute, killing us all.

I need a knife. There's a box cutter on the stage manager's desk.

I crawl across the floor, away from the inferno. The back wall is completely ablaze now, creeping closer toward Molly. She screams in terror.

"Hold on, Molly," I choke out. "I'll get a knife."

The lights begin to pop and go out as the heat intensifies. The crackling and roaring of flames drowns out almost everything else.

Everything except Molly's cries of pain and terror.

I drag myself across the floor, trying to stay below the smoke. It's too thick. I can't see. I can't breathe.

A hand grabs mine.

"We need to go," Cole coughs. "Hold on to me. I'll get you out of here."

"No! Molly. She's still stuck. We can't leave her."

Molly screams, a mix of fear, despair, and pain. I watch in horror as the inferno engulfs the ladder she had been tied to.

"Molly!" I yell.

"We have to go." Cole coughs uncontrollably. "We can't save her."

The flames grow hotter, moving in on us. We're moving too slowly.

We need to stand.

We need to make a run for it.

Cole pulls me up and we stumble toward the scene shop. I drag my damaged foot behind me, the stage crackling and popping around us. We scramble toward the back door, and Cole trips over something. He falls, taking me down with him. He gasps and scurries backward.

Josie.

She's dead. Her body a pincushion of nails. Her eyes stare at nothing, pupils blown wide in terror.

"Did you… kill her?" I can barely get the words out through the smoke that invades my lungs.

"No. I swear." He looks terrified. Like he's never seen a dead body before.

A flash of white drifts past as the thick smog closes in on us. It's impossible to see. I stand, pushing through the pain that emanates from my hip and my foot, unable to take my eyes off the frozen look of terror on Josie's bloodied face. I pull Cole up beside me, leaving Josie's body behind. We're wet, drenched in sweat from the unbearable heat that creeps toward us. The lights are all out. I can't see the door. We stumble, arms locked together, afraid to let go.

"We're almost there. The door is here somewhere." I stub my toe on the edge of the shelf containing the flats. I put my arms out in front of me to stop from falling yet again, and I lose my grip on Cole.

"Heath?" He's coughing uncontrollably.

I can't see. The smoke is thick and stabs at my eyes. "I'm okay. Follow my voice. I'm not going to leave you." I spin right and left, searching for him.

"Heath?" Cole yells over the roar of the fire. "I found it. This way."

I stumble toward the sound of his voice. A figure in white streaks past me, and the back door explodes open. Wind howls through the room, feeding the flames. Cole grabs my arm and pulls me through the door, flames licking at our feet. The door slams shut behind us.

Cole hauls me toward the front of the building, both of us choking for air. Blood streaks down his shirt, a nail still jutting from his right biceps. We stumble into the parking lot just as three police cars screech to a halt. My legs give out. I hit the ground, eyes burning with sweat and blood.

"Which one of you is Heath Ingram?"

"Me." I manage to barely raise a hand.

Guns are drawn on me.

"Place your hands on your head and don't move. Sir, step toward me, please. Are you okay? Are you hurt?" I hear the officer ask Cole.

"Yes, I mean no. Yes, I am, but not because of him. It wasn't him." Cole's voice is hoarse from smoke. "I know a young woman named Josie called you, but I called immediately after to tell you she was lying. She is the one who attacked us. She had a nail gun. She shot both of us. She started the place on fire. She's still inside. There's another…" His voice breaks. "Another young woman inside as well. We couldn't get her out. Heath didn't do anything wrong. We need an ambulance."

Cole sinks down next to me, running his hand over my head.

"Cole?" I can barely breathe. I'm weak. I've lost a lot of blood. My lungs burn, and my vision swims.

"I'm right here." His voice is gentle. "They've called an ambulance. Just hold on."

I try to answer him, but I can't. I can't stop coughing.

"You're going to be okay." He gently caresses my bleeding hand. "You are so brave."

The light from the burning building intensifies, lighting up the sky, casting Cole's skin in a sickly orange glow. I can barely keep my eyes open.

"Heath?" He pats me on the face. "Heath, don't leave me."

My body convulses as I'm wracked with another coughing fit. I do my best to focus on Cole's face. I'm so sleepy.

I glance over at the theatre. It's engulfed in flames now. A girl in white stands off to the side, watching it burn.

"Heath?" Tears escape Cole's eyes, cutting small rivers into the soot-smeared skin of his cheeks.

"I'm okay." I manage a whisper. "Everything's going to be okay."

EPILOGUE

Two Months Later

"Come on, slowpoke," Cole calls over his shoulder as he walks backward across the quad. "You're holding up the official tour."

I adjust my crutch and pick up the pace, my boot cast making a satisfying thunk with each step. The Oregon rain drizzles steadily, but neither of us seems to care. After everything we've been through, a little rain feels like nothing.

"You know I've already enrolled here, right? You don't need to sell me on it anymore."

"I know." He grins. "But this is the official tour so you know where all your classes are. And, it's your very own personal tour from your boyfriend. The only one that counts."

Boyfriend. The word still feels new, even two weeks later. We'd danced around it for weeks while the investigation dragged on. While reporters kept calling us asking about Josie's "blood bath" and what we'd survived that night. It's kind of tough to define a relationship when you're both considered suspects.

Not anymore, though. The investigators finally cleared us two weeks ago. Things can finally start getting back to normal. Dad's staying in Rock Harbor for now to help Vic design a new theatre. "Smaller and more modern," he'd told me on the phone. "And definitely not built on the old site."

No more ghosts. Just scars.

We have plenty of those.

"So, where to first, tour guide?" I ask as we reach the center of campus.

"Thought we'd hit the library, the student union, maybe grab some coffee…" He trails off as we approach a large brick building with "Theatre Arts" etched above the entrance.

My chest tightens. Even knowing this building is nothing like the Opera House, my palms start to sweat.

Cole stops walking, his hand automatically rubbing the spot on his chest where the nail barely missed his heart. He always does that when he's thinking about that night. "Auditions are today. Wanna go in and check it out?"

"No, it's fine. It's just a building."

I watch students flow in and out of the theatre doors, carrying scripts and water bottles, talking about callbacks and rehearsal schedules. Normal people doing normal theatre things.

"You sure?" Cole asks.

"I don't plan on stepping foot inside another theatre in a very long time."

He nods without trying to convince me otherwise. He doesn't point out that his major requires him to audition. To perform. That someday I'll have to choose between supporting him and my irrational aversion to theatres. He just accepts it.

"That's totally fair," he says. "Want to go get that coffee instead?"

"Yeah." I take one last look at the building. In the glass door's reflection, I catch a glimpse of someone in white, but when I look closer, it's just a student in a white raincoat.

"What is it?" Cole asks.

"Nothing. Just thought I saw someone."

"Still seeing her?" He places a hand on my back, glancing at the theatre.

"Sometimes," I say. "Let's go."

We turn to leave and Cole bumps my shoulder with his right arm. The one that doesn't still carry the outline of where the other nail hit. "So, what's the final verdict on your major?"

Until this summer, my dad wanted me to study engineering. I'd toyed with the idea of physical therapy, but after everything that happened, after seeing how therapy helped me heal, I changed my mind.

"Psychology." The word feels right in my mouth. "I want to help people who've survived trauma. People like me. Us."

Cole's entire face lights up. "That's perfect. You'd be amazing at that."

"We'll see."

We walk in comfortable silence for a while, rain pattering gently around us. I should call my parents later, tell them about my day. Things are different now. Dad asks about my class schedule instead of my nightmares. Mom texts about campus food and whether I'm remembering to do laundry. Real adult conversations instead of constantly watching my every move like I'm a fragile toddler. It helps that they both trust and adore Cole.

"Hey, Heath?"

"Yeah?"

Cole stops walking and faces me, rain beading on his dark hair. "I'm proud of you. For coming here, for starting over. I know it wasn't easy."

My cheeks warm despite the cold rain. "It helps having someone to start over with."

He smiles and takes my free hand. "Always."

For the first time since that night in the Jeep, since everything that happened in Rock Harbor, the future doesn't feel like something to survive.

It feels like something to live. To look forward to.

And it doesn't scare me.

Author's Note

All through my childhood, books were my escape. I grew up in a rural area where there wasn't much to do, so I needed something to keep my overactive imagination occupied. In sixth grade, I noticed my cousin reading *Comes the Blind Fury* by John Saul. She was several years older than me, but she happily handed it over when she finished (even though I was much too young). The book was about a girl who befriends the ghost of a blind child who had been bullied and killed years earlier. The ghost encourages her to get revenge on the classmates who bully her. It terrified me. It also completely captivated me. That was the start of my love for paranormal horror. Over the years I would go on to devour more of John Saul's books and love every one.

Years later, in my late twenties, I was working at a community theatre in Houston. When I wasn't at my day job, I was at the theatre—acting at first, then stage managing, and eventually directing. The building had been around for decades and collected set pieces, furniture, and other odds and ends donated by longtime supporters. If you're into paranormal stuff, you already know what that means: sometimes the furniture comes with a ghostly guest. And we had plenty.

Over the years, cast and crew swapped so many ghost stories that it was impossible to keep track. I heard and saw my fair share of strange things, but they never really scared me until one night in 2007.

It was Christmas Day. I hadn't left town because I was directing a show that opened right after the new year. I spent the day being lazy, but by that night I was bored. Around 10:00 p.m., I decided to head to the theatre and finish painting the set. I locked the doors, turned on the stage lights, and got to work.

That's when I heard footsteps upstairs. A shadow moved across the light booth, then toward the spot loft. I thought maybe my lighting designer had the same idea I did, so I called his name. Nothing. I called again. Still nothing.

Then the lights went out.

It was pitch black, and I had no flashlight and no clue where my phone was. I fumbled my way off the stage and into the lobby. The doors were still locked. My car was the only one in the lot. When I got back, the stage lights were on again. I started painting, trying to brush it off, until about ten minutes later when it happened again. This time I had my flashlight ready. I swung it around and caught the shadow of a man once more. The lights flicked back on, and he was gone. That was my cue to pack up and head home.

Three years later, I sat down to write a horror novel in the same spirit as John Saul's books. I wanted it to be a ghost story about a young man dealing with grief and his sexuality. I wanted to write the book I would've loved to find as a teenager. And I used that personal haunting as fuel.

When I first wrote *The Weeping*, YA was all the rage, so I wrote for that age group. In earlier versions, Heath was eighteen and reeling from an accident that happened on prom night. As I mentioned in the preface, I straight-washed him in later drafts because I thought that was the only way to sell the story. Cole didn't exist then. Molly was Heath's love interest (and she lived at the end). Catherine's journal was also much longer in that version, with pages of angsty, overwrought entries about Phillip (Heath's dad) and the baby. At the time I thought they added depth. Looking back, they were melodramatic and leaned on tropes that just didn't work anymore. In this revision, I cut them down to the handful of entries Heath actually reads. I also reframed what Noah did to Catherine, changed a few characters' names, and updated the dialogue so it felt more modern. I realize the book still reads a little "angsty YA", but the characters are just barely out of their teen years, so I guess it kind of fits. I'll let you decide.

The original book also ended differently. No epilogue, no hope. Just Heath fading in and out of consciousness outside the burning theatre, with Catherine's ghost being the last thing he saw. I thought I was being clever, leaving the ending ambiguous in true John Saul fashion. But when I revisited the book years later, I couldn't shake the feeling that Heath deserved better. The guy had been through hell. He deserved a little light.

So that's the story behind *The Weeping*. A little nostalgia, a little ghost fuel, and a lot of stubbornness about writing the kind of horror I craved as a kid. I hope this version gives you chills, but also leaves you with a flicker of hope—because if Heath can find it in the dark, maybe we can too.

Acknowledgements

Writing a book for the first time is no small feat. Rewriting it almost fifteen years later wasn't any easier.

There are so many people, living and gone, who helped make this book possible the first time around. It all started with "Frank," one of many ghosts at the old Country Playhouse in Houston, TX (now Queensbury Theatre), who thought it was funny to turn the lights out on me and knock things around while I stumbled through the dark.

More thanks to:

Susie T: stage manager extraordinaire, amazing artist, and fellow ghost hunter. Thank you for the late nights at the theatre painting sets, chasing ghosts, and sharing taco bowls and gossip. I miss those nights. Thanks, too, for reading the very first (very rough) draft of this story all those years ago and giving me feedback that was honest but encouraging.

Anne Z: another early reader who kept me going in 2010 with kind words and positive energy.

To all my current online writing and critique buddies who jumped in with feedback and editing help on such short notice—Ally, Clay, Justin, Claudia, and Lonnie B.—you're the best. And to everyone else in our crazy little group (there are too many to name, and I'd hate to leave someone out), consider this a blanket thank you. Over the years you've inspired me more than you know.

To my "booksta buddies": Scotty (fashionably_late_books), Jason (books_and_olfactory), Louis (bookmearead), Stellah (bookwormandcoffee), Dee (mel.a.nat.ed_nwellread), Jeff (jmkb-bookstagram), Danny (thatbookishbear), Samantha (saminfine-print), this.guy.books, spongebobbiii_books, and so many others—thank you for the support and the wild, welcoming bookish community you've brought me into. I haven't met you in person, but you're all amazing.

And finally, to my family and friends who keep inspiring, encouraging, and showering me with love every single day: thank you, from the bottom of my heart.

About the Author

Kallum Rytting lives in Portland, Oregon, with his adorable Bernedoodle, Hazel. He swears the scenery is unbeatable, the food is divine, and the weather is perfect (most of the time). When he's not reading, writing, or playing fetch, he's probably binging *Real Housewives*, *Drag Race*, classic TV reruns, or a stack of horror movies. You can find him on Instagram @kallum_rytting or sharing book reviews and promos on @just.read.it.already. *The Weeping* is his first novel.

9 781969 289095